COCAINE, CUPCAKE

Chester Gattle

This is a work of fiction. Names, characters, businesses, places, incidents, and institutions are either the product of the author's imagination or are used fictitiously. The author's use of names of actual persons, places, and agencies are incidental and are not intended to change the fictional character of the work.

For Missy Chan
You served as no inspiration for this book

All the world's a stage,
And all the men and women merely players;
They have their exits and their entrances,
And one man in his time plays many parts,
His acts being seven ages.

— William Shakespeare, *As You Like It*

The world's a stage,
But the play is badly cast.

— Oscar Wilde

One of the deep secrets of life is that all that is really worth the doing is what we do for others.

— Lewis Carroll

I.

Vicente had lost another ten kilos of cocaine. It was the second time in as many weeks. And just before that, the safe house in Paradise Hills had been hit. *How much was that?* he wondered. *Thirty, forty kilos? Gone. And some fentanyl. Don't forget the fentanyl.* It'd been a rough month.

At this point, he was lucky to even be alive. El Avispón, the boss of the plaza, was not a lenient man. He ordered men to their death for lesser mistakes, their naked bodies washing up on shore with pieces missing, some picked off by fish, others removed with kitchen knives and garden tools.

Vicente was clueless as to what he'd done to be in El Avispón's good graces, but he intended to stay there. He was now belly crawling through the dark, some fifteen feet underneath the desert, looking for the lost cocaine.

The shoulder-width tunnel hadn't been constructed for the passage of people, and he was struggling. Every couple of yards, the walls pinched in, and he'd get stuck. Only after a great deal of straining and squirming did he manage to pass through. *This is what hell feels like.*

The tunnel was one of many used by the cartel. It was an inconspicuous method of transport. The product (blocks of cocaine, boxes of counterfeit Oxy, bags of fentanyl, and bales of marijuana) was whisked under the border by a simple rope-and-pulley system. Vicente was following one such rig right then. Something had gone wrong, or that's what Bill and Marty of Bill and Marty's Convenience Store were saying. The last shipment, ten kilos of cocaine, had never arrived. Bill even sent Vicente a photo of the empty transport cart that'd pulled up beneath his store.

Vicente was skeptical. He'd been lied to before. Cocaine sold for twenty to thirty thousand dollars a kilo. It was only natural for there to be thieves along the supply chain, even if it meant stealing from the Cártel de Jalisco Nueva Generación (the CJNG), one of the most powerful cartels in the world. Vicente was sure Bill and Marty never imagined he'd go into the tunnel to prove them liars—these things were prone to collapse—but there he was, crawling inch by inch through hell, looking forward to seeing their faces when he emerged on the other side empty handed.

But then his hand bumped into something cool and slick in the dark. He drew his fingers across the side of a cellophane-wrapped bundle. He reached around and touched another bundle, then another. "They weren't fucking lying," he muttered. The cocaine was all there, pushed neatly against the side of the tunnel. *Good for Bill and Marty.* They weren't the thieving sons of bitches he thought they were.

Vicente unrolled a garbage bag he'd almost not brought along and shoved the bricks inside. He then paused, thinking. He was about halfway through the tunnel. He could return the way he'd come, but without room to turn around, it'd be a slow belly crawl backward. Alternatively, if he continued ahead, an easier progression, he'd have to deal with the border crossing to get home. Amid the sound of silence, he considered his options. Finally, he grasped the bag tightly, said "Fuck it," and reversed course, shifting hips and knees, elbows and palms—left, right, left, right.

The ceiling, a tenacious, oppressive beast, pressed

and clawed at his back. He concentrated on drawing long, calm breaths, but with his feet leading the way, claustrophobia quickly crept in. He realized now what the migrants he'd recruited to dig the tunnel had been talking about. It'd taken them weeks to dig through, and at the end of every shift, they'd been forced to backtrack, enduring this tortuous process. Granted, they got a free pass north for their work, so their fear had an offset, but for Vicente, well, Vicente had his cocaine, but he was shitting himself. He kept kicking the walls, knocking dirt loose. The whole thing, he imagined, was going to collapse. *I'm going to die.* Not that he feared death. He didn't really care if he died. He'd lived a rough twenty-one years. Death would be a welcome release, if he was being honest, but the process of dying? *That* was bad.

He imagined a low, deep groaning in the earth around him, a grating of shifting stone, a rustling of sand. Except, he realized, he wasn't imagining it. There *was* a trickling of sand. He couldn't see the wispy flow of grains—he couldn't see shit—but he heard it and felt it, just beyond the bridge of his nose. He quickened his pace. Then the earth opened with a rip and a roar.

The dirt and rocks poured over his hands and up his tattooed arms, razor-like bits cutting and slicing his skin. But as suddenly as it started, the rush came to a stop; the dirt settled at his biceps, just below the hem of his sleeve. Dead silence. "Jesus fucking Christ," he huffed, his breath deflecting off the dirt no farther than the length of a brick of cocaine.

His arms stung. His left wrist ached, sharp and vivid. *Probably broken.* But the earth was quiet now, and he could breathe, so no need to panic.

The bag of cocaine was fully buried, though. He hooked his fingers into the plastic and pulled. Sand and stones and whatever other organic matter there was in the desert scratched and dug at the lacerations across his arms.

He ignored the burning and pulled; he had to get the bag.

A low groan arose from the earth, and the pressure on his arms intensified. The tunnel had only paused in its collapse. He released the cocaine. Straining his back and wiggling side to side, he tried to pull free from the dirt, but there was no give. The tunnel held him tight.

In the darkness, the moan and murmur of the awfully weary space grew.

II.

Jacob White made it through most of the day without his suicidal thoughts growing beyond mere background noise. The drive from Minneapolis to 3M's headquarters in Maplewood wasn't delayed by any incompetently slow drivers; no one had taken his unofficial parking spot near the lot's outer edge; and he had walked uninterrupted to his workstation in the Carlton Science Center, where he buckled down and ran chemical treatability analysis for the duration of the morning. At noon he found an empty meeting room overlooking the 3M lake and munched on a sandwich before accepting the inevitability of an afternoon slog consisting of three meetings and a conference call. But still, only background noise. Then came rush hour traffic.

The clumsiness of the other drivers was maddening, and he wished a plague of unfortunate events on them all. Multiple times, he considered jumping the median for a head-on collision to end the misery. Where was a tanker truck when you needed it? But that westbound lane was backed up as well; even if there was a truck nearby, the head-on collision would've been nothing more than a head-on love tap. Maybe he'd get a little whiplash. Definitely no sweet release of death, though. He bit his tongue and endured the drive, like always.

When he arrived at his apartment, he parked with a sigh and went upstairs. Missy was on the couch, decked out in bright-green lululemon, feet up on the cushion and a laptop balanced on her knees. He flopped down beside her, nearly tipping the computer from its perch.

"You go for a climb?" he asked.

She nodded. "There's a new climbing gym on Central. Pretty nice."

"Got three more rejection letters today."

"Start an Instagram account," she told him for the thousandth time.

"Bleh. Rather kill myself."

Missy gave a snort of skepticism.

Jacob stood from the couch and looked at the balcony. "Sixth floor. That's high enough, yeah?"

She glanced up, her expressive brown eyes all he could see. He loved those eyes. They'd been together for nearly seven years, having met by chance at freshman orientation, and like that first day, he was still absolutely captivated with her gaze.

"Go up to the roof just to be safe," she said. "You don't want to risk it and only get paralyzed. I'm not taking care of a cripple."

Jacob gave a firm nod. "You want a picture before I go? A before-and-after? Put it in one of those frames that says, 'Memories.'"

"No, it'll go on Instagram," Missy said, lifting her phone.

"No," Jacob groaned. "It's just for you. Don't put it online."

"You can't stop me. You'll be dead." She gave him an evil toothy grin that lifted her cheekbones and compressed her eyes to the point that only her black eyeliner was visible.

"Fine," Jacob acquiesced, and sat back on the sofa. "Not going to do it then. Not contributing to your online nonsense." He kissed her cheek. "I think the dream's dead, though. Like *really* dead. Torn to bits and smeared across the highway. That shit is *dead* dead."

"You sound pretty convinced."

"There's this White House secretary that's getting a book deal now. She was there for like two weeks. *How* does that get published?"

"It's what people read," Missy said as if it were obvious. "It's scandalous. People love the drama."

Jacob leaned forward and lifted Missy's tea from the coffee table. "I'm getting buried in rejections." He took a sip.

"If you want a cup, I can make you a cup."

He took another sip. And another.

"Seriously. Don't drink it all."

He had one more long sip.

"Stop," Missy whined.

"What? I'm creating scandal, drama. Don't you love it? Maybe I'll write a book about it."

"No, don't love it." She grabbed her mug.

"Where's Quincy?" Jacob searched around for their pug. "Quincy?"

The fawn-colored dog emerged from underneath Jacob's writing table beside the couch and cocked its head.

Jacob grabbed Missy's phone near her hip and snapped a photo of the dog. He cropped and filtered the image. "Can I put this on your Instagram?" He showed her the phone.

The muscles in her temples tightened. "You didn't post that, did you? Did you?"

Quincy had gotten cherry eye, an infection and subsequent inflammation, under his lower eyelid, two weeks earlier. There was now a raw, oval mass, like a tiny cherry, popping out and obscuring his vision. Quincy would need surgery. But the dog was undeterred; his squishable face was still smiling.

"No. Relax." He tapped the screen and showed her he was only in the photo-editing app.

Missy snatched the phone and deleted the photo.

"Come on," he mumbled. "I was going to post it as #*UglyPug*." Jacob reached down and gave Quincy a pat on his head. "So ugly. But you can still live with us. We accept your hideousness."

Quincy sneezed and the protrusion squirted out a little. Jacob jerked his hand away.

"That thing is so nasty." Missy rested the phone back near her hip and drank her tea.

"Sorry, Quincy. You're too gross for Missy's Instagram."

"Put him on *your* Instagram," Missy argued. "Pet photos are very popular."

"Not getting Instagram or Twitter or Snapchat."

"You can't build your brand without an active social media presence."

"I don't need to build a brand," Jacob said. "Just need to publish my book."

"So you don't care if anyone buys it?"

"People will buy it."

"Not if you're not out marketing yourself."

"I'll market it in other ways."

"I don't get why you hate this so much."

"It's vapid, shallow, toxic. Rewards only the narcissistic. It's ego pollution."

"Thanks," Missy mumbled.

Jacob took her hand and gave it a light squeeze. "I didn't mean it that way. I'm just saying the kind of person who would read my book isn't the kind of person who's on social media. I don't get the point of needing to post, especially when it annoys me so much."

"You'll have to get over that. No publisher wants an author who refuses to promote on social media, even if your audience isn't on social media, which, I can assure you, they are."

"That's actually a little depressing."

"That's just how it is." Missy went back to her computer, pecking at the keyboard with one hand while the other held her tea.

Jacob picked up her phone. "Just looking at your Instagram. Not going to post anything," he promised, glancing through the accounts she was following. Unblemished faces. Fashionable bodies. Blue skies. Enticing food. Everyone was *so* busy, *so* happy, *so* interesting. He didn't want these characters in his life. And even if he did join the fray, what was he supposed to post? A picture of himself sitting in rush hour traffic? *#SurvivedDailyCommute* A picture of him touching Quincy's prolapsed cherry eye? *#UglyPug* There weren't enough filters to make his pictures worth memorializing. He just wasn't social media material. People wanted to follow glamour and fame and success, and they wanted to see it on a daily basis. His life's successes could be counted on one hand: a great SAT score, acceptance into the FBI Academy, and a job offer from 3M. Yet, even those had their darker underside: every top university he applied to rejected him; he dropped out of the academy because he couldn't pass the physical requirements; and 3M reassigned him to a position of drudgery and frivolousness. *#HateMyJob* He contributed nothing. "Loser," Jacob mumbled.

"What's that?" Missy asked, not looking up from her computer.

"Nothing." Jacob continued to scroll through her account, thinking about his latest failure, getting his book published. *Hopeless, hopeless, hopeless.* The novel he'd written *was* good. *Why doesn't an agent want it?* "I should just self-publish."

"Ugh." Missy looked at him, her lips curled in disgust. "Losers self-publish."

"Exactly."

Missy shook her head. "Just keep emailing agents." She leaned over and set her tea on the coffee table, her long black hair just missing the cup. "J.K. Rowling got rejected like a hundred times."

"Rowling got an agent right away."

She sighed. "Stop trying to make yourself feel bad. She got rejected a lot." Missy took her phone from him and gave it several taps. "Here. Look at this." She turned the screen around for him to see.

Before he glanced at it, he mumbled, "Don't believe everything you read on the internet."

Missy yanked the phone back.

"I saw it," he lied. "One of your motivational posts: 'Shoot for the stars, 'cause even if I miss, I'll land among them.'"

"It's 'Shoot for the moon, 'cause even if you miss, you'll land among the stars,' you dolt."

Jacob shrugged. "What'd it really say?"

"Nothing. Alicia posted a comment."

"What'd she say? Show me."

"Doesn't matter." Missy swiped the screen and mumbled, "She's such a green-tea bitch."

Jacob started to reach for Missy's tea again.

"Don't," she warned with a sideways glance.

He paused his hand midair and stared hard into his girlfriend's eyes. Then he raised his eyebrows and gave a wild grin, slowly moving his hand toward the mug. "Drama..."

"Don't do it." She stared back.

He touched the handle and wrapped his fingers around it.

"What are you doing?"

Unblinking, he lifted the tea and gave a long, slow sip.

Missy feigned exasperation. "You little bitch."

Jacob set the mug back on the table. "I'm a green-tea

bitch."

She grabbed the mug and held it close to her chest. "Maybe you should write a book about tea thieves."

"*Matcha Mischief*."

"*Bubble Tea Break-In*."

"*Break-Ins*. With an *s*," Jacob corrected. "Needs to be a series. Publishers want something with legs. Probably why my book isn't getting any attention. Just a one-off piece of hot garbage."

"It's not garbage. Don't say that. It's a numbers game, and you know it."

"I'm an outlier."

"No, you're not. Just be positive."

"You sound like my mom."

Missy chugged her tea, set her laptop aside, and got in his face. "And what's wrong with that?"

Jacob saw the minefield before him and didn't take another step. "I really thought people would like my book."

She wrapped an arm around him. "People will. It's an amazing story. You just need to catch a break. It'll happen."

"Maybe when I'm dead, yeah."

"It'll happen soon," Missy went on. "Do whatever it takes." She stood up, set her mug on the kitchen island as she passed, and disappeared around the corner. "Start a Twitter account. Or Instagram. Get your name out there," she instructed from the bathroom.

"Why don't you do that for me?"

"You can't afford me." The bathroom door shut.

Jacob went to the balcony. Six stories up would be more than enough. He had his exit plan if he needed it.

The turd fell from beneath Quincy's curly little pig tail and settled into the grass. There appeared to be a paper clip glistening within it. Jacob leaned close for confirmation. *Yep, paper clip.* "You're lucky, Quincy. Damn lucky that didn't tear your soft puppy guts apart."

Quincy wasn't listening. He was watching some dogs across the way yip at each other. Jacob sighed, inverted a plastic bag, and grabbed the still-warm deposit. With a quick twist and a loop, the foul bundle was secured. There was no disposal bin nearby, so he tied the bag around Quincy's collar. "You carry it," he muttered, leaving the bag of stench dangling just below Quincy's chin. In the colder months, Jacob didn't actually mind carrying the bag, it warmed his hands, but during the nicer months, Quincy could carry the load.

The sun was dropping behind the downtown skyline, and Jacob led the dog up the observational hill to catch the last bit of the day's rays. There was a disposal bin at the top, and Jacob released Quincy from his burden before taking a seat on a bench. Quincy perched himself beside Jacob and lorded over the park, surveying the commoners below with a quiet magnificence, as if he hadn't just carried his own crap up the hill.

Jacob hunched over, rested his elbows on his knees, and buried his head in his phone, scrolling through *The New York Times*, eventually settling on the "Books" section, where he reviewed the latest rumblings within the industry. The top blurb was about a new nonfiction novel: a kidnap victim's harrowing tale of perseverance: *Syndrome* by Scott Holm. Below that, a cookbook by a six-year-old who had a YouTube channel, and below that, an immigrant's journey from pauper to millionaire. The rest of the page he'd already seen, so he flicked the browser from the screen.

Nonfiction was getting published a lot these days. Tales of hope, power, purpose, and drama. It was everywhere. The market was flooded. But still, even with the glut, new nonfiction books continued to get published every day. *Because that's what the market wants.*

He bit his fingernails and glanced around the park. There were a half dozen people, some on blankets in the grass, some on benches near the walking paths. All were reading. The industry data said five of them were reading nonfiction. And the one reading fiction was reading something by a mega author like Rowling, Patterson, Brown, or King. An active social media presence wasn't going to help with that. "I've written a really good story, Quincy. Don't even care about the money. Just want it out there, in front of people, getting them talking, thinking."

A couple of motorcycles rumbled down the street. "Sunshine boys are out today," Jacob said, watching the riders pass an ice cream shop that had a line trailing out the door. A homeless man in an oversized parka wandered near the people waiting their turn for the frozen sugar rush. He stopped and tried to talk with a young skinny-jeaned couple. They ignored him, pretending to be engrossed in their selfie shots, so he continued on, bopping and jiving to a soundless beat.

There were a lot of homeless people scattered about that evening, Jacob noticed. At least seven from his vantage point. Not that that was unusual this spring. In comparison to last year, though, the numbers had skyrocketed. He and Missy wouldn't have moved to the neighborhood if the homeless people had been around then. Or more specifically, *Missy* wouldn't have moved. He didn't care so much. A summer in middle school spent volunteering at a soup kitchen had given him some perspective.

Charlie, a homeless man Missy worried was becoming too friendly toward them, was making his way up the side of the hill, ignoring the circular walking path and cutting through the grass.

"Hey, J. Hey, Q," the man said as he got near. Charlie reached out a wrinkled, sunburned hand and gave Quincy a pat on the head. "Nice out, huh?"

"Really is." Jacob smiled. He glanced up at his

apartment; Missy wasn't in sight. "Have a seat," he offered, pulling the panting Quincy close so there'd be room on the bench.

"Hmm, yeah, don't mind if I do." Charlie dropped his rucksack, gave his mangled beard a straightening tug, and sat with an oomph, the smell of dry rubber—not all that unpleasant—wafting up from within the layers of fabric he'd draped himself with. Charlie scanned the park while giving Quincy a few more absent-minded strokes.

Jacob eyed the rucksack in the grass. It was decorated with distressed pins and patches, most of them honoring the Marines. He'd never asked, but he assumed Charlie was a vet. He vaguely remembered a conversation they'd once had about the VA Medical Hospital, so he didn't think the jump in logic was too big to make.

"Everyone's out tonight, aren't they?" Charlie muttered. "God's treating us. Nobody wants to miss it. Not even Whispers." He chuckled like a mall Santa.

The image of Charlie cleaning himself in a suburban mall bathroom before pulling on his red suit and going out to greet soccer moms and their demon spawn for holiday photos made Jacob laugh as well.

Charlie grew serious. "Whispers is going down fast." He was staring at the man in the oversized parka who'd passed the ice cream shop a few moments earlier. The man was now having a heated argument with a tree.

"He okay?" Jacob asked.

"Let's just say he sees things through a different filter."

"Should we do something? Call someone?"

The man slapped the tree.

Charlie shook his head then pulled out a half-smoked cigarette hidden in his beard and lit it. "Whispers'll be happier if he's just left alone."

"If he needs help..."

Charlie puffed on the cigarette. "Some people don't

want help. Refuse it even if you give it."

"Yo, Charlie! You see Calvin?" a harsh voice called out from behind them.

Charlie didn't turn around. He just lifted his face to the sky and answered, "Not today. Haven't."

"Need to talk to him." A squat man, maybe twenty years old, with a heavy drooping brow circled the bench, the intense smell of weed and citrus (*Pledge?*) emanating from him. "Where is he?"

"Can't say," Charlie told him.

The weed and Pledge and cigarette smoke combined into a vicious cocktail that was too much for Jacob, and he started coughing.

"Oh, hey, Mitch," the weed-Pledge man said, giving Jacob a slap on the shoulder. "You don't sound too good. You need a hookup?"

Jacob lifted his eyes to meet the man's placid stare. Maybe he wasn't twenty. *Could still be a teenager.* The overly large, untied sneakers certainly made him look childish, like a toddler wearing his father's work boots.

"That's not Mitch, D," Charlie corrected him.

"How many times I have to tell you? It's Dwight, not D. I'm no D," the man growled.

"And he's no Mitch," Charlie added.

Dwight's brow drooped even lower, shrouding his eyes in darkness, as he studied Jacob. His face was extraordinarily wide, like a dinner plate. "No?"

Jacob's throat spasmed again from the fumes. He shook his head. "No, I'm not."

"Well, fuck me." Dwight leaned closer. "You want a hookup anyway?"

Assuming he was referring to drugs, Jacob quickly said, "I'm good."

Charlie exuded another cloud of cigarette smoke, driving away any remaining aromatic hints of the park, earth, nature, trees, and grass. He pointed to several people milling about behind the ice cream shop. “Is that Calvin over there?”

Dwight turned and looked. After a second, he muttered, “Your eyes suck.”

“Yes, yes, they do.” Charlie gently dabbed the lit end of his cigarette on the bench, snuffing it out. He shoved it back into his beard, then stood and gave Quincy a pat. “Enjoy the rest of your evening, puppy.”

Dwight leaned back on his heels as if Charlie had tried to hit him. “Wait? Where you going? You got a problem?”

“I always got problems, Dwight.” Charlie picked up his rucksack and slung it over his shoulder.

“I think you got a problem with me. You and this guy were talking all casual. Relaxing. Having cupcakes. Now you gotta go ’cause I come over?”

“Cupcakes?”

“It’s a metaphor,” Dwight explained.

“Analogy,” Jacob corrected him.

“Just time to go,” Charlie said, ignoring them both and turning away.

“No. Hold on a minute. I don’t like this vibe you’re leaving me with.” Dwight reached out, placed a hand on Charlie’s shoulder, and brought him back around.

The conversation was morphing into a confrontation. Jacob lifted Quincy from the bench and set him on the short, worn-out grass between his feet, then stood himself.

“Oh? You too, Cupcake?” Dwight muttered, dropping his hand from Charlie’s shoulder.

“What’s with the cupcakes?” Charlie asked.

“I call everyone a fucking cupcake,” Dwight argued.

“Not me, you don’t.”

“’Cause I don’t like you enough.”

Jacob tugged Quincy’s leash, eager to leave the men, their argument, and their pungent odors.

Dwight kicked at Quincy, missing mostly but still clipping the toe of his sneaker across the pug's rump and making the dog yelp. "Go. All y'all. I don't give a shit." He raised a fist, pretending he was about to swing. Jacob flinched. "That's what I thought, Cupcake. Get out of here."

Jacob scurried down the hill, ignoring the path, cutting through the grass like Charlie had on his way up. Quincy huffed and grunted the entire way.

When they reached the safety of their apartment's lobby, Jacob stopped and gave Quincy a gentle squeeze. The pug was winded; his eyes bulged from his squishy face. Jacob took pity on the chubby little guy and picked him up, carrying him the rest of the way.

"There you go," he said, as he set the pug down inside the apartment. Quincy scuttled off into the kitchen, where Missy was standing, brewing herself a cup of green tea.

"Hi, Quincy," she sang. "Is it nice out?" She bent over to give the pug a kiss on his head. "Why's his butt dirty?" She brushed at his fur; Quincy backed away from the touch. "What happened to him?"

Jacob stopped at the edge of the kitchen, keeping his distance. "Had a little run-in."

"With some homeless people?" Missy accused as she knelt and pulled Quincy over for a closer inspection.

"I don't know. Maybe. He didn't really look homeless."

"What happened? What'd you do?"

"Nothing. We were walking away, and the guy kicked him."

"Kicked *Quincy*!" Missy hugged the dog and glared up at Jacob. "I told you to stay away from them. Why don't you listen?"

Jacob made an attempt to kneel and wrap his arm around Missy, but she quickly stood, grabbed her tea, and left the kitchen. "Quincy, come."

The dog followed her into the bedroom, and she shut the door.

Jacob remained bent over for a second, then sighed and stood. The couch would be his bed tonight.

It was four in the morning when Jacob pushed the blanket to the floor and sat up. He couldn't sleep. The couch was a bit too short and lumpy. He grabbed his phone and started browsing Facebook, the one social media platform he hadn't absolutely shunned. Not that he actually liked it any better than the others. He'd just signed up for it back in high school when the concept of social media was new, and he hadn't known any better.

He scrolled through the page, trying to cure his insomnia. An old buddy announced he was relocating for a new job. Another posted about nearly dying from a battle with painkillers. Someone's kid was turning two. An irate tirade against the president. A barbecue meet-up. A donation request.

An email notification flashed at the top of the screen, so he clicked it. A literary agent based out of the UK was turning down his novel. She assured him tastes were subjective, though, and what wasn't right for her didn't mean it wasn't right for someone else.

"No," Jacob said, "it's not right for anyone. Appreciate the canned optimism, though."

He stood up and paced in the darkness, thinking. No one, absolutely no one, was willing to take a look at his novel. *Why? Is it the email query?* He'd rewritten that thing a dozen times before deciding it was good to go and sending it to a few agents, but then he didn't get a single response, so he rewrote it a dozen more times and sent it out to a new batch of agents, but still, he got the same non-responses. He was almost starting to think his story wasn't good enough to be published.

But not yet. He was just getting lost amid the mountain of queries the agents received every day. Dozens and dozens of queries. It was endless. Everyone thought they could write, and agents were inundated with their hot, stinking piles of...*cupcakes. Cupcakes? Where did that come from?*

He remembered. The guy from the park. That guy was a hot, stinking pile of cupcakes. If there was ever a time to know karate, or boxing, or just a good takedown maneuver, that would've been it. The asshole had kicked Quincy. He should've grabbed his leg, then shoved him hard down the hill. That would've been great. But with his luck, the guy would've pulled a gun or something. *Screw it.* The fantasy dissolved. Jacob kicked a blanket lying on the floor instead.

Down the hall, Quincy started scratching at the bedroom door. Missy slept like a log, so the noise wouldn't wake her, but in the absolute quiet only the dead of night can bring, the grating of tiny claws on bare wood was too much for Jacob.

He escaped to the balcony where the steady rush of the Mississippi River passing over the lock and dam a quarter of a mile away provided relief. He leaned over the railing. The full moon cast a soft glow across the treetops in the park. Someone was walking on the far side of the park, the streetlights betraying his presence as he passed under them. Jacob sang, "I hurt myself today..."

"Gonna serenade me?" a hoarse voice spoke.

Jacob jumped, nearly dropping his phone. On the next-door balcony, his neighbor, Curly Burly, was stretched out on a lawn chair wearing only his boxers. Jacob's face flushed, partly from being caught singing, partly from the sight before him. Curly Burly, with his spots and moles and sags and folds, wasn't a pretty sight, even in the dull glow of the moon. The man was too old for bodily demureness, though. The old hipster professor embraced what nature had done to him and remained splayed out for all to behold, ignoring the blanket that'd fallen from the chair while he'd been sleeping. Jacob tried not to look too closely, but he might have caught sight of a fuzzy ball poking out from a particularly scrunched-up segment of the underwear. "Ah, Jesus. Hey, CB," Jacob muttered, turning back to the park.

"Tryouts over at the Guthrie this week. Might be a musical. You could be the lead," Curly Burly offered.

Jacob chuckled. "A dream come true."

"How's the writing coming along?"

"Plenty of writing. Not much else."

"Oh, you focus on your writing, and the rest will come. It's like a turd that won't drop. Just let it be and gravity eventually gets it for you."

Jacob searched the park for something to replace the image of CB with a dangler.

"Who you sending your queries to?"

"Agents. New York. LA. London."

"I only got an agent after I proved myself with an independent publisher."

"Might have to go that route. Just really thought I could get an agent."

"Good writing gets noticed. Always does."

Jacob wasn't sure about that. He leaned over the railing and peered at the sidewalk below. A man was up in arms about some perceived slight the world had placed upon him. "This homeless guy is going crazy."

CB picked up the blanket that'd fallen and covered himself. "You're not supposed to call them homeless. You say they're 'home challenged.'"

"Serious?"

CB giggled. "No. Wouldn't doubt if that becomes a thing, though. You read about the one who got sliced by an industrial mower over on Hiawatha and Lake?"

"No. Sliced?"

"He was lying in some tall grass against the retaining wall there, burrowed deep like a damn toad, no doubt drugged out of his mind, and—*shink*!—the maintenance worker never saw him until the wall was sprayed with blood. It's still stained a pinky hue, if you feel like checking it out."

"Be crazy if the maintenance guy actually *did* see him, but some sick urge told him to go for it."

"That's dark. Make for an interesting short story," CB exclaimed. "Internal monologue of that split second where he's deciding, 'Should I veer or not?'" He chuckled then drew serious. "Mark my words, that won't be the last nasty death we see with these people. Some sweet old lady or young kid is going to get killed by one on a bender. Mark my words. Need to throw their butts in jail and force the drugs out of their systems. The city's just too lily-livered to do what needs to be done. You been finding needles in the park? I have."

"Yeah, we've seen some." Jacob watched the homeless man make his way down the street, amble back a little, swerve around, and pause at the corner, shoulders hunched and hands in his trench coat like he was pouting. Jacob aimed his phone at the man and snapped a photo.

"Pisses me off," CB said. "My first novel was about a couple of homeless guys. You know that?"

"Didn't." Jacob inspected the photo he'd taken. There wasn't enough light. He couldn't see much. "Been reading your recent stuff mostly."

"Set in the 1950s. Hobos. That's what they were called back then. Not homeless. Just down-on-their-luck, well-meaning men. But today...they're a different breed. Drug addicts. Mentally unstable. Truculent. Intemperate."

"So that first book was with an independent publisher?"

"It was. Doubt it'd even get published today. People want authentic stories. Even if it's fiction, it needs to be authentic. And I was never a hobo, so it wasn't 'my story.'" Curly Burly thought for a moment. "You writing about a world you're not part of?"

Jacob said, "Don't think so," but he'd wondered about that. He'd actually wondered about almost every conceivable issue that could even remotely affect his chances of getting published. And it was driving him crazy. The current frontrunner was his obscurity. He didn't have industry connections. He didn't have a body of published work. His queries were sent out unsolicited and got summarily tossed to the slush pile, the stack that only got attention when an agent had nothing better to do for ten minutes. He needed a way off that pile. He just couldn't figure out how. He was a horrible networker. His short stories were okay but too personal to publish. He had no interesting backstory or hook. He wasn't doing anything. He *wasn't* anything. *Might as well just give up. Climb over this railing and jump. Take the fast way down to the homeless guy.*

A police car circled the park then slowed as it passed the homeless man. Jacob took a couple of photos, hoping to capture the moment when the police hit their lights, but they didn't even stop; they left the man alone. "You ever see the cops arrest these guys?"

"They won't do that. Not with the city council leaning over their shoulders like they do. Should, though. Overdoses are out of control. And giving cops Narcan is no solution. Just brings the addict back to OD another day."

"Here you go," Jacob said, grinning as he showed CB his phone. "Got a photo of the cops driving right by the guy."

CB erupted with an annoyed harrumph. "Put it online. On Twitter or something. Shame the city for their indiscretions."

Jacob smirked. "You know Twitter?"

"How old you think I am?"

"You're a grandpa, aren't you? You're old."

"Maybe, but my phone's newer than the one you've got there."

Jacob smirked. "Touché."

"Put it on Twitter," CB pressed.

"Should I?"

"Damn right, you should. *#OpioidCrisis*! Get the word out."

"Opioid crisis," Jacob repeated as he glanced out at the park, thinking of addicts and homeless and death. *Oh, my!* That would be a dark departure from the beautiful food and filtered selfies flooding social media. He kind of liked it. And Missy did want him to start building an online presence. *There you go, Missy. People love drama? Well, bask in the glorious, drama-filled world of deadly addictions and mental health issues.*

"Opioid crisis," he said again as he thought of the man who'd mistaken him for some guy named Mitch earlier. He should've recorded that conversation. That would've been a good first post for a Twitter account. *#YouWantAHookup?*

There'd be other opportunities if he wanted to try recording something. The homeless, the addicts, the dealers were everywhere. He could gather all the content he wanted right across the street. *Dozens, hundreds, thousands of posts.* He'd been standing on the balcony for just ten minutes (in the middle of the night, no less), and he'd gotten a few photos. *People love drama. Drama, drama, drama.* His account could be like a car wreck; everyone would want to look.

Maybe an agent would take note of his manuscript then. Missy said agents wanted authors with active social media accounts and established platforms. If he had thousands of followers—even if they were pulled in with some unrelated dark and dangerous subject matter—that should still count for something.

So perhaps his dream wasn't dead and smeared across the interstate just yet. Traffic was heavy, and the dream was walking the painted line, awfully close to death, but it hadn't yet caught the sharp edge of a bumper. He could try it; he had no other ideas, so why not? #*OpioidCrisis*

III.

In the morning, before Missy got up, Jacob sat on the couch and called his sister, a police officer in Wisconsin. His social media idea was expanding into something a little more significant, and he needed to pick her brain. "Emily, what's up?"

"Nothing. Leaving in five minutes," she warned.

"Yeah, no, that's fine. That picture you sent me a few weeks ago of your partner with that bag of meth?"

"Yeah."

"Did that bust get in the paper?"

"Didn't look."

"Usually it does, though, right?" he asked.

"Usually."

"How'd you find the drugs? You get a tip?"

"Got an addict to rat him out."

"A CI?" he clarified, remembering the term from his FBI training at Quantico.

"A snitch, yeah."

"The FBI called them CIs."

"Good for them."

"You ever get tips from regular people?"

"Eh. Sometimes. What's your point? I've gotta get going."

Jacob came clean. "Thinking of turning in a dealer."

Emily groaned. "You know a dealer?"

"Might. Not sure. He offered me a hookup."

"A hookup? He was just hitting on you."

"A hookup. Not *to* hook up. Was about drugs...I think."

"If you don't know what he was talking about, don't waste anyone's time. We get enough bullshit tips."

"I could probably figure it out."

"That's worse. Now you want to be a vigilante?"

Jacob hadn't considered himself the vigilante type, but he liked the idea. "I'm Batman," he growled.

"I'm not joking. You don't know who these people are. Some are small-time losers selling on the corner, but others are major players. Heads of street gangs. Enforcers. You don't know—they could even work for the cartel."

"Like in *Narcos*?"

"I don't watch *Narcos*," Emily said.

"Where'd the meth you found come from? Mexico?"

"Some distributor in Eau Claire. Maybe came up from Mexico. Which is my point. Don't mess around with this."

"I'm not going to do anything stupid."

"Heard that one before," Emily muttered.

The bedroom door opened; Quincy's paws clicked across the hardwood floor. Missy appeared in the kitchen, eyes half open, hair a mess. She glanced over the kitchen island at Jacob and gave a tilt of her head. She pointed to her ear and mouthed, "Who's that?"

Jacob gestured to a picture of him, his sister, and their parents on one of the floating shelves behind the couch. He rarely spoke to his mom, and his dad had passed a decade earlier. *You get one guess*, he thought.

Missy nodded and turned to the cabinets. She struggled to reach something on the top shelf then spun around and quietly asked, "Can you help me?"

He went over as Emily continued, "These aren't jaywalkers. Drug-dealing brothers shoot each other over territory, and fathers sell their babies to sex offenders to get deals done. They'll go after anyone. They shot a cop in Oshkosh a few years back."

"Who shot a cop?"

"A street gang with cartel ties. The cop was taking bribes from them. He tried to stop, so they shot him."

"Whoa. Cool," Jacob said. "That'd be awesome if I uncovered a crooked cop."

Missy was pointing to a large mixing bowl. He pulled it down and set it on the counter.

"Thanks." Missy smiled. "I want to make pancakes together." She gave him a sweet stare, seemingly having forgiven him for the incident that had relegated him to the couch for the night.

"That wouldn't be awesome," Emily scolded. "These people are psychopaths. Please don't say that's awesome. The cartel is worse than Al-Qaeda, ISIS—"

Jacob cut her off. "I get what you're saying. I saw *Breaking Bad*. The cartel is crazy dangerous, but I'm not going after them. This guy just hangs around the homeless in the park."

"You don't know that."

But he did. He was pretty sure of it, and even if he started to suspect he was wrong, he could ask Emily to look the guy up, check out his background. He still liked his plan, even if she adamantly did not, so he said, "I'll let you get to work."

"I'm not exaggerating with this," she stressed.

"I know. I know. Thanks. Be safe." Jacob waited until Emily said goodbye, then hung up.

Missy plucked a couple of eggs from the fridge. "What was that about?"

"There's a guy in the park who's dealing drugs. Wanted to ask about reporting him."

"Oh, you should. Absolutely." She split the eggs over a pile of mix and stirred.

"Probably will the next time I see him."

Missy gave a huff and yawned wide.

Jacob snagged a chunk of the pancake goop and flipped it down her gullet, yelling, "Yawn Stop!"

Missy's gag reflex kicked in as the mix struck the back of her throat. Her eyes went wide, and she started to heave.

Oh, shit. Shouldn't've done that.

She grasped the counter and gave one large cough, expelling the bits of mix across the cabinet doors. "What the fuck?" Still braced against the counter, she glared at him.

"It's called Yawn Stop," Jacob said. "When someone's yawning, you toss something into their mouth." He'd seen the trend on Twitter and Instagram during the night.

"Really? Haven't seen that one yet," Missy mumbled. "But pretty sure you're supposed to record it, so that's a fail." She reached into the bowl and dug a finger into the mix.

Jacob knew her intention and grabbed for her wrist before she could execute the plan. He missed, knocking her arm against the side of the bowl. Over the edge of the counter it went, clattering at their feet. Eggy powder exploded across the floor, and Quincy went running for safety.

"Missy!" Jacob whined.

"That was *your* fault." She tiptoed away from the mess, shaking bits of congealed slop from her feet and ankles. "You're so clumsy sometimes."

Jacob stared at the mess as Quincy returned, sniffing and licking at the outer edges of the splatter.

"No, Quincy," Missy scolded him. She bent over and pushed the pug away. Quincy tried to return, and she pushed him again. He grumbled and tried a third time.

“Take him out, can you?” Missy reached up and pushed Jacob toward the door down the hall.

“Yeah. Sure.” Jacob quickly washed off his legs in the bathroom, then took Quincy from the apartment, leaving Missy to wipe up the mess he’d apparently made.

Jacob and Quincy crossed the street to Gold Medal Park, navigated the summer joggers, avoided the homeless people lying on benches, and found an open spot in the grass near the base of the small observational hill. Jacob searched around for discarded syringes; there were none. He snapped a photo of the most dejected homeless person he could see and put that online instead: *#OpioidCrisis*. One of his posts from the previous night had gotten a like. *Nice.*

Quincy had a tennis ball from the apartment, and Jacob grabbed it from his mouth, asking, “You ready?”

The dog hopped and crouched and shook his butt. Jacob flipped the ball high into the air. Quincy watched it rise, reach the top of the trees, and begin its descent. He toddled underneath and snapped for it, but his cherry eye messed with his perception, and the ball hit him on his broad, wrinkled forehead with a thump. Quincy stared at Jacob, baffled. “Go get it,” Jacob encouraged. The dog bumbled away like a pudgy little dump truck.

Jacob glanced at his apartment, thinking he should’ve stayed to help clean up. *Too late now.* Quincy brought the ball back, and Jacob kicked it across the grass this time. They played fetch for the next half hour as Jacob figured it best to give Missy time to eat her breakfast (whatever that ended up being) in peace. He watched the pug go back and forth, back and forth through the trees. Jacob didn’t even notice the pungent aroma of weed and Pledge until Dwight was right there beside him.

“Mitch, what you looking for today?”

Jacob looked at Dwight, unsure whether he should correct him. Emily's warnings repeated in his head: *working for the cartel, worse than Al-Qaeda, psychopaths*. But that didn't apply to this guy. Dwight was certainly a dealer of some sort, but to Jacob he actually looked mildly retarded. Dwight also was swaying and fidgeting so much he seemed more interested in the location of the nearest toilet than getting a deal consummated at any cost. Sure, Jacob was a bit unsettled around him, but he wasn't afraid of him. The only thing Dwight could attack was his sense of smell.

Dwight grabbed the ball Quincy had dropped at Jacob's feet and gave it a toss. Quincy let it go and took a seat beside Jacob.

"Want a teener? Or a little more for the weekend?" Dwight reversed his baseball cap, letting the sun shine over his broad nose, heavy cheekbones, and wide chin. His similarity to Quasimodo was uncanny. "Want two teeners?"

Jacob was going to let this play out. Maybe there'd be something worth posting. He pretended to search his pockets. "Didn't think I'd run into you. Don't have any cash."

Dwight rubbed his nose, snatching something from the edge of his nostril, and gave it a flick. "Go get some. I'll wait."

"You'll wait?" Jacob studied Dwight's clothes. The police would want a detailed description. *Yes, Officer, a dark-yellow hoodie. No, nothing on it. No logo. Baggy blue jeans. Really baggy. They puddled around his ankles. Shoes? Jordans. White. Untied with the tongues sticking out.*

"Yeah, I'll wait. Go check," Dwight instructed.

"Yeah, sure, okay."

"You can leave your dog here. I'll watch him." Dwight turned his cap back around.

Jacob said, "Oh, no, that's okay. He's been out long enough. I'll go check if I have some cash." He turned and led Quincy away, snatching the tennis ball from the grass as they passed.

"Don't make me wait."

"No, I won't. Will come right back. If I'm not back in a couple minutes, just go. It's fine." Jacob looked over his shoulder. Dwight shrugged and pulled the hoodie over his cap.

Jacob hurried Quincy across the street and around the side of their building, out of Dwight's sight, where he could call the police. But he paused. He should record something for social media. Get a photo at least.

"Come on, Quincy." Jacob rushed up to their apartment. He'd snap a photo of Dwight from the balcony. He could also record the arrest. *Bird's-eye view.* He opened Instagram, Snap, Twitter, and Facebook as the elevator took them to the sixth floor.

Missy was standing in the bathroom, applying her makeup.

"Come look at this," Jacob called as he power walked to the balcony. He scanned the park near the base of the hill. It took a moment, but he spotted Dwight leaning against the side of a young oak tree, watching people pass. Jacob took a few photos.

"Look at what?" Missy stood next to Jacob. Her hair was finished and curled, but her makeup had only been half applied.

Jacob pointed to Dwight. "See that guy? Yellow hoodie by the tree?"

"Yeah."

"He's the drug dealer. Tried selling me some again just now."

Missy shook her head. "This place sucks. You didn't sign the renewal yet, did you?"

Ignoring the question, Jacob continued, "He asked if I wanted a teener."

"Call the police." Missy stared at Dwight in disgust.

"Exactly. Going to record the arrest, then put it

online."

"Don't do that. That's stupid."

"Why?"

"You don't put that kind of stuff online."

Jacob showed her the posts he'd already put up. He pointed to the like that'd been given. "And see?" He pointed to the top of the screen. "Got a follower too."

"That's nothing."

"I'm doing this because you wanted me on social media," he reminded her.

"Not what I was saying." Missy locked her eyes on the hooded man in the park. "What was he selling?"

"A teener. Think it's slang, like maybe a tenth of an ounce or something."

"A tenth of an ounce isn't a lot."

"Probably has more."

"You see more?"

"No."

"What'd you see?"

"Nothing."

"So you don't even know if he has anything? What if he was just trying to rip you off?"

Jacob paused, reevaluating. Emily had warned him about bullshit tips. Still, he refused to give in. "Just because I didn't see anything doesn't mean he doesn't have anything."

Missy rolled her eyes. "Give me your phone. You're not calling."

Jacob twisted it away. "Fine. I won't call now. I'll figure out what he's got, and then I'll call."

"No. Stay away from him," Missy said.

"Why? You want me on Twitter and Instagram and all that, don't you?"

"Post your stupid pics of the homeless. Waste your time. I don't care." She glared at him. "But *don't* mess around with a drug dealer. Don't." She spun around and marched inside.

Down in the park, Dwight shuffled from foot to foot and stretched his arms. He finally had enough of waiting and walked away, disappearing around the hill.

Jacob pulled one of the plastic chairs close and sat, scrolling through the photos he'd taken. There was one particularly crisp shot with the dealer slouched over, hands shoved in his pockets. He looked like he was scheming. Jacob put it up on Twitter and Instagram. *#OpioidCrisis #Dealer #Minneapolis*

If this new post also got him some attention, he might still try to get the dealer arrested. He had to take advantage of the situation. Missy would be pissed, but he didn't care; he had nothing else to try, so she could just suck a dick. "You're the one who says, 'Do whatever it takes,'" he muttered. "'Shoot for the moon.' Your words, Missy. Not mine."

Missy had been working at 44th Parallel Digital, an online marketing firm, for a little less than a year. It was her fourth agency in five years. Her strategy was to self-promote, hopping around, going after opportunities wherever they arose. It was working well. She was now an executive project manager. More responsibility, more pay, more client face time. She was loving it. And with this latest upgrade, she got to attend big client events, such as today's get-together at Target Field. The entire party deck, high up in left field, had been reserved for employees, friends (meaning clients or prospective clients), and family to see the Twins play the Tigers.

Jacob was desperately wishing for a torrential downpour and a game cancellation, but luck wasn't on his side. It was a beautiful, sunny Saturday—upper eighties and zero humidity. He and Missy parked in 44th's employee lot six blocks from the stadium and made their way over.

Missy, clutching her Louis Vuitton tote, turned to him and said, "You'll look people in the eye and smile, right?"

He took a breath to pause before answering, because of course he knew that—who didn't?—and if he didn't take a moment, he'd only make some snide remark about forced interactions, faked niceties, and reshaped personalities. He hated these things. He looked people in the eye and smiled at writing seminars or book conventions where the interactions were pleasant and engaging, but these corporate events drove him mad. Missy didn't understand. The artificial atmosphere was reasonable and maybe even a little amusing to her. Missy's voice was already rising to a sickly sweet, chirpy pitch, and the two of them were only just walking up to the stadium's ticket gates. So to pacify her, Jacob let out his breath, widened his eyes to a Nicholas Cage madman level, grinned wide, and stared hard into her face. "It's SO nice to see you!"

She rolled her eyes. "Be normal, please."

His face dropped. This was going to be oodles of fun. *Like last year's holiday party.* He'd been feeling particularly down about his writing that day and mostly stared at his feet the entire time, just following Missy around, thinking through plot points. Missy's coworkers laughed about it afterward. She'd been horrified.

"I'll be normal," he said as they entered the stadium. The elevator to the party deck was off to their right, and in less than a minute, they were upstairs. *Go time.*

The elevator doors opened. Clusters of people, cold drinks and small plates in hand, were everywhere. Country-pop music hooted over their voices and hollow laughter. A bartender, encircled by a thirty-seat bar in the center of the deck, hurried around in his protected bubble pouring drinks. *Good God.* Jacob followed Missy into the madness.

As she progressed across the deck toward a group

that included her boss, she gave several excited greetings to coworkers. Jacob tried to put on a happy face as they sidled their way into the cluster, but he was struggling.

Missy's boss, a Hugh Jackman look-alike named Kyle, put an arm around her shoulders, pulled her close, and introduced her to a frumpy specimen standing across from him. "Lester, want you to meet one of our best project managers, Missy Chan." The music and the crowd were so loud he had to shout to be heard.

Missy smiled wide and shook Lester's hand. "Hi. Nice to meet you. I really like your shirt."

Lester tugged the collar and grinned. "Well, thanks. Wife bought it."

Jacob took a half step toward Lester, thinking he'd be introduced as well, but he was ignored.

"Should let her dress you every day," Kyle hollered.

Jacob stepped back as the group laughed.

Kyle continued. "Missy's one of the team members I'm sending to that conference next month I told you about. The Social Media Strategies Summit. She's on a panel."

"Is that right?" Lester gave a slight tilt of his head toward Missy. "Where is it? Someplace you can enjoy the sights? New York? Chicago?"

"Oh, she won't have time to enjoy any sights. She'll be working the whole time," Kyle joked.

Missy laughed. "That's true."

The others in the group—there were seven of them—gave a chuckle as well. Jacob managed a milquetoast grin.

"I honestly can't quite remember what city, but I want to say San Francisco," Missy told Lester.

"Ah, great city. That'll be fun." He took a sip of his drink and scanned the crowd.

Jacob tried to amuse himself by guessing what Lester's clear drink might be. *Water? Vodka? Gin?* Lester looked like a guy who'd never turn down an alcoholic drink, especially if the tab was going to someone else, which it was today, so it had to be either vodka or gin. The man's floppy driving cap gave him a British vibe, so Jacob settled on gin. Looking to confirm such astute observational skills, Jacob lifted his hand to get the man's attention, but again, he was ignored as Missy stepped in.

"Who've you been working with at 44th?" she asked with a wide smile, regaining Lester's full attention.

Jacob lowered his hand, hooking his thumb into his pants pocket.

"Well, Kyle and I've known each other for about five years." He tipped his glass at Kyle. "But not really working with anyone just yet. Still trying to think about my digital strategy."

"Sure. My specialty is social media, so if you want to bounce anything off me, feel free to call." She pulled out her business card and handed it to Lester.

Lester accepted the card, but he said, "I've been chatting with Alicia about some of that actually, but I'll keep you in mind."

"Okay, great. Alicia's coming to the conference with me," Missy said. "I showed her a bunch of panels she should attend."

"She just got added to speak on the panel you're on," Kyle told Missy.

Missy's happy demeanor skipped a beat. Jacob saw it, although he doubted the others picked up on the twitchy blink and momentary droop of the smile. He knew she didn't want to be sharing her panel, but she said, "That's great. This'll be her first panel, won't it?"

"Yup," Kyle said. "You two will hit it out of the park. No pun intended."

The group gave a hearty laugh, but Jacob couldn't muster it. He looked down at his feet.

Missy gently elbowed Jacob. "Smile," she whispered.

"Ha." Jacob faked a grin and tried to think of something to say before someone could interrupt him again. He blurted, "So did you know a pun is also called a paronomasia?"

The group blinked as one.

"Didn't know that," Kyle said. "Hey. We got plenty of food and drinks." He motioned to the bar and a buffet table near the elevator. "Help yourself."

Jacob looked at Missy, who said, "Go check it out."

"Yeah, sure. Hope the food's not *a-foul*." Jacob waited for the group's laughter, but they just stared.

Missy cleared her throat. "How'd Alicia get on the panel, Kyle? Someone drop off?"

"Yeah, she was an alternate."

"Didn't know that."

Jacob slunk away from the circle and made a beeline to the bar where there was an open stool near the bartender. "Jack and Diet Pepsi, please." He pulled at his collar, venting.

The bartender didn't look up from the drinks he was pouring. He just gave a quick, "Yep, be right with you." He finished the pours and carried the dripping glasses to the other end of the bar, swiftly sliding them over the counter to a waiting couple. He then bent down and grabbed two Coronas from a case, popped the tops, and handed them to a blond woman in a low-cut T-shirt. The hem of the woman's neckline rested atop her cleavage at an odd angle, and Jacob knew she'd taped it in place. *With 3M's tape.* He'd recently worked on a project to improve the tape's adhesive performance in warm weather. The marketing department plastered images not too dissimilar to that of the woman across the bar, just with a more carefully placed hem, on all their advertisements. *Cover up only what you want to cover up.* Jacob's boss later reported that the tape was outselling the previous version by a quarter of a percent, which was incredible growth for something so mundane as tape. *Thanks to you, woman with the Coronas.*

Jacob let out a sigh. *Such a pathetic contribution to the world.* He couldn't wait for the day when his book was published. Then he'd have done something he could be proud of.

He turned from the woman. On the other side of the counter was a row of glasses filled with cocktail garnishes: orange wedges, lemon slices, lime twists, and cherries whole. Jacob watched a fly crawl around the rims, lapping up the juices. *Don't let Missy order anything with a garnish.*

A small sign next to the garnishes warned that the bar was cash only. Jacob dug into his pocket, thinking it might have been a good thing the bartender had seemingly forgotten about him. His fingers graced the edges of a couple of bills, but when he pulled them out, they were the two twenties he couldn't spend. They were his good luck charms, the last gift his grandpa had given him before passing away the year prior. It'd been a birthday followed by an un-birthday. He was totally misusing Lewis Carroll's notion of an un-birthday, which was defined as any day not your birthday, but he thought one's death much better suited the term.

He shoved the bills back into his pocket. Missy likely had cash, but he didn't want to bother getting up. He had his seat. He didn't have to talk to anyone. He was content. He stared at the TV hanging over the bar, watching the start of the game. Inevitably his mind wandered, as it was apt to do, and he found himself thinking about the drug dealer in the park, and then a website he'd bookmarked of a recent DEA drug assessment report. He pulled out his phone, went to the site, and downloaded the two-hundred page report, passing the time reading through the meaty document.

• • •

The baseball game was nearly over when Missy stepped beside Jacob and said, "We can go whenever you want."

Jacob was nearly at the end of the DEA's report, but instead of taking a moment to finish, he hopped off the barstool. "All right, let's go." He glanced out at the stadium, the bright-green field, the cheering crowd, and took a panoramic photo. "One sec," he said as he posted the photo of the 39,000 people to Twitter with the caption: "This many people died in the US last year from an opioid overdose." *#OpioidCrisis*

He showed Missy, who shrugged, then grabbed her hand and navigated them through the crowd and out the stadium. When they were alone on the street, Missy whined, "I can't believe Alicia is on my panel."

"That sneaky bitch," Jacob huffed. He meant it as a joke, but Missy was pissed.

"Yeah. Green-tea bitch. No one at 44th even trusts her."

"No one?"

"Anyone who's worked with her knows she can't be trusted," Missy said.

"Was she there today?"

"Yeah, I saw her once."

"Say hi?"

"No, I stayed by Kyle and those guys the whole time. Lester's going to be a big client. I'm sure of it. Who'd you end up talking to?"

"Not sure. Just random people," Jacob lied. He hadn't looked up from his phone for more than a few casual glances.

"It's good you're talking and getting to know people at my work."

"Yep," Jacob said, wondering why it mattered when she switched firms faster than he got haircuts. "But anyway," he mused as they reached their car and climbed in.

Missy quietly buckled her seatbelt, deep in thought.

After the stadium, the silence was bliss, and Jacob didn't say another word as he drove from the lot. In a few minutes, they were passing Gold Medal Park. Standing alone in a cluster of trees was Dwight.

A teener, Jacob had learned, was a sixteenth of an ounce of cocaine, or about three and a half grams. Just a tiny little pile of powder. And if that was all Dwight had been carrying the other day, Jacob figured it was a good thing he hadn't called the cops. There was nothing to brag about for busting a dealer with a teener in his pocket. If he was going to boast about his vigilante efforts, he needed to catch Dwight with ten times that, at least. And he had an idea of how to do just that. But first he needed more content. He needed more photos, and maybe even a short video of the dealer in action. He really wanted to establish that he, Jacob White, was indeed tracking the dealer, and that he, Jacob White, was, without a doubt, responsible for the dealer's arrest. No one should be able to refute his involvement or say he'd just been in the right place at the right time.

Jacob turned into the garage. "I'm sure Quincy has to go out," he said as he stopped in their space.

"Probably. Can you take him out? Please?"

Jacob nodded. "Sure." When he and Missy were upstairs, the apartment door barely opened, he called out, "Go to the park?" The dog came running, and Jacob clipped the leash to his collar and made a 180.

He'd lied to the dog. He wasn't taking Quincy to the park. They stood on the side of the apartment, only peeking at the park across Second Street at the park. Quincy pulled on his leash, but Jacob held him tight. "Use the bushes here," he said, guiding the dog into the decorative shrubs running the length of the building. Quincy sniffed and sniffed, eventually locating a suitable splash pad to do his business while Jacob continued to eye the dealer loitering among the trees across the street.

Dwight was a compact, broad-shouldered man who

looked a bit like a meatball. A tough, retarded meatball. The dealer picked his nose and flicked away the treasure. Jacob giggled, sorry he hadn't been recording. He took out his phone, ready for the next opportunity.

The dealer glanced around then left the shelter of the trees, heading for Second Street. There was a car coming down the street; Jacob started to record. It seemed Dwight was going to meet the driver, but the two didn't so much as glance at each other. Dwight stood in the bike lane until the car had passed then continued on, angling toward Tenth Avenue where Jacob was hiding.

"Quincy, let's go." Jacob hurried the dog back inside. A thin rectangular window beside the door provided an inconspicuous bay from which to watch the dealer pass. As Dwight went up the street, Jacob pressed his face against the glass, straining to keep his eyes on him.

He had to follow him. He had to know where he was going. Even if it was just to circle the block, he had to know. Because no matter what it turned out to be, it was still content for his social media accounts. And maybe Dwight was going to his car, or maybe he lived nearby. That would be *very* interesting. Jacob had to find out. *But Quincy.* There was no time to take the dog upstairs. He had to leave him. "Fuck it," he mumbled and tied Quincy's leash to a fire extinguisher mounted on the wall. Missy would kill him for this, but he had no choice. "Just stay, Quincy. Stay."

The dog sat, and Jacob pulled the door slightly ajar. Dwight was just down the block.

"Stay Quincy," Jacob told the dog once more before creeping outside. He leaned against the brick building and pretended to scroll through his phone while he glanced sideways at Dwight. The dealer crossed Tenth and rounded the corner, disappearing down Washington Avenue.

Jacob bounced from the wall and bolted after him. He hadn't run at a full sprint in years, not even at the FBI Academy had he pushed himself like this, and his muscles didn't know what the hell he was doing to them. But once he reached Washington and saw Dwight was just down the block, he slowed, matching Dwight's saunter from a safe distance.

At the next intersection, Dwight crossed Washington and proceeded up Chicago Avenue. Jacob couldn't reach the corner before the light changed, and because Washington, a six-lane street, was much too busy to scamper across against the light, he could only stand there muttering, "Come on, come on, come on."

Dwight was a full block ahead of him now. He was approaching the light rail station. Jacob finally got the walk signal and broke into a sprint again as Dwight stepped onto the platform.

A train was coming. Jacob pushed his little-used muscles into overdrive. Huffing, he reached the station as the Blue Line train slowed to a stop.

There were no turnstiles or gates at Minneapolis' rail stations, only ticket kiosks, and Jacob hurried right by, scanning the platform, a strong scent of urine (but no Pledge) wafting from a nearby empty rain shelter. The train's doors opened. Amid the crowd, Dwight's dinner-plate sized head appeared then disappeared into the train. Jacob jumped through the doors closest to him; no ticket, no problem.

A sea of Navy blue, scarlet red, white, and Kasota gold, the colors of the Twins, surrounded him. The baseball game had officially ended, he realized, and everyone was heading home. He tried to locate Dwight at the other end of the car, but there were too many people. He had to get closer. With the train pulling from the station, Jacob wiggled and squeezed his way through the bodies, inching toward the back.

He smelled the dealer before he saw him. The weed and Pledge combination was unmistakable, even amid the complicated, aromatic brew of the baseball crowd. Leaning against a plastic partition, one hand grasping the overhead rail, Dwight stood, staring at the back of a man wearing a Mauer jersey. Jacob stepped aside until only Dwight's white Jordans were visible.

His phone vibrated, and he lifted the phone to his ear, careful not to elbow the man beside him. "Hello?" he answered, not looking away from Dwight's shoes.

"Where are you?" Missy yelled.

The train was screeching around a curve, and a family was laughing uproariously beside him. "What's that?"

"Security brought Quincy upstairs just now."

He heard that bit. "Oh, shit. I forgot."

"Where are you?"

"I'll be right back."

"What?"

"I'm on the light rail. I'll be right back."

"Why'd you leave Quincy?" she demanded.

"I love you too," he said, and hung up.

The train stopped at Cedar Riverside Station; Dwight's shoes remained where they were. Jacob kept still. His phone vibrated again. Missy. He let it go to voicemail. He'd deal with the Quincy shitstorm later. He was on a mission, full-on Bourne mode, cue Moby's "Extreme Ways." The train moved on down the line, arriving at Franklin Avenue, and the Jordans went out the door.

"Excuse me, excuse me," Jacob said as he battled through the crowd, finally popping out onto the platform with a stumble. To his left, Dwight was approaching. "Shit." Jacob turned and began walking. The dealer was eight steps behind him. Jacob was certain he'd been spotted. This was trouble. His heart raced; he wanted to run. He sidestepped in front of an elderly man, then a bulbous woman and hid behind her girth. *A good spy uses whatever tools happen to be at his disposal.*

A northbound train approached on the opposite

track. *Abort!* Jacob skipped over, ready to jump on and escape. From the corner of his eye, he watched as Dwight continued on. The northbound train stopped, and the doors opened. Jacob half-stepped inside. He glanced back at Dwight. The dealer seemed oblivious to his presence. *He really didn't see me?* Jacob gazed around the empty car, reconsidering his escape. *Dwight didn't see me, did he?* The warning lights on the door flashed. He hadn't even recorded a single second of post-worthy video. Had he really come this far for nothing? *Re-engage!* Jacob hopped back out onto the platform.

Dwight was strolling on ahead, hands in his pockets, head down. Jacob resumed the chase, Jason Bourne once more. The camera, he imagined, was just over his shoulder, following in a jerky, chaotic manner to create a sense of raw, harsh suspense.

He brought his phone to eye level, pretending to text, but the phone's camera was snapping dozens of photos. At the end of the platform, there was a great cluster of bushes doing a poor job forming a barrier between the station and the parallel street. A well-worn dirt path ran from the platform's end, through a gaping hole in the center of the bushes, and out the other side. Dwight turned down this path, passed through the porous shrubbery, and continued on his way.

Jacob held back for a moment, then cut through the leafy mass himself. He didn't know this street, a crumbling, pothole-filled avenue lined with decaying single-story warehouses. Franklin, the perpendicular cross street down a block, he'd driven on. And the heavily trafficked Hiawatha Avenue somewhere nearby, its steady hum of vehicles easily discernible, was a familiar face, but this street he'd never even noticed before.

It was still and quiet. Except for Dwight. He was moving on through, so Jacob set aside his qualms and went after him, snapping photo after photo. He'd put some filters on the pictures later to really highlight the moody, dramatic nature of the situation. People would love it.

Near the end of the block, a homeless couple was huddled together near a chain link fence, lighting each other's cigarettes. Behind them, several military-style tents stood, each as long as a metro train car. Jacob now knew where he was. This was where the city had put the homeless camp. He'd heard about it—Minneapolis's hastily erected answer to a flood of homeless people who had pitched tents and flimsy huts along Hiawatha Avenue, turning the roadside into a colorful patchwork of plastic in April. Curly Burly had even ranted to him about it: "Enforce the law! Tear the damn tents apart! Send the squatters scattering!" The city council decided to be more empathetic; the industrial tents were erected and the homeless people invited in. And it worked, to a point, but many of those in the group were struggling with addiction problems, and they wouldn't move unless they were assured the housing was provided without the threat of prosecution. The city agreed not to search personal belongings, and Curly Burly was sent into a tizzy. Alternatively, Jacob was sure it pleased Dwight. The dealer was heading straight for the homeless couple.

A dented Impala was parked across the street from them, and Jacob snuck behind it. He held his phone aloft and continued taking pictures. The homeless couple, layered in clothes (wind jackets over stained sweaters over torn shirts), became tense and hopeful and desperate and afraid when Dwight came over. The man spoke a few words to Dwight as the dealer drew nearer and nearer until they were almost nose to nose. The bundled man tried to step back, but he bumped against a shopping cart stacked with rolled blankets and stuffed plastic bags ready to burst.

Dwight shook his head as the man continued to talk (*Plead his case?*). With a move so quick that Jacob was sure his camera only caught it as a blur, Dwight spun the man around in a flutter of clothes, and pulled his elbow up behind his back. The homeless man cried out, and the woman let out a yip.

Jacob tapped and tapped his phone, capturing the scene. To his surprise, and mild delight, the man made a countermove, dropping to his knees, letting his arm twist at an odd angle in Dwight's hands, then giving a sudden shout and rolling away in the dirt. He quickly stood, facing Dwight with his knees slightly bent and muscle-less legs tensed, ready to sprint away.

But Dwight only jammed his hands in his pockets and shrugged. He said something, and the man eased up. Dwight gave the man a pat on the shoulder. *Friends again?*

The man nodded, went to his shopping cart, and dug through his belongings, eventually finding a handful of dollar bills. He gave the money to Dwight. In return, Dwight pulled a closed fist from his pocket and shook the man's hand. A small bit of plastic transferred between them. *There's that teener.* Dwight left the couple and walked through the camp's gate, disappearing inside the nearest of the tents.

Jacob stayed where he was, unwilling to continue the pursuit. He set his butt on the curb, leaned back, and took a breath. His heart was racing. He scrolled through his photos, grinning. He had some really good shit.

He had no pictures of the camp itself, though, and that wouldn't do, so he pulled himself up the side of the Impala and peeked over the trunk. With several taps on the phone, he had what he needed.

"Hey," the homeless man yelled. "Hey! You spying on us?"

Jacob dropped out of sight and laid on his side, gazing under the car. Across the street, faded sneakers and frayed sweatpants stepped from the curb and started toward him.

"Hey! Get out here," the man shouted. The couple shuffled their feet, kicking up pebbles that pinged against the Impala's hubcaps.

Jacob bounced to his feet, thinking he could feign innocence. "Hey. What's up?" He gave a quick wave.

The couple paused at his sudden emergence, but their fragrance of cigarettes, vinegar, and urine continued ahead of them to greet the spy.

Jacob rubbed his nose, then drew his hand through his hair. "How's it going?" He smiled.

The man grinned but not in a display of friendship. The stringy walrus whiskers hanging over his lips fluttered. The woman beside him had no teeth. She mashed her gums, bulging her lips with each harmless bite.

"What's up?" Jacob asked, continuing to grin stupidly. "Something wrong?"

"Fucking right something's fucking wrong," the woman blasted. She waved in annoyance at an oily strand of hair dangling between her eyes, but in doing so, she dragged the ashy end of her cigarette across her forehead, streaking it like she'd just been to Palm Sunday mass.

Jacob smirked. Emily's warning of the cartel was missing its mark. *Worse than ISIS...* Jacob pointed at his forehead. "You got a little something..."

The woman didn't understand. She pursed her lips and hissed, "You wanna get your ass beat?"

Jacob laughed nervously. "No." She wasn't ISIS, but a threat was still a threat.

"So what the fuck you doing here? Keeping tabs on us?" the man growled.

Jacob searched his pockets for some cash. *That'll calm them down.* He only had his two twenties and three quarters. *The quarters will have to do.* He flicked the coins at the woman. "Here."

She flailed her arms as the coins pelted her. "Ack!"

"You shithead," the man shouted. "Come here!" He leaped at Jacob, the hazy, yellowish whites of his eyes leading the charge.

"Rape!" Jacob cried. He had read once that nobody responds to a woman's calls for help. Instead she should yell, "Rape!" Jacob slipped around the man's scabby hands. "Rape!"

The man pulled back. "What the fuck?"

"He's raping me!" Jacob turned and sprinted down the street, zigzagging around the potholes, his arms pumping wildly at his sides, his calves burning.

"Get back, you little shit!" the woman yelled.

Jacob dove into the shrubs and rushed the platform. The arrival screen over the tracks said the northbound train to downtown wasn't due for another five minutes. *Shit.* He didn't have five minutes. The couple would catch him and do unspeakable things to him.

The southbound train was pulling up, though. With no hesitation, he hopped on. He could switch trains down the line. Right now he just needed to escape.

The crowd from the baseball game had thinned some, and he stepped to the far side of the car and peered out the window, looking for the couple. Blocking most of his view was a trackside billboard. The text read, "Addiction problem? We're here to help. No judgment." A number to call was listed at the bottom. Jacob took a picture. *#DrugTroubles*

The doors closed, and the train crept from the station, passing the shrubs at the end of the platform. The homeless couple was nowhere in sight. Jacob sighed and took a seat to inspect his photos.

IV.

Vicente was subjected to the tunnel's threatening groans for ten long minutes. But in the end, there was no second collapse, and he eventually pulled himself free with the help of a thickening layer of sweat and blood across his arms. When he finally emerged, ass backward, and climbed up into the stash house, he splashed himself with cold water until the bloody sludge was gone and his fingers were numb.

Twenty-four hours had since passed, and he was now back at the tunnel's entrance, still needing to get the cocaine. He'd told El Avispón what had happened, and the cartel boss had given him two choices: recover the cocaine or cover the $200,000 loss. Vicente could not cover that much cash, so here he was, standing in the empty back room of the stash house again. Beside him, the six-foot-eight Benedicto "Bravo" Ravoi was looking down at the chipped-out circle in the concrete floor where they'd just sent a petite migrant woman who'd been willing to fetch the cocaine for ninety pesos.

With spindly fingers, Bravo gave his temple a scratch. "Think she'll find it?"

"No. It'll collapse again." Vicente had given the woman a gardener's spade and a warning: "Dig slow."

"What's the point then?"

"Have to try," Vicente said. He knelt next to the hole. It was dead silent. "Who was this going to again? Who ordered it?"

"The mechanic in Imperial Beach."

"Phil?" Vicente gave his arms a careful rub. Both were stitched up and bandaged. His wrist was also heavily wrapped to prevent further strain.

"Phil," Bravo confirmed.

Vicente waved his hand over the tunnel, disturbing the still air. "Wish we hadn't sent him anything in the first place."

"He's got a serious buyer," Bravo said. "Could be big money."

"Phil's a mechanic, not a distributor. Should've just worked with the buyer directly. You see he's got an Instagram account? Posts all the time. The three C's: cars, cash, and—"

"Cunts?" Bravo smirked.

"No. Cats. He has a bunch of cats." Vicente continued, "He's got a few thousand followers. You know he's going to post something stupid one of these days. Get himself arrested."

Bravo grunted.

Vicente stood and rested against the wall.

"How far you think she's gotten?" Bravo asked.

"No idea. She'll be faster than I was, but it's a long way."

"You think we can clear it out? Keep using it?"

"I'm not using this anymore. It sucks. It's too small."

"Shit's piling up," Bravo reminded him. "We need it."

"It's too small," he repeated. "I'll have a tunnel over in Nueva Tijuana done. Soil's better there. Denser. More compact. We can make it bigger. Big enough for your huge ass."

"Major project," Bravo muttered.

"Migrants," Vicente said. "Dig like goddamn rabbits."

"They're tired these days. Coming up from Guatemala, Honduras, El Salvador."

"They're still desperate."

"How many were there this morning?" Bravo asked.

"Three, four hundred. Lot of women and kids."

"Sex traffickers."

"Fucking Americans," Vicente mumbled.

"Could use the tunnel to start moving them."

Vicente shook his head.

"It's decent cash. How much cocaine we lose in the last month?"

"Not happening," Vicente insisted.

"That was Castor who hit our safe house up there," Bravo warned.

"I know." Castor was a wild card. No one knew who he was. Maybe an ex-cop. Maybe a vigilante. Maybe just a psycho. But nonetheless, Castor liked hitting safe houses. He killed everyone inside, stole the cash, and dumped the drugs. When Castor hit their safe house the previous month, El Avispón swore revenge and posted a half million dollar bounty on his head, but so far, Castor was still running loose. *A different problem for a different discussion*, Vicente thought. "That girl must be there by now," he grumbled, peeking into the tunnel.

"You got shit to do?" Bravo asked. "Go. I'll watch."

Vicente did have shit to do. A lot of shit. The cartel's product was in high demand, higher than ever, and if the American FDA kept handing the cartel gifts like they did with their crackdown on painkillers—limiting the availability of OxyContin, codeine, and hydrocodone without actually dampening the demand—the cartel's business would only grow. It was a modern-day gold rush, and he wasn't going to miss the opportunity. If he kept producing, despite the recent setbacks, he'd rise up the ranks and make his mark. He left Bravo to watch the tunnel until the faint, low rumble of the inevitable collapse was heard.

V.

A week passed, and Jacob recovered from having the shit scared out of him at the homeless camp. The content he'd captured for social media from that little adventure had been worth it, though. He had fifty new Twitter followers for his trouble. He'd also gotten fined by the Metro Transit Police for not paying the fare. They'd been checking at the Lake Street Station. They scanned his driver's license, logging the infraction, and sent him on his way. The two-hundred-dollar ticket arrived in the mail four business days later and was now hidden under a notepad on his writing desk. Missy was still furious he'd run off and left Quincy tied to a fire extinguisher, so he certainly wasn't going to let her see the ticket.

On the screen of his laptop, an email from an agent popped up. A glimmer of excitement rose in his chest. He'd forgotten he'd queried this agent. It was like discovering an overlooked gift under the Christmas tree. The gift turned out to be a sweater vest from Grandma. The agent was rejecting his novel.

When he first started sending sample chapters to agents, Missy told him to print out the rejections and tape them to the wall around his desk. "For motivation," she said. He didn't do it. He couldn't handle staring at that every day. He was already depressed with reading the rejections once; he didn't need to cover the entire wall with them.

It really was shocking, though; there were just so many of them. There was no explanation for it. His story was a clever modernization of his favorite novel, Stephen King's *The Shining*. It perfectly subverted expectations for what horror could be. And it examined universal, relatable themes. It even commented on many topical social justice issues. And the twist at the end came out of left field. No reader would predict the entire story had been from a dog's perspective. So what was wrong with these agents? Why didn't they like *The Shedding*? One agent even called the story fraught with racist overtones. Dogs, cats, and squirrels were racist? Unbelievable. But even if that were true (which it wasn't), that could still be a good thing. If it got people talking about the issues, then great. Let it come across as racist.

Jacob groaned and pushed away from the desk. He couldn't let the rejections get him down. *It could be worse.* He'd actually thought about quitting his job after finishing the novel. He'd been *that* confident in its success; he'd been all ready to embark on his new career. That would've been an inexcusable disaster.

But then again, if he had quit 3M, it would've afforded him time to properly focus on finding an agent and getting his book published. By keeping his day job, he wasn't truly committing to the dream. He was half-assing it, and all the rejections were the proof.

Jacob stared out the balcony door. It was one of those Minneapolis summer days that was absolutely flooded in sunshine, greenery, and life. It drew everyone outside. At least everyone who had a pulse and a relatively healthy emotional state. He only had one of those, but then he caught sight of someone very interesting in the park, and he jumped up from his chair and went down the hall.

"Stay here," he told Quincy lying near the door. "Missy's still not letting me take you out. Sorry, buddy. Be right back."

Jacob cruised through the park, focused on his target, imagining himself again as Jason Bourne, efficient and resolute. He hadn't seen the dealer since he'd disappeared into the homeless camp. He was now sitting on a bench, forearms on knees, staring at the ground between his feet. Without hesitation, Jacob took a seat beside him. *Ah, weed and Pledge.*

Dwight slowly cocked his head sideways. "Cupcake, you fucking left me out to dry last week."

"Couldn't find my cash, Cupcake."

Dwight scowled. "Don't call me that."

"Yeah, yeah, sure. Okay." Jacob gave a goofy grin.

"So what do you need now?"

"A lot. How much can I get?"

"Don't know. You got cash this time?" Dwight looked away.

"I think I want a pound."

Dwight lifted an arm and rested his hand on his thigh to get a better view of Jacob. "A pound?"

"Big party." His eyes settled on Dwight's biceps. The man could knock him out with one punch if he caught him square. But like Jason Bourne, maybe he had unbelievable combat skills that a bout of amnesia had made him forget. Maybe he was an expert in Jeet Kune Do. Jacob didn't want to test that. *Focus.*

"Listen," Dwight said. "I'm your guy for this shit. You know that, right?"

"Yeah, I know." Jacob slapped him on the back, trying to play the part of Mitch, the friendly buyer.

"You really need a pound?"

"Massive party. Huge." Jacob grinned.

Dwight nodded. "I get that, but really? That much? You get caught with that and you're in prison for fucking life, Cupcake."

"Well, yeah, exactly."

Dwight eyed him suspiciously then laughed. "I can't tell if you're fucking with me or not, but I'm not getting you a pound of cocaine, Cupcake."

Jacob's plan was slipping away. "I'm not joking. Lots of people at the party. You think I can't afford it?"

"I think you can't imagine how much a pound really is. You serving up an entire strip club? I've never sold a pound to any motherfucker in my life."

"How much *you* think I need then? Going to be seven or eight people."

"Fucking Christ, Cupcake. It's like you've never done coke before."

That's true.

"Why you want a pound for seven motherfuckers?"

"Eight," Jacob corrected him.

"Eighty! Doesn't matter. You trying to kill them?" Dwight stood from the bench and paced, looking ready to walk off.

"Some for later," Jacob quickly suggested.

Dwight shook his head. "No, no. You know coke goes bad, right? No way you'll get through a pound, even in a year. Not your skinny ass."

"You ever seen *Scarface*?" Jacob shaped his hands around an imaginary pile of cocaine.

Dwight burst out laughing. "I'll get you ten teeners. And when it's 'later,' you come back to me for more. I'm not getting you a motherfucking pound. Shit."

Ten teeners sounded acceptable. "Fine."

"When's this party?"

"Next weekend."

Dwight extended his fist for a bump, and Jacob

leaned out with his. "I'll take care of things," Dwight promised. "Be a couple days."

"How much is it?"

"Price of your teener times ten, Einstein."

Well, shit. He had no idea what that was, but he supposed it didn't matter. He wasn't actually buying anything. "Where you getting it? Where's it coming from? The cartel?"

"The cartel?" Dwight laughed. "This is Minnesota, not Mexico."

"It could come from there, couldn't it?" That was what Emily had told him.

"You don't need to know. I got my people, and you'll have it in a few days."

Jacob nodded, assuming Dwight's nondisclosure was an admittance of having no cartel connection. *See Emily? It's safe.* "So how long you been doing this?" he asked, fishing for whatever info he could get for social media before the dealer was hauled away to prison.

Dwight studied the park around them. "Been selling to you for a couple years now, haven't I?"

Jacob had no clue. "When you'd first start, though?"

"Ten years ago maybe. Busting my ass a long-ass time."

"You were young."

"Nine or ten, yeah."

"You always sell teeners?"

Dwight brushed the question aside. "How much you want today?"

"I'm good. Nothing."

"Mitch." Dwight frowned. "You're going to be like that?" He sat down next to Jacob. "Come on. I gotta eat. What do you need?"

Jacob smiled sheepishly. "No, really. I'm okay."

"Cupcake." Dwight sat up straight, puffing his chest, and stared at Jacob. "I came all the way down here, 'cause I knew you'd be in need."

Jacob shook his head meekly. "Yeah, just not today." He peered up at the apartment buildings surrounding the park. The balconies were empty. The windows dark. "Just got things to do."

"Oh, now you're making me angry." Dwight rose from the bench and clapped his hands in front of Jacob's face to get his full attention. "Okay. How about this? You buy nothing today, and you get nothing tomorrow. How about that? Fuck your party."

Jacob considered the ultimatum, buying time by swallowing hard then gently coughing. "Um."

Dwight's icy stare persisted.

"You really want me to get something?" Jacob asked.

"I *need* you to get something."

"Okay." Jacob dug into his jeans and pulled out the contents of his pockets: keys on an Avengers keychain, his cellphone, a Visa credit card, and...

Dwight grabbed the two twenties.

"No, that's not—"

"That's not what?" Dwight pressed Jacob, daring him to say more. "Not what?"

"Not..." But Jacob wouldn't finish the sentence. Dwight was ready to snap. He kept his mouth shut, biting his tongue, and watched the last gift his grandpa had given him disappear into Dwight's pocket.

The dealer looked briefly around the park. Seeing no eavesdroppers or police, he took a cellophane-wrapped ball from his other pocket and shoved it into Jacob's palm.

Jacob wrapped his fingers around the tiny bundle. *Oh, shit.* And just like that, his grandpa had bought him a teener of cocaine. *Happy birthday, motherfucker. Get wrecked.* But now he knew how much a teener cost, and by extension, how much ten of them would cost. Not that he intended to actually make the purchase, but it was good to know. He'd post it on Twitter. *#TeenerForForty*

"Get out of here," Dwight instructed.

Jacob did as he was told, rising from the bench and heading toward his apartment. "Oh," he muttered, turning back. "What about the teeners? When *exactly* will you have those?"

Dwight looked at him like he'd lost his mind. He hurried over, whispering harshly, "Are you fucking stupid? Did you really just fucking call that out?"

"What?"

"It's fucking amazing you haven't been arrested yet. When you do, you don't know me." Dwight pointed a finger straight into Jacob's face. "You don't know me, right?"

"Of course. Sure."

"I swear. If you ever rat me out, I'll fucking kill you." Dwight was dead serious.

"What about the stuff, though?" Jacob whispered.

Dwight shook his head, looked down at his feet, then back at Jacob. "In a couple days. I'll be around. Just be watching." With another shake his head, Dwight hurried out of the park.

"Couple days," Jacob repeated to himself. *Fine.* He'd be watching. For now, though, he needed out of the park too. He had a teener in his pocket.

With each step toward his apartment, the ball of coke pressed against his leg, calling for his attention. The noxious little gremlin wanted to be let loose, and he shook with panic. He nearly tripped twice just crossing Second Street. What the hell was he doing? He wasn't Jason Bourne. He was Mr. Bean. He cursed his grandpa for his mistimed heart attack. Had he just died before, rather than after, his birthday, there wouldn't have been a gift. No gift, no twenties, no cocaine.

Jacob rushed through the lobby, head down, certain the front desk attendant would know what was happening if their eyes met. Up in his apartment, Jacob considered flushing the teener down the toilet as he passed by, but he continued to the living room, where he pulled the cellophane ball from his pocket and cradled the cocaine in his hands, studying the white powder. Maybe he could hold on to it. Maybe he could find a use for it. Take some photos of it or something. *Can you post drugs on social media? What do the terms of service say? Who the fuck knows?* Whatever the case, the shit was expensive. Cost him the last gift his grandpa had given him. He might as well make use of it somehow.

He shifted to his writing desk and pulled his laptop close, typing "Does cocaine expire?" into Google. After some browsing, the consensus seemed to be that cocaine could last for years, if not decades, so long as it was sealed tight and kept dry. *Dwight's a liar.*

Jacob grabbed the ball and was giving it a solid twist when the apartment door opened. Missy's sneakers squeaked, then there was the snapping release of the pug's leash.

"You're free," Missy announced.

Jacob frantically searched for a place to hide the cocaine as Quincy's toenails clicked across the hardwood floor, barreling down the hallway to find him. There was a gap in the coffee table between a leg and the tabletop. He wedged the ball into the space and quickly sat back at his desk.

Quincy rounded the corner, then Missy, wearing her workout/climbing gear. Quincy launched himself up on Jacob's lap.

"So exhausted." Missy flopped onto the couch, glancing at his open laptop. "Writing?"

"Researching." Jacob nonchalantly shifted Quincy off his balls. "Looking to see if cocaine expires."

"You're going to get on some government watch list."

"Already am, I'm sure," Jacob said, eyeing the coffee

table, thinking maybe he should get rid of the cocaine before the Feds came storming in.

"Guess it doesn't matter if you can show them it's for a book."

"But it's not."

"Well, it's to get publicity for a book. Same thing." Her face then lit up. "What if you *did* write a book about this?" She considered the idea. "Yeah. What if you did? All your social media stuff could build up to a book release."

"I'm trying to get my novel published, not write something new."

"Keep working on that. But you can write this too. It could be like one of those Michael Lewis books. Write about the opioid crisis. That would *definitely* get published."

"Definitely? Like *The Shedding* is definitely not getting published?"

"Be honest. That's nichey. It'll get published *someday*, but drugs have mass appeal."

Jacob shrugged.

"And...maybe if you publish this, it'll be easier to get *The Shedding* published. Quick—let's think of a title." Missy leaned toward the desk and grabbed the notepad, exposing the ticket from Metro Transit. She scanned the paper. "Two hundred dollars? Are you kidding me? You didn't pay your fare?"

"Just forgot."

She didn't believe him. "Was this when you left Quincy downstairs? It was, wasn't it?"

He nodded.

She groaned. "You're such a dolt."

"I'll pay it."

"Your money's my money." Missy picked up the ticket. "At least get something out of this. You take a picture?"

"I did."

"Post it?"

"I did."

She smiled. "Good." Grabbing a pen, she said, "Let's think of a title."

Stephen King used cocaine early in his career. Cocaine fueled Robert Louis Stevenson's six-day bender that produced *Dr. Jekyll and Mr. Hyde*. Hunter S. Thompson tried cocaine and anything else he could get his hands on for *Fear and Loathing in Las Vegas*. Jacob's neighbor, Curly Burly, even dabbled in various drugs to get his creative juices flowing. How much of an influence any of this had on their final products was debatable, though. There were plenty of authors who'd done the same thing but were—and would be—forever unknown. Talent was born of time and care, not snorted through a rolled-up dollar bill. But still, Jacob was tempted to see what the teener would do for his productivity, especially now, because he was struggling with how to start this new book on the opioid crisis.

The frustration had been quick to form and reluctant to depart. Unlike *The Shedding*, he couldn't muster the motivation to dive into this story. He didn't have much to say, which was to say, not a lot had happened to him. There was still a long way to go, a lot more to develop, and working on it now seemed inefficient and premature. The thing also felt commercialized, like he was putting together a marketing piece, not crafting a tale with weight or purpose. It was an insult to the medium. At least with social media, his motives and musings weren't desecrating sacred ground. In fact, the whole point of social media was to be one big marketing cluster fuck.

He'd left his desk about an hour ago without having made much progress with the still-untitled book. He had half a mind to abandon it. Missy kept hounding him, though, reminding him to keep at it, pushing him to memorialize what had happened before some of the finer details vanished.

There was no danger of that. The finer details had already been plenty memorialized on social media—either that or they were filed away on his phone, queued up for release. He didn't need to memorialize them on the typed page. What he needed to do was collect more experiences, and he was standing on his balcony, about to do just that.

Jacob lifted his phone and spoke into the camera. "Heading across the park to get the dealer arrested." He swung the camera around so it could look down on Gold Medal Park. In the center of the park near the base of the observational hill, Dwight was on a bench. He'd been there for about five minutes now.

He zoomed in on the dealer, held the camera steady for a moment, then ended the recording. He'd post that once everything was said and done. He hurried back through the apartment, Quincy trotting after him. The dog tried to follow Jacob out, but he nudged him back inside. "Later." Quincy plopped down and scowled as the door closed.

Jacob recorded his walk to the elevator, riding it down, then crossing through the lobby. He'd edit that into a cool, quick transition. Once he posted the big reveal of the dealer being arrested, he expected his follower numbers to explode. He wouldn't even be surprised if they jumped fivefold in the next twenty-four hours. This would be big. And then maybe he could start referencing his robust social media presence in his next round of queries to agents.

He walked over to the lobby's floor-to-ceiling windows that faced the park. Dwight was a good forty-yard dash away. Not that there'd be any running today, but still, Jacob subconsciously stretched his legs before snapping a photo of the dealer. The Jordans were on again, the laces undone and the tongues sticking out. In one of his pockets, there'd be ten teeners. Jacob called the police.

"There's a man selling drugs in Gold Medal Park,"

he told the operator. "Dark blue T-shirt, jeans, an old school Minnesota North Stars hat. White Jordans."

"Is anyone in immediate danger?" the operator asked.

"No, ma'am. He's just sitting on a bench. Southwest side of the park."

"Can you give me his physical description? Height, weight?"

Jacob provided the details, reassured the operator no one was in danger, then promised to call back if anything changed before a squad car could arrive. He hung up and took another photo of Dwight. His heart beat faster. He bounced on his toes, waiting and watching, pressing his face against the glass to look up and down the street for the police. He checked his phone. A minute hadn't even passed. He crossed his arms then uncrossed them to take another photo. He wanted a tighter shot and zoomed in, but the resolution become all grainy.

Dwight surveyed the park, trying to mask his watchfulness with an exaggerated stretch of his arms. The dealer stood. *Shit. Shit. Don't go anywhere.* He shoved his hands into his pockets and tilted back on his heels. Looking, scanning, then moving. He took two wide steps around the bench and headed toward the cluster of trees he seemed to like.

From the lobby, the sightlines were terrible, and to make matters worse, there was a metallic sculpture the size of a cargo van set amid the trees, which Dwight decided to stand right behind, perfectly blocking Jacob's view. *You're fucking kidding me.* Jacob sidestepped along the glass, trying to regain his visual, but there was no good angle. He gave it a moment to see if Dwight would reemerge, but the man remained where he was.

"Fuck." Jacob rushed from the lobby, through the back hall where he'd left Quincy tied to the fire extinguisher, and out the side door. *If the police come now...*

Jacob sprinted to the corner. Dwight was there in the cluster, alone, leaning against the sculpture. Jacob sighed and glanced at his phone. Two minutes had passed.

He peeked around the corner, scanning Second Street. There were cars, but no police cars. *Where are they?* The Hennepin County Jail was just seven blocks east of the park. And there were always squad cars parked outside the building. *Send one over!*

Dwight pushed from the sculpture and sauntered around it, inspecting its abstract lines and sharp angles. He went out of view again. *Damn it. Damn it!*

With no time to waste, Jacob snuck across Tenth Avenue for a better angle. A utility box near the curb offered some cover, and he knelt beside it. He could see Dwight again. As he tried to take another photo, waiting for the camera to focus, the dealer turned in his direction. Jacob didn't notice. His eyes were fixed on his phone. Only when the camera finally focused did he see Dwight was looking straight at him.

Jacob pretended to tie his shoes. He then stood and nodded at Dwight. *Coming, buddy.* Jacob smiled. The dealer waited.

Jacob could've thrown up, the adrenaline coursing through his body creating a thick soup of nauseousness in his belly. He swallowed hard, drew a breath, and forced his legs to move, crossing Second Street into the park. He didn't dare look for the police. Dwight would notice, and somehow he'd know what he was searching for. Jacob also didn't want to see them now anyway. They'd arrest him too. *But wouldn't that make for an interesting twist to the tale?* The title for his new book suddenly came to him: A Vigilante Tale. But there was no time for that string of thought. "Hey, Dwight." Jacob nearly choked on the words. His mouth was numbingly dry. He coughed slightly. "What's up, dude?"

Dwight chuckled. "Not much. How you doing, *dude?*"

Jacob shrugged. "I'm good." He kicked a stick and watched it settle against the sculpture. "So," he said, turning to Dwight, "you got my stuff?"

"I got things settled for you, yeah."

Jacob had no money on him. He slowly reached into his pocket anyway, acting like he was going for the cash.

Dwight grabbed his wrist.

Jacob nearly pissed himself. This meatball drug dealer knew what was going on. His mind raced, looking for some appropriate response. Where was that expert Jeet Kune Do hidden by the Jason Bourne amnesia? *Not there.* So maybe then the homeless man's dead-opossum escape technique?

"I don't have it on me, Cupcake," Dwight hissed.

"You don't?"

Dwight let go of his wrist. "You think I'm carrying that around? Fuck that shit." He laughed. "Keep your money in your pocket."

Jacob's face flushed. Behind Dwight, on the other side of the park on West River Parkway, a squad car was creeping up the road. Jacob couldn't hide his horror.

"Don't fucking worry," Dwight muttered. "1779 Humboldt."

Jacob shifted his attention back to Dwight. "Humboldt? Humboldt Avenue?"

"Pick up your shit there."

"There? That where you live?"

"Tomorrow at three."

Jacob watched the squad car round the corner and proceed along the park's southeast side. He had to get Dwight out of there. "All right, well, fine then." He clapped his hands in feigned satisfaction. "We're good. I'll go there. We done? You want to go?" He took a casual step toward Second, but Dwight didn't follow. "Let's head out," Jacob suggested. He grabbed the edge of Dwight's sleeve and gave it a tug. "Come on."

But Dwight had spotted the squad car. He swiped Jacob's hand away and stood his ground.

The squad car turned onto Second, and sounded the siren.

"Oh, shit," Jacob yelled.

"Calm down," Dwight muttered, eyeing the police as they pulled to the curb.

"We should... Let's..." Jacob stuttered as so many incomplete thoughts rushed through his head. The one that finally settled him was Missy's voice. She was telling him to post, post, post. He liked that and pulled out his phone and started to record. *This could be something.*

The officers stepped from their car and walked toward them. "How's it going, guys?" the closer of the two asked. He looked to be a twenty-year vet. Casual, composed, confident, and slightly overweight, with a mustache from the eighties that Burt Reynolds would've appreciated. He glanced at the phone in Jacob's hand, ignored it, and turned to Dwight, scanning the dealer up and down. His partner, another force veteran, adjusted his aviator sunglasses, then circled the car.

"What you want?" Dwight muttered.

Officer Mustache looked at Jacob. "How you doing, Chief?"

Jacob couldn't tell if the officer knew he'd been the one who had called in the tip. He hoped to God he wouldn't ask. "I'm good. All good." He tried to smile.

"Ah-uh. You mind putting that away?" The officer gestured toward the phone.

"Keep recording," Dwight instructed.

The officer smirked, lifting the mustache. "Okay. You two mind emptying your pockets for us?"

"You got no cause," Dwight shot back. "This is straight-up harassment. Straight-up motherfucking harassment. Keep recording," he told Jacob.

The officers took Dwight's behavior in stride.

Officer Mustache turned to Jacob and asked, "*You* want to empty your pockets?"

Jacob kept the phone held high, but he did as asked with his free hand, carefully turning each pocket inside out, revealing nothing but lint and a set of keys. No cash.

Officer Aviators nodded and turned to Dwight.

"You got no right," Dwight repeated.

"You're in a public park, and we have probable cause," Officer Mustache said.

Officer Aviators agreed. "What if I told you we saw you dealing?"

"No fucking way." Dwight shook his head. "I wasn't doing shit."

"We can, and will, search you if you don't empty your pockets," the officer added.

"Fuck this shit," Dwight hissed.

Jacob turned the camera from the officers to Dwight and back as they stared at each other. Jacob was torn between wanting to diffuse the situation and letting it run its course. It could erupt into something spectacular. But if it did, he wouldn't be the hero he was trying to become. He'd just be a witness. *But still, better than nothing, isn't it?*

Dwight scowled at the officers, then gave in and pulled out everything in his pockets. He tossed the contents at the officers' feet. There were no drugs. "Happy, motherfuckers?" He held out his bare hands in vindication.

The officers scanned the items in the grass. Officer Aviators looked back at Dwight. "Why don't you two move on?"

Jacob nodded and started to go, but Dwight said, "This is a public park. I can be here. *We* can be here." He grabbed Jacob by the arm.

Jacob froze. "It's okay. We can leave."

Officer Aviators smiled. "Go somewhere else, or we'll write you up."

"For...?" Dwight huffed.

"Public nuisance."

"Fuck you guys. What about him? And him? And him?" Dwight pointed around the park at the scattered homeless people. "Public nuisances."

"We'll talk to them next," Officer Aviators promised.

Dwight let go of Jacob's arm and knelt, gathering his belongings. "I'm coming back when you fuckers leave."

"If you do, we'll arrest you," Officer Mustache said.

"Arrest me then." Dwight stormed past the officers. "See if I give a fuck," he shouted as he left the park.

The officers looked at Jacob. "Stay away from him," Officer Aviators advised.

Jacob gave a quick nod, put his phone away, and hurried across Second Street. By the time he reached the far curb, the officers were already back in their squad car, driving off. Dwight was watching from down the block, and as Jacob crossed Tenth Avenue toward his apartment, the dealer came back. Jacob knew he was in trouble. Dwight had put it together. There'd been no cash in his pockets. Things weren't adding up.

Dwight intercepted him just outside the apartment door. "You have anything to do with that?"

"No," Jacob exclaimed. "No. Why?"

"You didn't do something stupid, did you?"

Jacob shook his head.

"Talk to someone you shouldn't have? You sure?" Dwight glared hard into Jacob's eyes.

Jacob vigorously shook his head. "No. Absolutely not."

Dwight gave a quick snort. "You probably did something and don't even fucking know."

"I'd know. Haven't even been out much," Jacob added. "Been binging on Marvel movies all week."

Dwight leaned around Jacob to scan the park. "See? That's why I don't fucking carry ten teeners with me."

"Yeah. That was smart." Jacob cleared his throat. Maybe Dwight hadn't recognized the disconnect between his behavior and the empty pockets, so he asked, "Still on for tomorrow then?" *Please say yes.*

Dwight nodded.

"1779 Humboldt?"

"Yeah. In Kenwood."

"Yep, Kenwood." Jacob knew the neighborhood. He'd grown up in that part of town. His mom still lived there, just a couple blocks from Humboldt, in fact. He'd have to tell her who her neighbor was. That'd knock her self-righteous ego down a notch. "Your place."

"Not my place. A stash house."

Woah. Even better. Jackpot!

"Three o'clock," Dwight reiterated.

Jacob nodded while doing his damndest to remain stone-faced and keep the grin at bay. He had just gone from ratting out a dealer to finding a *stash* house, and in Kenwood of all places. He was *absolutely* going to be a hero. *Holy shit.*

Dwight glanced back at the park once more then headed away toward Washington without another word.

Jacob's grin went wide. This was going to be big. Not only was he going to get the attention he needed to finally get his book published, but this drug book wasn't sounding so bad now either. This was a proper adventure.

What amazing luck. Two books, both in bookstores within a year. *How did things turn around so quickly?*

VI.

As Jacob went back to his building, his grin turned into a scowl. He really should've known better. Of course Dwight wasn't going to bring four hundred dollars' worth of drugs to the park. What made him think such a thing? He was lucky the mistake hadn't turned out worse.

But then again, wasn't that how it usually happened? His screw-ups never led to total disaster. They certainly *seemed* like they were going to, but he always pivoted, adjusted his plan, and avoided the real trouble. Did that make him smart? Clever? People *thought* he was smart. Ever since grade school, he'd been told he was smart. But that hadn't translated into anything of substance. Just a mediocre, middling existence where nothing truly bad happened.

Nor did anything truly good happen either. Still, he had hope. Hope that he abused like the veins of a heroin addict with his constant mistakes. Yet it remained, punctured and torn, but there. It kept his suicidal comments just that, comments. Missy liked to think the inspirational Instagram posts she always showed him were helping, but those only made him gag as if he'd sucked down a spoonful of grocery-store frosting. *That shit is so fake.* He didn't need that. He just needed to keep trying, to keep pushing for something (like his book), and hope would be there urging him on. In a way, it was a self-perpetuating existence.

It was hope that had him pushing the down button at the elevator. Instead of going to his apartment, he went to the garage. He needed to check out 1779 Humboldt before tomorrow. Preparation was key.

He was going to generate so much attention for this. Then it'd just be a short wait until *The Shedding* was published. Hardcover, paperback, eBook, audio, everything. It was finally going to be available to the world. *What'll the cover look like?* He hadn't actually given it any thought. It'd been a secondary concern, but maybe he needed to start thinking about that now.

He passed Sebastian Joe's Ice Cream Café and a twinge of guilt struck him for not asking Missy to come along. She adored Sebastian Joe's. But then he would've had to have come up with some reason for why they were in the area that certainly wasn't to scope out a stash house. That was too much trouble. And besides, he remembered, the last time they'd stopped at Sebastian Joe's, it'd been a disaster. They'd run out of his favorite flavor; some little shit no one would claim as their demon spawn kept trying to look up Missy's skirt; and as they left the shop, the day's freakishly strong wind had knocked both their cones from their hands. It was a good thing he hadn't brought her along. She could find other places to take seventy-eight photos of desserts to help build on the carefully crafted narrative that she had a sweet life. *Pun intended.*

He continued down Franklin Avenue and parked near the Lake of the Isles. The homes surrounding the water were a mixture of old and modern. The old, early-1900 mansions, had been preserved with care, while the new, sleek glass structures, had been built on the graves of the less-than-redeemable properties.

Jacob stepped from the car. Rain clouds had gathered in what'd previously been a pristine sky, but they weren't dark enough to cause much of a fuss. He left his umbrella in the trunk and started to record himself walking from the lake.

"This is supposedly a stash house. Haven't been here before. Let's go check it out." He swung the camera around to capture the neighborhood beyond the lake's perimeter. "This area used to be a swamp. A lot of these homes were built after the city drained it in 1900 or something. The Mary Tyler Moore house is somewhere around here. Some people make a big deal out of that. It's from an old TV show. Before I was born, so..." He came up on Humboldt Avenue and stopped the recording to snap a photo of the street sign.

The houses on the treelined avenue were all set back a precise fifteen feet from the sidewalk, creating the perfect amount of grassy space for a six-year-old Jacob and his friends to play football on for hours. The sidewalk and the front of the house were the out of bounds. The walkways that led from the sidewalk to the front door, bisecting the lush lawns, were the end zones. Over the years, the trees had grown thick and tall. It looked almost impossible to throw those long bombs now. Not that there were many young kids around these days. The neighborhood was filled with empty nesters.

Jacob passed a gray-and-white Tudor where his best friend had lived. *What happened to that guy?* They'd been friends until about college, and then things just kind of faded. He'd met Missy by then, though, so it didn't matter. Most people would take a picture of the house and post it: *#ThrowbackThursday*. He didn't bother. He was moving on to 1779.

He couldn't remember the people who'd lived in it when he was younger. *How long's it been a stash house?* He faintly recognized the sea green siding and its wraparound porch.

As he passed, he gave it a sideways glance, slyly

recording a short video. It seemed peaceful enough. The first-floor windows, looking out on the porch, were dark, and the windows on the second floor had their curtains pulled. Nothing to see.

A light rain started to fall, so he pocketed his phone and continued to the end of the block where he paused at the corner. The neighborhood was lonely and still, coming alive only during the holidays when family came back home, or in this case, when there was a stash house to bust.

Jacob gazed back down the block. He wanted another peek at 1779, a closer look. This was going to get his name out there, and he wanted a little more detail on the house. He didn't expect Dwight would let him record videos and snap photos tomorrow.

The trees rustled against one another as a gust of wind portended an approaching thunderstorm. To the east there was an alley off Douglas Avenue, and Jacob headed for it, curious to see what the backyard contained.

A flaking white privacy fence surrounded 1779's property. He glanced through a gap in the wooden slats. The grass, shining in the sprinkling rain, had recently been mown. *Dwight appreciates a nice lawn.* A brick patio near the back door was decorated with a wrought iron table and chairs and a sturdy grill. *And a good barbecue too.* There was even a small, well-tended garden near the fence. *And fresh tomatoes and parsley?* This didn't look at all like a stash house. But then again, he had no idea what a stash house truly looked like, did he? Maybe they looked precisely like 1779. Hiding in plain sight.

Jacob peered through a window of the one-car garage to his left. A ladder, shovels, a rake, and other lawn-care tools were lined up against the walls. The space in the center of the garage was clear, the car that usually sat there absent. He turned back to the house. Seemed like no one was home. *Take a closer look?* If he saw any drugs or money or guns, he could just call the police right now. No need to wait until tomorrow.

That seemed easy, so Jacob placed a hand on the gate, surveyed the alley up and down to make sure he was alone, then pushed. The gate held. He pulled. It didn't open. *No problem.* The fence was just a foot taller than he was. He grabbed the top of it, planted a foot against the side of the garage, and hoisted himself up. As he swung his leg over, a board snapped, then another, and he went tumbling head over heels into the yard with a gasp and a thump. He quickly scrambled to his feet and froze, examining the world, listening for trouble. Nothing happened.

He checked himself for injuries. Other than his pants, which were torn, he was fine. His right pocket hung against his thigh, exposing his briefs. He lifted the flap to cover himself, but it flopped back down the second he let go.

The rain was coming down in earnest now. It smelled great, but it was cold, so he hurried across the yard and pushed himself against the side of the house where the overhang offered a little cover. Above him was a window, and he glanced in. The kitchen. *No one there.* He brought his head up a little higher to get a fuller view. Across the room was a table pushed against the wall. A neatly folded newspaper and a coffee cup were atop it. The laminate counters circling the kitchen were similarly clear of clutter except for a row of ceramic containers marked "Sugar," "Flour," and "Coffee" beside the sink. Next to that, a stainless-steel fridge was covered with crayon drawings and family photos. There were no stacks of cash or mounds of cocaine.

"What the fuck?" Jacob muttered. He reached for his phone but grabbed his exposed briefs instead. "Oh, goddamn it." His phone was lying in the grass amid white splinters, getting soaked. The phone was supposed to be waterproof, but still, he didn't believe the marketing. He raced to it, wiping it dry as best he could with a shirt that itself was becoming dotted with raindrops.

He snapped a picture of 1779's backyard, testing the camera. It worked. The resulting photo looked fine too, and the screen responded to his touch. *Good enough.* He slipped the phone into his other pocket, flipped the latch on the gate, and stepped into the alley.

Having found nothing of interest and destroyed more than he ever should have, he had to get out of there. But before he left, there was one more thing he could check. A garbage can was out near the corner of the garage, and he lifted the lid above his head, protecting himself from the rain, and poked around the trash. Thinking back on his FBI training, he remembered (Missy's excitement at him not making it through. "The pay sucks," she'd said.) that trash could be a valuable tool in evidence collection, so he went at it with gusto, rifling through the empty food cartons, used tissues, spent coffee grounds, and unidentifiable piles of goo and congealed fat. He dug his arm in as far as it would go, and for his troubles, he found nothing even moderately incriminating. "Fuck." He slammed the lid down.

The rain was now coming in whirling sheets, soaking him through. He glanced at his dripping arms. *At least it's washing away the shit from the garbage.*

"Is it getting bigger?" Missy asked Jacob.

"Keep touching it, and yeah, it'll get bigger."

Missy pulled her finger away from Quincy's cherry eye. "Wasn't touching it. Just giving him his drops."

"Could it cover his whole eye? One nasty red glob?" Jacob sat at his desk and examined Quincy resting on the couch next to Missy. He'd changed his clothes and explained to Missy he'd been caught on the nearby Stone Arch Bridge when the rain hit. "If it does, we should take him out for Halloween. Make him a zombie dog."

Missy smirked. "That'd be the *only* time I'd post

something about his cherry eye." She pointed at her LV tote beside the coffee table. "Can you give me that? Brought you something from work today."

Jacob picked up the bag from the floor and handed it to her, then watched as she pulled out a few sheets of paper and set them on the table.

"Here. Look," she said, scooting to the edge of the cushion. "Sit." She patted the sofa next to her, waited until Jacob shifted over from the desk, then said, "It's the latest study on today's most popular social media accounts and how they've become so influential."

"'Cause they all have a pretty face and lots of whip-creamy Starbucks drinks?"

Missy pointed to a line chart showing the growing difference between the post frequency of an average user and an "influencer." "Beauty doesn't matter," she said. "Posting does. More than it ever has."

"Couldn't quantify dumb luck and the power of the idiot masses?"

She ignored him. "These influencers created content every day, every hour sometimes, and they were relentless about it. *That's* what people follow. Whoever posts the most gets the most."

"So you want me to go get Starbucks every hour?"

Missy rolled her eyes. "No, you still need to keep your messaging consistent. But I'm saying post all the homeless pictures you can."

Jacob showed Missy the photos and videos he'd accumulated but not yet posted. "So don't wait to post these then?"

"Right. Get them out, but don't just dump them all," she added. "Do a post every other hour or something."

That'd be simple enough. "Sure."

Missy gave him a gentle poke in the chest. "You're lucky you have me. The agents who've passed on you are going to be so sorry."

"They won't even remember they passed. They get so many queries. Twenty or thirty a day." *Such long odds.* Jacob snapped a close-up of Quincy's butt, chuckling to himself as he gave his phone a couple of taps.

"Did you post that, Jacob?"

He nodded.

"No. Delete it. That's spam. Stay on message. Your followers will leave."

"But it's funny. Butt humor."

"It's not the brand you're building. Be consistent." Missy pulled her phone from her bag. "I got my fifteen hundredth follower on Instagram today. How do you think that happened?"

Jacob shrugged. "Luck?"

"Post frequency and..." She showed him her account. "See? All these selfies? It's all about makeup. My followers come to me for my makeup posts." She scrolled through her history.

"#Blessed?"

"Yeah. I'm blessed. It's part of the upbeat messaging my followers like."

"Here. How about this?" Jacob edited his post of Quincy's butt to include #Blessed. He showed Missy the update.

"Why don't you take this seriously?"

"I'm just joking."

"No. You're not. You're making fun of me."

"Okay, okay, sorry." Jacob deleted the post. "There. It's gone."

Missy didn't care. She got up and went to the balcony.

"Uh-oh, Quincy." Jacob followed Missy outside, his metaphorical tail tucked between his legs. "Hey, I was just joking."

She was sitting one of the plastic chairs facing the park. The storm had passed, but the clouds remained.

Jacob pulled the other chair over, sat down, and grasped her hand. He took it as a good sign she didn't pull away. "I didn't mean to upset you."

"There's a homeless guy down there with a pile of shit," she said. "Take a picture of him."

Jacob spotted the man bundled in rags and took a photo. He showed her. "Is that okay?"

"Yeah. Post it with #*Minneapolis* and #*DrugAbuse*."

"#*OpioidCrisis*," he added.

"Good."

He squeezed her hand. "Thanks."

"I know what I'm doing. You're lucky to have me."

"I know."

Missy's sat up straight. "I'm going to get vice president at 44th soon. I know it."

"Really? High-five." Jacob held up his hand, and Missy swatted it.

"I mean, it's not totally determined yet, but Alicia isn't going to get it. No way. She's incompetent. You know that."

"I do," Jacob confirmed.

"And I've been making sure Kyle sees all the things she screws up."

"And highlighting everything you do well?"

"It's obvious what I do well," Missy said. "I'll get the promotion before my trip. Be good to have 'VP' on all the conference material."

"For sure."

The rain had coated the park in an earthy fragrance, and Jacob breathed long and deep. He was tempted to tell Missy about the stash house and the attention he was about to get on social media for helping the police seize the piles and piles of drugs that would be found there, but he held his tongue. She wouldn't approve; she'd try to stop him. Even though they'd both heard about Emily's big find last year, where she and her partner had recovered thirty kilos of cocaine, ten kilos of meth, and $250,000 in cash, and all the attention she'd received, Missy would tell him to stay away. So he'd tell her tomorrow. Then she'd have nothing to worry about. It'd be over, and they could work together to come up with a social media strategy to maximize the views and capture more followers.

For now, he just listened as she talked about the upcoming conference.

Jacob had to use a sick day, a sick day he didn't have, to be at the stash house that afternoon. He wasn't going to get fired for playing hooky, but 3M was old-fashioned, and there were other punishments beyond a simple firing for those who didn't toe the corporate line.

If everything went well enough with the stash house, he hoped it wouldn't even matter what happened at 3M. If he got the attention he thought he might from the house, he wouldn't be far from a book deal or two, and at that point, he'd just quit 3M anyway. He wasn't about to waste any more of his life there. He needed out. No more studying the life-cycle characteristics of plasticizers, stabilizers, and polymers.

Jacob parked at Lake of the Isles again and recorded a quick video for social media, then he hopped out and made his way north along the shore.

The wind whipped at the water's surface and brought tears to the corner of his eyes. Admittedly, he was a little scared, but not *that* scared.

The plan was to go into the stash house, verify the drugs were there, then leave to get the cash, which he'd "left" in the car. He'd say he was just being careful or that he didn't know who'd be there, so he'd felt better leaving the money behind. Of course, once he was out of the house, he'd call the police. Simple.

He'd read up on cocaine the previous night. At least, as much as it related to what a user would know about it. He wanted to *really* play up the part of Mitch for this last encounter. He also couldn't be sure who else would be there, and what, if anything, they'd ask of him. So he had studied:

> ***Effects:*** *euphoria, dizziness, muscle twitches, restlessness, increased heart rate*
> ***Common street names:*** *blow, bump, coke, dust, nose candy, snow*
> ***Mixed with:*** *cornstarch, talcum powder, sugar, miscellaneous drugs*
> ***Packaged as:*** *teeners (1/16 oz. or 3.5 grams) and eight balls (1/8 oz. or 7 grams)*
> ***Servings:*** *twenty to thirty bumps per gram*
> ***Length of buzz:*** *ten to thirty minutes per bump, for a nonheavy user*

Jacob felt good, confident, ready to go. To get his blood flowing, he did a brief shadow-boxing session as he proceeded down the street. An old woman and a scruffy terrier emerged from a nearby house and stared. He dropped his arms, shoved his hands in his pockets, and smiled sheepishly before hurrying on by.

The next block was 1779. A beast of a man in a Harvard University hoodie and sunglasses rounded the corner and walked up to Jacob. "You heading to 1779?"

Jacob stopped and gave him a confused stare.

"Are you?" the man pressed with a patience-less voice.

"Yeah, I am." Jacob swallowed and looked back for the woman with the terrier. She'd gone in the opposite direction. No one was around. He turned to the man. He looked like a bodybuilder. His pecs pressed tightly against what would've been a loose hoodie on anyone else. A tattoo of a dragon with a skull in its mouth crawled along the left side of his thick, veiny neck. Jacob pulled his hands from his pockets and rubbed his palms across his chest, wiping away the sweat.

The man placed a hand on Jacob's shoulder. "There's nobody at 1779. Where'd you park? We gotta go get what you're picking up."

"What? No," Jacob whined. He'd done all that recon. He'd dug through the trash. His pants had gotten torn. "Why can't we go there?"

"There's nothing there, champ."

"But that's the pickup spot."

"To get you. The pickup spot for *me* to get *you*."

Jacob didn't get it.

"Let's go," the man said. "Where'd you park?" He turned Jacob around and guided him back down the block.

"Over by Lake of the Isles," Jacob answered. "What're we doing?"

The man dropped his hand from Jacob's shoulder now that he'd gotten him to fall in step. "You and I are driving over to Theo Wirth. Dwight's meeting us by the volleyball courts."

"Oh, okay. Cool," Jacob said, trying to act like he was fine with this turn of events, but in actuality, he was struggling to keep from pissing himself. He finally understood what Emily had been telling him about drug dealers. Dwight wasn't much, but this guy was another breed.

Jacob unconsciously repeated Missy's mantra for success (*Do whatever it takes*) to push out thoughts of this Vin-Diesel-man-beast stuffing him into his trunk, driving out to the country, and rolling the car, him included, into a lake. *Do whatever it takes!* "That's it. The Honda Fit," Jacob mumbled.

"Why'd you park so far?" the man grumbled.

"I don't know. It's nice out," Jacob lied with a stupid chuckle as the wind whipped at his face, bringing tears to his eyes again. Although the wind wasn't entirely to blame for the tears this time. His plan had completely gone to shit, and he was in outright panic mode. He had parked so far away because he didn't want to be anywhere near 1779 when the police arrived. *What's the plan now?*

Jacob unlocked the Honda, and the man squeezed in, making the Fit look like a plastic Tikes Cozy Coupe. He couldn't even sit up straight.

"Sorry," Jacob said as he buckled himself in. "Didn't think I was going to be driving the Hulk around today."

The man scowled...

...and growled? Jacob grew tense. "Just a joke. No offense. Hulk's cool. Hulk's like the strongest Avenger, so that's a compliment. And he's smart too." Jacob gestured at the Harvard seal on the sweatshirt. "Harvard Hulk."

"Let's just go," the man said.

Jacob started the car. He'd forgotten what he'd been listening to on the drive over, and Taylor Swift's "22" blasted from the speakers. "Oh, sorry." He quickly tapped the dash screen to mute the song, but the screen wouldn't register his touch. *Sweating too much.* The chorus hit: "I don't know about you, but I'm feeling twenty-two..." Jacob tapped and tapped, streaking the screen with sweat.

"Where's the volume knob?" Harvard Hulk asked.

"There isn't one." Jacob sighed. "Just the screen."

The man watched Jacob fumble and swipe for a couple more seconds then said, "It's fine. I listen to this all the time."

Jacob pulled back. "You like Swift too?"

"I'm not a twelve-year-old girl. Just have one."

"Oh."

"Drive."

Jacob put the Honda into gear and pulled from the curb. His embarrassment quickly subsided, replaced with an odd curiosity about a drug dealer raising a kid. *What wild shit has she been exposed to in her life?* He imagined a house with drugs and weapons and cash hidden all over. Open the cupboard for a box of cereal, find a stack of money. Reach under the sink for a new roll of toilet paper, find a gun taped under the sink. Harvard Hulk's daughter was the real-life equivalent of *Breaking Bad's* Walter White Jr.

Well, Jacob figured if he could somehow still execute his plan, he'd get that mess out of her life. She'd go through her teenage years with her father in jail, but that was fine. *It'll build character.*

Jacob eyed the seal stretched over the man's large chest. "You went to Harvard?"

The man stared out the window for a moment, then said, "Wife did."

A daughter who liked Taylor Swift, a wife who'd gone to Harvard, and him, a muscle-bound drug dealer. The equation didn't balance. Maybe Harvard Hulk was a chemistry high school teacher. If that were the case, then which *Breaking Bad* character was he? *Walter's DEA brother-in-law, Hank? Hank dies in that story.*

The song "22" turned into "Blank Space" then "We Are Never Ever Getting Back Together." As "Gorgeous" began, the man pointed up the road. "There." On the left, alone in a narrow dirt lot, was a black Cadillac Escalade.

Jacob licked his lips and parked the Honda beside the SUV. With the push of the ignition start/stop button, the poppy, chirpy music finally ceased. The man opened his door and squirmed out, stretching long and hard. "Fucking Christ," he groaned. He rapped his knuckles on the Escalade's roof. "Dwight, wake up."

The door opened. From within the SUV, Dwight said, "Wasn't sleeping."

"Sure you weren't."

Dwight waved the man aside and dropped from the Escalade. He reached back and pulled a metal baseball bat from the SUV. The dealers, standing side by side, turned and looked at the Honda.

VII.

The construction of the tunnel in Nueva Tijuana had begun. In a windowless room, a steady stream of fine dust was drifting up from a hole in the floor the size of an oil drum (the cartel's preferred vessel for transporting bodies). Against the back wall were two wheelbarrows ready to be filled with earth, having just been emptied in the backyard a moment earlier.

Vicente stood over the chipped concrete rim of the hole, peering down at one of the migrants he'd promised could stay north of the border if he dug his way there. The eight other migrants he'd hired, all men in their early twenties, no older than he was, were just out of sight, hacking away at the earth beneath the house, dragging along a floodlight that cast monstrous shadows, flitting and flicking, around the tunnel's entrance.

"Please, yes, come have a look," the migrant said. He clutched a rung on the ladder poking from the hole and shook it to demonstrate its sturdiness.

Vicente went down where the air thickened and tasted of burnt oil. When he turned around, his brow furrowed.

The tunnel, which would be several hundred yards long when finished, was just a rather large hole. He stretched his arms to his sides, touching both walls. This wouldn't do. "Wider," he told the man. "Another yard."

"Sure. Sure." The man nodded.

Vicente stepped forward, ducking. Bravo and his twin brother would need to bend themselves in half to come down. "Make it deeper. Another yard."

"Sure. Okay. No problem."

"And smooth this out," he directed. Every surface was jagged and sharp. It was a torture chamber, not a tunnel. Vicente pointed at his arm, showing the man his barely healed skin. "It cuts like a razor."

The man stepped close to inspect the wounds. "Oh, okay."

Vicente spotted several fresh slices on the man's own arms. "You know what I'm talking about."

The man nodded.

Vicente studied him for a moment, trying to determine if his point had truly hit home. This was important. El Avispón was considering using the tunnels, and this one specifically, to transport people under the border. Whether the idea had come from Bravo or was of his own volition was unclear, but the idea was there now, and Vicente had to plan accordingly.

He still intended to try and dissuade El Avispón of it, but it was likely a fool's efforts. As Bravo had said, the traffickers were getting terribly desperate. The flood of migrants at the border, while initially making it easy to get trafficking victims across, was now a mass so bloated and so out of control that everything was at a standstill. The traffickers, unable to wait, were offering large sums of money to anyone who had a viable path north. And El Avispón wasn't one to pass up an opportunity.

Vicente wasn't either, but human trafficking was hard to stomach. Drugs were one thing; he'd send drugs all day long. But people were...well, people were people. And they were unpredictable and unwieldy. What if someone got claustrophobic in the tunnel? What if they were noisy? Border Patrol was always listening. And even if they did get across, what were the logistics then? They weren't bricks of cocaine that could be stacked against a wall until the buyer arrived.

But most of all, forget the unpredictability, forget the logistics, these trafficking victims were mostly kids. He'd committed a remarkably high number of gruesome, soulless acts in his life, but it took a special kind of raw savagery to traffic kids.

Or so he thought, because now, here he was on the precipice of doing just that. El Avispón had told him to do it, and that was what he'd do. There was no saying no to El Avispón. Ever.

Vicente touched the sharp point of a stone jutting from the wall and reiterated his request, "Smooth it out." He didn't need kids coming out the other side all sliced to hell.

The man nodded, and Vicente turned back to the ladder, momentarily forgetting the tunnel wasn't as large as it should be. He scraped the ceiling with his head, and a handful of dirt and sand fell across his shoulders. His heart skipped a beat, the memory of the previous collapse still fresh. This soil was sturdy, though, and everything held.

Still, as he climbed out, he mumbled, "Support beams. We need support beams down here."

The migrant said, "Sure. Okay."

VIII.

Jacob didn't see the bat in Dwight's hand until he stepped from the Honda and circled around to meet the men between the vehicles. Dwight leaned on it as though it were a cane, resting the barrel in the gravel with a hand cupped over the handle.

Behind Jacob was a hiking trail that disappeared into the shadows of the heavy woods. The trees, bold and green from the previous day's rain, leaned out over the men and their vehicles with eager curiosity.

Not that there would be much to see. Jacob had no cash on him. No deal would be consummated. He'd decided he'd go through the actions, make it look like he was ready to close the deal, then try the forgotten cash trick. It'd piss Dwight off to no end, but that was all he could come up with. Either that, or he could just make a break for it. Seemed a bit too late for that now, though. In any case, he had a sick curiosity to see where this all went, for good or ill. At least then he could say something *had* happened.

The bat was an interesting twist. He imagined Dwight knocking out the Honda's windows, breaking the mirrors, and taking out the headlights. *Does insurance cover drug-dealer attacks?* he wondered. Jacob gestured toward the bat. "That an Easton? Looks like an Easton."

"It's a bat," Dwight said dismissively.

"Well, yeah," Jacob grumbled. "Easton's a brand."

Dwight handed the bat to Harvard Hulk. "Let me get you a bump." He reached into the Escalade.

Jacob didn't realize the comment was directed at him. He was distracted, craning his neck to see the SUV's license plate. Once he drove away, he'd call the police and give them the number. Regrettably, that meant he wouldn't be around to witness the arrest, but at least it'd happen, and then he could get his social media blitz on the road. He had a lot to post. He'd been holding much of it back, waiting for this moment. Overhead the sky was darkening. Another summer thunderstorm was drawing near.

"Yo, Cupcake. Here."

Jacob turned from the license plate. Dwight was an arm's length away, holding out a house key. On the tip was a tiny pile of white powder. "What's that?" Jacob asked.

"A fucking bump," Dwight huffed.

Jacob smiled. "Oh, no. I'm good."

Dwight looked over his shoulder at Harvard Hulk. "I'm good?"

The man smirked.

Dwight shifted back to Jacob. "Take it."

Jacob gave it a second's thought then shook his head. "It's the afternoon," he argued. "I'm not taking a *bump* right now." *That should settle it*, he thought.

"Well, you are. 'Cause I'm not selling you this much coke without you telling me you're good with it."

Jacob grinned, spotting his way out of the mess. "Then don't."

Dwight cocked his head and squinted, processing the response.

Jacob figured it was time to get in his car and leave.

But Dwight spoke up. "Don't waste my fucking time. Take it." The key remained suspended between them.

Harvard Hulk stepped closer, the university seal

across his chest staring Jacob in the face, his fingers tightening around the bat.

Taking the bump didn't seem to be a choice. Jacob pinched the bridge of his nose, thinking, thinking. *What's the worst that can happen?* People did cocaine all the time. Stephen King, Patrick Bateman, Tony Montana. The little illicit mound of powder teetering on the edge of the key seemed harmless. Whatever happened, he could post about it. Get another follower or two. And when he tried it, he could tell Dwight the quality wasn't any good. That'd be that!

So he leaned forward. *Count to three and then do it. One...* He'd never done any illegal drugs in his life. Hadn't even smoked a cigarette. Now it was straight to coke? The pile was a little more overwhelming up close. Would it even fit up his nose? *Two...* Dwight's breath flowed over the top of his head, gently agitating his hair. Harvard Hulk was off in the periphery, a huge mass of crimson. Jacob lifted a finger, pressed it against his left nostril, hovered his other over the powder, and... *Three!* He inhaled as hard as he could, as if clearing his sinuses of a thick, snotty clog.

The cocaine stung the edge of his nose, then up it went, to the center of his face where it lingered between his eyes, drawing tears. Jacob gave several whooping coughs. His knees went weak, and he almost buckled over. He forced himself to stand up straight, hands on hips, blinking away the tears. It had to be obvious he hadn't done cocaine before, so he said, "Oh, it's good," and gave Dwight a thumbs-up. *Why the fuck did I say that?* He wasn't supposed to say that.

"No shit," Dwight snarled, turning to the SUV and grabbing a rolled-up paper bag. He handed the bag to Harvard Hulk and took back his bat, which was, in fact, an Easton, Jacob noticed.

As he composed himself, clearing his throat and drawing a breath, he mentally scanned his body, checking for signs of the cocaine's effects. He didn't feel much of anything. Just his nostrils burning. *Maybe that wasn't really cocaine.*

"So?" Dwight asked, raising his brows and pursing his lips.

Cash, Jacob remembered. *But there is no cash. But he said the cocaine was good, so...* "Yeah, cash," Jacob mumbled. "Cash for the blow, white fluff, devil's dandruff." A rumble of thunder resonated in the distance as the storm approached. Jacob's heartbeat quickened. He shook his hands and bounced on the toes of his feet. He felt as if he could run a marathon, as if he could lift weights for hours, as if he could fight a dozen children (or midgets, whichever arrived first) and not break a sweat. He waved his hand in a "follow-me" gesticulation and proceeded to the back of the Honda. "Cash for the devil's dandruff," he repeated, opening the trunk. He dug around a pile of old hockey gear. "Used to play hockey with my friends. Don't have any friends anymore. Just Missy."

"What about your coke party?" Dwight pressed. "They're not friends?"

"Oh, yeah. Sure." Jacob grabbed an ice skate and considered whether the blade was still sharp enough to slice Dwight's neck. *Possibly.* With the amount of energy flowing through him, he could likely cut his head clean off. *Schlink.*

But all the blood. Where would that go? He'd have to clean it up, and it wouldn't be easy getting it out of the gravel. Gravel was hard to clean. That thought confused him, so he let go of the skate. His mind was racing; a thousand unrelated ideas and concerns were trying to be ordered into reason; and he had no idea where to start. "What was I looking for?"

"My money," Dwight reminded him.

Jacob nodded and pulled out many forgotten items. The ice skates. A half empty bag of sidewalk salt. An old sweatshirt. Wrinkled dress pants. Fast-food wrappers. But no cash. "I had it," Jacob claimed. "Right here." He pointed at an empty space in the trunk.

"You don't have it?" Dwight groaned.

Jacob stepped from the car. He threw up his hands. He smiled. He was feeling fucking amazing.

"This a game to you?" Harvard Hulk growled.

"Oh, no," Jacob replied quickly. "No game. This is real life." He pinched himself. "That hurt. Real life. Fact."

"Then where's the money?" Dwight asked. He pounded the bat against the gravel.

Jacob snapped his fingers. "The shelf in the closet at home. I'll go get it." He started to gather the items from the ground and toss them back into the trunk.

"Hey, Shawn?" Dwight hissed.

Harvard Hulk gave a grunt.

"You know that part in *No Country for Old Men* when Chigurh tells the guy to hold still as he sticks the cattle gun against his head?"

"Yeah..."

"And the guy's so stupid, he doesn't move? You know that part?"

Jacob was kneeling, collecting the fast-food wrappers, when the barrel of the bat settled against his shoulder blade. He froze, a crumpled Burger King logo staring up at him. A moment passed where all he heard was his own feverish breathing, fast and hard. He couldn't tell if it was from the cocaine or the bat on his shoulder. He looked up at Dwight.

The dealer stared back, ready to settle a wrong. "Hold still," he said and lifted the bat over his head.

Jacob wasn't stupid. He tried to scramble to his feet and run, but then the bat came crashing down. It smacked with a hollow thunk against his right shoulder. Something gelatinous popped. He cried out and dropped to a knee. Dwight brought the bat down again, striking the same shoulder flush and square. The collarbone splintered. Shards of bone sliced through the surrounding muscle like glass. Jacob collapsed to the dirt. The Honda's tailpipe, in the shape of an O, matched his own look of shock. He tried to hold up his hand, plead for mercy, but he couldn't lift his arm. Dwight hit him again. And again. And again.

Jacob was on the verge of unconsciousness by the time the beating ended. Dwight clutched the bat and took a deep breath, his face shining with sweat. He glared at Jacob. "I'll kill you next time," he warned.

Jacob groaned and lay unmoving on his side. His right arm drooped from his shoulder like a cooked noodle over the edge of a pot. He couldn't move his fingers. His body had endured so much trauma his brain wasn't accurately registering the pain. The first few strikes had been crippling, but now things were just tingly, fuzzy. He was sure he looked like he'd been hit by a truck, but he really only had a strange, loopy sensation shaking around in his head. *Maybe the cocaine's keeping the pain at bay.* Jacob carefully tilted his head to look at Dwight and Harvard Hulk. "Thanks for the bump," he said as the thunderstorm rolled in and the rain started.

"Fuck you." Dwight tapped the bat against Harvard Hulk's hip. "Let's go."

Jacob croaked an unintelligible reply, which the men ignored. They climbed into the Escalade and sped off, flicking gravel across Jacob's face. The smell of weed and Pledge faded. *#OpioidCrisis #MinneapolisDrugProblem*

Jacob rested his head on the ground as the sky broke open, and the rain came down in sheets. He wasn't going to even try moving. *Let the rain come. Wash away my sins.* He started to cry. The bump of cocaine muted much of the pain, but it couldn't make him forget the failure that was his life. It couldn't keep that eternal frustration at bay. It couldn't tell him why it was so impossible to contribute even a shred of value to the world or why fate continually spat in his face. But maybe, for some reason, he deserved this, he thought.

"Fucking opioid crisis," he grumbled just before he passed out.

A motorist eventually spotted Jacob laying like road kill in the mud and gravel. The sixteen-year-old had gotten his driver's license the prior week and was driving around to get a feel for what it was like out in the rain by himself. Had he not been so wide-eyed and terrified, he might've passed right by like the others before him, but he spotted the curiosity through the torrential rain and pulled over. While he waited for the police, he took some photos of the splayed-out man and put them on Snapchat. He added the title of the Dr. Seuss book his parents had recently given his brother for high-school graduation: "*Oh, the Places You'll Go!*"

IX.

Jacob spent much of the evening in the hospital, unconscious. A surgeon repaired the displaced comminuted fracture in his shoulder and upper arm, but it was a crapshoot as to how it would heal. His mobility and range of motion would likely never be the same.

Just after 2:00 a.m., Missy took him home and helped him to bed. Standing at his side, arms crossed, she studied the massive spica cast that ran from elbow to shoulder then across his chest, around his hip, and finally up his back where it reconnected with itself.

Jacob was awake, staring into the dark hallway.

"So what happened?" Missy asked for the fifth time.

Quincy hopped up on the bed, and Jacob pulled him close with his good arm, thinking how best to deliver the story. He had to be careful about it; he had to be calculated with his words. He was a writer; it wouldn't be that hard, but he was also on a heavy dose of OxyContin. The pain that'd come once the cocaine wore off had been the worst he'd ever experienced. The Oxy now flowing through his blood provided wonderful relief, but there was still a deep, persistent bitch of a pounding that coursed from shoulder to chest. He couldn't let that distract him while he spoke. *Don't mention the cocaine. The bump never happened.* The emergency room knew about the cocaine, but thank God for HIPAA. They kept that detail to themselves. So he started to tell Missy what the plan had been.

As he spoke, she took a photo of him and the cast. He stopped and watched her mess with the phone's screen. She looked at him. "I'm listening."

"Did you post that?"

"On Facebook."

"'Cause you want sympathy?"

"*I* want sympathy? No."

"I think so."

She shook her head.

"That's not on point," he reminded her.

"It's Facebook. That's just whatever."

"You want sympathy."

Missy's lips pursed inward. She was biting her tongue given his condition.

So he moved on, continuing his story, skipping over the cocaine and making up something about the pain he should've felt as the bat smashed apart his shoulder.

Missy began to pace, arms crossed tightly against her chest. He wrapped things up, and she asked, "Are we safe?"

"Yeah, why?"

"Did those two get arrested?"

Jacob wasn't sure how to answer that without creating further alarm. He glanced at his cast; Missy had chosen an ocean-blue color for him, a shade brighter than his eyes. "Even if they haven't yet, I think this settled things."

"He could've killed you," Missy said, the reality of the situation really starting to settle in. "Oh, my God."

"He wasn't going to."

"You don't know that."

"He would've just beat my head in if he wanted to kill me."

Missy wasn't having it. She perched on the edge of the bed, shaking her head. "You're crazy."

"I'm trying to get my book published. Do whatever it takes," Jacob reminded her. "That's what you always say."

"Oh, no, don't put this on me," Missy huffed. "I told you to stay away from him." She stood up, glaring at him.

Jacob stared back, refusing to say anything more. He'd made his point, and he was sticking to it.

Missy shook her head. "You're unbelievable." She went to the closet, grabbed her LV tote, and stuffed a change of clothes in it. She then stormed from the bedroom and down the hall. The door opened. Quincy jumped from the bed and hurried after Missy.

"Where're you going?" Jacob called out.

"I can't be around you right now."

Jacob was quiet. *What'd I do?*

"Quincy stay." The door shut hard, and the lock clacked in place.

Jacob lurched to his side, wincing at the pain, and grabbed his phone from the nightstand. He typed out a text but held off on sending it. He should wait. He should give her a moment. *If she texts first...* That would be bad. So he'd wait four minutes.

Quincy returned looking rejected and took Missy's side of the bed, curling into a ball, letting the soft purple comforter fold in around him.

Two minutes passed; the phone vibrated. "Shit." He grabbed it. The Caller ID didn't say Princess Peach, Missy's self-assigned nickname, though. It was his mom. Missy had given her the news. *Probably for spite.*

"Hi, Mom," he answered.

"Are you okay? Do you need me to come over?" his mother cried. "I'm going to come over."

"No. Please, don't. I'm fine. There's nothing for you to do."

"I'm coming over."

"Don't."

"Are you sure?"

"I'm sure."

"Where'd this happen? Have the police arrested anyone?"

"North side," Jacob lied, offering an answer that'd conform to her world-view. Theo Wirth was supposed to be safe; she'd believe the lie more than the truth and therefore wouldn't ask questions. "They're still looking for the guys. I didn't see them. Just random."

"Thank God you're okay."

"Hmm."

"I would suggest you keep out of the north side from now on."

Jacob rolled his eyes. *That's what you suggest, huh?*

"You're not going to work tomorrow, are you?"

"Going to try."

"You shouldn't."

"Don't have any sick days to take."

"I think they'd understand."

"I'm fine," he reiterated.

"Well, I still want to come over and check on you," his mother said.

He knew she wouldn't. She said she would, but tomorrow, she'd remember she had a committee meeting or a dinner she just absolutely couldn't cancel.

"Tell Missy not to make you supper. I'll get you something."

Jacob considered making a snide comment about Missy walking out, but his desire to end the conversation was greater, so he said, "Fine. I'll tell her."

"Okay. Get some sleep. I'll be over tomorrow."

She wouldn't be over tomorrow.

"Love you. Call if you need anything."

"I will. Love you too." He hung up and texted Missy. "*When are you coming back?*"

"*Not. Went to Jenny's. Staying the night.*"

"*I'm sorry.*"

She didn't reply.

"Fuck." Jacob stared across the room, wondering why she had to be like that. He'd done nothing to her, and she had to be such a... He assumed the worst. She was going to leave him. Another failure.

He groaned and focused on the pain rippling across his shoulder and chest. *Take it all in. Suffer for your incompetence.*

Which reminded him he needed to contact his primary doctor. The ER nurse had said his platelet count was low, and he should get it checked out. *One more thing to suffer through.* He sent Dr. Chaniara a message through the clinic's health portal then turned to Google for a faster answer.

"Ah, fuck," he muttered. Low platelets could be the result of a disorder such as leukemia. *Wouldn't that be poetic?* Tears gathered in his eyes for the fifth or sixth time that day. He'd lost count. *Fucking cancer.* He wanted to cry, but no, he wouldn't get sucked down that rabbit hole of despair. He shook his head, then chuckled aloud. "Don't care. Bring it on, you motherfuckers."

He held his phone aloft and took a selfie. *#MinneapolisDrugs #Cocaine #GotJumped*

Unable to help himself, he ventured over to Missy's Instagram. He stared at her smiling face, wondering if their relationship had just ended. It was a good thing he could barely move, because after scrolling through her posts for the next hour, that balcony six stories up sounded very tempting.

Jacob barely got a minute of sleep, for all the obvious reasons. The cast was also itchy as all hell. *Six weeks of the fucking thing.*

Week one, day one: a workday. He lurched out of

bed and carefully tested his body, collecting data points on which movements caused pain and which didn't. Unfortunately, nearly everything did. *That's why I've got the Oxy.* He threw one down the pie hole.

The morning routine was a struggle. His hand, dangling out the end of the cast like a trapped animal, was put to work on occasion, to hold an empty mug or a spoon, but beyond that, it was quite worthless. Pulling on socks had him reaching and stretching at painful angles. Buttoning pants was a joke. And for all the shirts Missy had bought him, he couldn't manage to get one over the cast. A baggy red-and-green Christmas cardigan tucked beneath a pile of empty shoeboxes was his only choice. Tediously, each button was fastened, and he took a breath. *Six weeks.* He finally headed out the door, his shoelaces flopping about, threatening to trip him with every step.

When he reached the garage, he didn't see his Honda. "Missy..." Of course she took the car. He went upstairs to the lobby and booked a forty-five-dollar Uber. While he waited, he sent Missy a good-morning text. She'd be at work. She wouldn't reply, and he didn't need a reply. He just had to show her he was thinking of her.

The Uber driver pulled up and gave a light tap of the horn. Jacob was double checking the make and model of the car when he noticed just over the hood, in the park, a familiar yellow hoodie. Dwight was near a bench talking with Charlie, the homeless vet. *Dwight's got balls.* The dealer must've thought it completely out of the realm of possibility Jacob would've ratted on him. Surely, a beating of that severity deserved discretion. But Jacob neither knew the rules of the drug world, nor did he care. He was, and still was, desperate. He wanted an arrest. He *needed* an arrest.

Jacob canceled the Uber and called the police. The driver received notification of his canceled ride, gave Jacob the finger, and sped off. Jacob ignored him, listening for the operator to pick up, and when he did, Jacob identified himself. Before he could say another word, the operator asked if he was calling concerning his assault. "Yes, sir. The man who attacked me is in Gold Medal Park right now. Just off Second Street. Yellow hoodie. Jeans. White sneakers."

"Are you in any immediate danger?"

"No, I'm in the lobby of my apartment building."

"Okay. Stay where you are. I'll send a squad car over. Be just a minute. If anything changes, call us back."

Jacob thanked him, hung up, and quickly flipped his phone to video mode. He started the recording: "There's the guy who jumped me. He's the drug dealer." Jacob focused in on Dwight, who suddenly drew tense, then shoved Charlie.

Jacob put the camera on himself. "Don't worry. I just called the police. This'll be good." He winked and turned the camera to the park.

Dwight gave Charlie another shove and the vet went stumbling over a bench.

"Oh, shit," Jacob grumbled.

Dwight stepped beside Charlie lying in the grass and kicked him in the ribs.

The park that morning wasn't busy, but it wasn't empty either. *Someone's going to help Charlie.* Jacob was sure of it, but the few who were close only watched in mild shock, and the others farther off either didn't notice or pretended not to notice as they stood over their dogs, studiously watching them do their business.

Dwight continued to wail on the defenseless Charlie. The beating wasn't as bad as Jacob's had been (there was no metal bat), but it was still plenty brutal.

Jacob had to stop recording. He couldn't watch. *But what kind of vigilante does that? So pathetic. Shoot for the moon!* He raised the phone up high, still recording, and raced out of the lobby toward the park. "Dwight! Dwight!" He rushed through the trees, rumbling awkwardly in his cast. "Dwight!"

The dealer halted in midkick, looked at Jacob, and

laughed. And laughed. "Nice fucking sweater."

"Leave him alone. I'm recording you," Jacob warned, stopping on the other side of the bench.

Dwight's beady eyes shifted to the phone. "Give it to me." He took a step toward Jacob, palm raised, leaving Charlie curled up in the grass.

Jacob backpedaled.

"Give it," Dwight repeated, circling the bench.

Jacob went on matching Dwight's steps until the dealer had had enough. He stopped and pulled a gun, pointing it at Jacob.

The bystanders cried out and scattered. Jacob froze.

"Give it to me, motherfucker."

"This is live," Jacob lied, shaking the phone.

"Then the world's gonna see a little bitch Cupcake get shot." Dwight pulled the trigger. But not because he'd meant to. Charlie had launched himself into the dealer's back, and Dwight accidentally squeezed the trigger as the two tumbled to the ground.

The bullet sailed over Jacob's head.

"Motherfucker!" Dwight yelled, kicking and shoving Charlie aside.

Jacob turned and ran. With his freshly broken bones and bulky cast, though, he couldn't have outrun a drunk.

Dwight got to his feet and caught Jacob before he'd even escaped the park, shoving him hard in the back. Jacob went flailing. His shoelaces sealed his fate and sent him face first to the sidewalk. The impact electrified every overworked nerve from shoulder to elbow, and he screamed. The phone went sliding into the street.

Dwight casually walked past him and grabbed the phone. "Just a fucking video recording, you bitch." He raised it high and threw it against the curb. With a swift kick, he sent the pieces skittering over a sewer grate, where they tottered for a moment then vanished. There was a faint splash.

"You asshole," Jacob hissed.

"Call me that again," Dwight dared him. He stepped onto the sidewalk and glared down at Jacob, gun held against his hip.

"Asshole," Jacob repeated, and grinned the biggest shit-eater grin he could manage.

Clearly not expecting such defiance, Dwight stared incredulously at Jacob then shook his head. "Your funeral."

A squad car, lights flashing, no siren, skidded to a stop behind them. The officers jumped out, guns raised. "Drop the weapon!"

Dwight's eyes went wide. Then his adrenal glands kicked into overdrive, and he bolted across the street up Tenth Avenue.

"Freeze! On the ground!" the officers yelled before taking off after him.

Jacob kept still as the officers rushed past, their boots thumping over the sidewalk, handcuffs clinking against their belts. As the three men sprinted toward Washington Avenue, Jacob picked himself up with a painful groan. He had to get after them. No way could he miss a second of the action.

Up the block, Dwight stumbled as his shoe caught an uneven bit of sidewalk and slipped from his foot. He nearly fell, windmilled his arms, regained his balance, and sprinted on with one white sneaker and one white sock. He was still faster than the cops, and certainly faster than Jacob. He was going to get away. *Dammit.*

At the intersection of Tenth and Washington, Dwight popped out from behind Gold Medal Wine and Spirits and bolted into the six-lane street.

The semi hit him dead center, lifting him clean out of his (one remaining) sneaker. The driver slammed on the brakes. The tires locked and skidded, fighting against the forward momentum of ten tons of metal and frozen bakery goods.

Dwight slipped down the chrome grille and disappeared under the truck, rolling and bouncing as the undercarriage ripped and tore at his limbs. His head caromed past the front tires by the width of a teener. For a moment, Jacob thought there was a chance—an infinitesimally small chance, but still a chance—the dealer might survive, but then came the back tires.

The seventy-five-pound, nine-inch-wide tires met Dwight's meaty head with glee, pinning it to the pavement, climbing halfway up, then popping it like a beetle underfoot. White, pinkish matter squirted across the street.

The police froze; Jacob froze; and the truck came to a stop. The intersection was littered with the dealer, a single upright shoe by the crosswalk the start of the vicious trail.

Jacob chuckled then vomited the Fruit Loops that'd taken him so long to prepare that morning.

One of the officers reached for the radio on his shoulder. "Officer 168. Suspect struck by motor vehicle at Tenth and Washington. Need units for traffic control. Send the chief and the ME."

An hour later, Jacob was in another Uber heading to work. Physically he was fine. Legally he was in no trouble. Emotionally...he needed to work on that. He distracted himself by fiddling with the old Samsung Galaxy he'd stashed away after upgrading to the phone that was now in the depths of the Minneapolis sewer system. Missy had told him to toss the Galaxy, but he never had. *Just in case.* Although the "just in case" he'd envisioned had been something more along the lines of dropping the phone on the floor or into the toilet while taking a shit, not having a drug dealer smash it to bits.

He shook his head as he tapped the Google Photos app. The cloud storage service was supposed to automatically back up photos and videos, but he had a bad feeling it hadn't caught everything. And sure enough, when it opened, the most recent—and possibly most important—video wasn't there. He refreshed the app several times, but it never showed. It was gone. As consolation, he posted the photo from the lobby of Dwight and Charlie mid scuffle. *"Called the cops on the guy in yellow." #DoingWhatICan #DrugDealer*

Jacob rested the phone in his lap and took a deep breath. *Is this enough for a book?* It didn't feel like it. A lot had happened, but his gut told him he was only about a third of the way through. There needed to be more; the stakes needed to be raised.

The driver spoke up. "Sorry about this route. I can't take Washington. It's blocked up for some reason."

"Some guy was hit," Jacob told him.

"Oh. But it's totally blocked off. They're not letting anyone through."

"You've seen the deer on the interstate when they've been hit by a semi? It was kinda like that. They're picking him up with shovels."

"Shit."

"Yeah." Jacob snickered as the thought of un-birthdays came to mind. Today was the dealer's un-birthday.

"So what happened there? Your arm? Get hit yourself? They hitting everyone in this neighborhood?"

"Got jumped. Couple a guys and a baseball bat."

"Whoa. Fuck, man. Crazy."

Jacob elaborated by telling him the same story he'd given his mother. "Now stuck wearing this for six weeks."

"Wild. You on painkillers?"

Jacob nodded. "Oxy."

"Be careful with that. Hard-core," the driver warned.

"I'll take it for a couple more days, then that's it."

"Good idea. What's the dose?"

"It's strong. I think forty milligrams."

"Had some myself. Took a bad fall a year ago. Messed up my back. Doctors don't like to prescribe much of that in this state. I had to fight to get a prescription."

"I got lucky then," Jacob said. "Didn't even have to ask for it."

"Well, look at you." The driver laughed. "No offense."

"None taken. I know I'm a mess."

"Let me give you a piece of advice. If you have any extra pills when you're done, hold onto them. They're amazing for headaches. Just a tiny bit, and you're golden."

Jacob chuckled. "I think I'm good with Tylenol for a headache. Probably just flush the extra."

The driver watched the road for a moment, glancing up at Jacob several times. "If you're going to just flush it, I'll take it. My back still gives me fits."

"I can't. Sorry, man." Jacob told himself not to forget to post this little encounter. *#OpioidCrisis*

"Happy to buy it off you. A buck a pill?"

Jacob smirked. "Not for sale. Sorry."

"You wouldn't get in trouble."

Jacob thought about Dwight smeared across Washington.

"Name your price," the driver tried.

Emily had told him the street value of Oxy was about a dollar per milligram. But he wasn't naming his price. "Sorry," he repeated.

"Yeah, no, that's cool. Respect," the driver responded quickly. "Never can be too careful. I mean, look at that cartel boss who got extradited. DEA's cracking down."

"They are."

"Can you imagine?" the driver mused. "He went from having billions to max security."

"Bet he gets a book deal out of it."

The driver laughed. "I don't read, but I'd read that."

A tinge of jealousy rose up in Jacob's chest.

"The stories he could tell. Bet it gets ugly down there in Mexico with him gone. And then, all these states are legalizing marijuana. Cartels are going to be making some moves."

Jacob nodded. "Interesting times."

They eventually reached 3M's headquarters. The driver stopped at the Carlton Science Center and glanced in the rearview mirror. "You sure you don't want me to take those Oxy for you?"

Jacob smiled and repeated one last time, "Sorry." He went inside to find his boss. They had to work out how to best manage his workload given the spica cast.

Afternoon rush-hour traffic, Jacob found, was decidedly more tolerable in the back of an Uber. He stretched his legs, pulled out his Galaxy, and read some emails. Top of the list: another agent was rejecting his novel. *Surprise, surprise.* The next email informed him there was a message on the clinic's health portal, so he followed the link. Dr. Chaniara wasn't concerned about the low platelet count (*good*), but he didn't think there was any harm in seeing a specialist (*fuck*). Jacob quickly but reluctantly scheduled an appointment with a hematologist as the Uber went from St. Paul to Minneapolis.

When he got to his apartment, he found it quiet. Missy wasn't home, and it didn't appear as though she'd been home. *Still at work. Maybe. Hopefully.* He found Quincy curled up on the bed and had to physically pull him from the comforter's embrace to take him downstairs for one of his thrice-a-day offerings to the shrubbery gods.

Once Quincy's bladder had been emptied, they

wandered among the joggers, dog walkers, daydreamers, and ice-cream eaters of Gold Medal Park. The place was oddly serene. Not a single homeless person or spaced-out addict. The two dozen or so benches that attracted them like Quincy to the comforter were empty. Despite the park's new (original) look, Jacob wanted to leave. He wanted to see the park from up high.

"Let's go out on the balcony," Jacob said, an idea for a Twitter post forming in his mind.

Quincy knew the word "balcony" well; he gave a soulful look up at the apartment. And when they got back upstairs (*still empty, no Missy*), the pug proceeded without prompt down the hall and sat near the glass door, waiting for Jacob.

"Just a second," Jacob called out as he hung Quincy's leash on the peg near the closet and grabbed the white sneaker he'd brought back earlier in the day. "There. Go," he told the dog, pushing the door open. Quincy went to work sniffing the railings, ensuring the balcony still had his, and only his, scent. Jacob set the sneaker on one of the plastic chairs and walked to the railing. He held up his phone, centered the park, and captured the peaceful summer moment. It didn't even need a filter.

He scrolled through his picture album, found one of the less-gruesome images of Dwight's un-birthday, then juxtaposed it against the unfiltered photo of the park. *#MinneapolisProblem #CleaningThingsUp* He added a third hash tag for the hell of it. *#Blessed*

"That'll work." He sat. Across from him on the other chair was the white sneaker. He had grabbed it on a whim. *A morbid memento?* It'd just been lying on the sidewalk behind the crowd that'd gathered. The police had gotten his statement and given him a once-over for injuries, then he wormed away through the pack and found the shoe right there, lonely and forsaken, so he picked it up. It was an Air Jordan 3 Retro, all white with a baby blue sole. The laces, a darker blue that matched his spica cast, were looped wide and loose through the eyelets. He'd put the oversized shoe in the apartment then gone to work, intending to post a photo of it later when he had the time. But now the sneaker had an accusatory look about it that was giving him pause.

Jacob grabbed the sneaker and gave it a sniff. No real smell, just a touch of that ever-present weed-and-Pledge combo that'd clung to Dwight like a robe. He set it between his feet and went back to his phone. His mom had texted. She had a committee meeting; she couldn't bring dinner over. He didn't bother texting back. Instead, he went to Twitter to continue contemplating the merits of posting a photo of the shoe. He noticed he had a couple new followers. One of them, @pugD3AL3R, had a profile pic of a herd of pugs. Jacob chuckled and showed Quincy. The dog studied the image for a moment, but lost all interest when the balcony door opened.

"Missy!" Jacob jumped up and hugged her with his good arm.

"I'm still not happy with you," she groaned as Quincy circled them.

"I understand." Jacob squeezed her tight, and she finally caved, hugging him back. "Are you hungry? Did you eat dinner?" he asked.

"Haven't. Just came from work."

"I'll make you something." He hurried to the kitchen.

"Just some noodles." She sat on the couch, summoning Quincy with a pat of the cushion.

"Sauce?"

"Butter and salt."

"BS noodles coming up." Jacob grabbed a bag of pasta from the cupboard and tore it open with his teeth. "Are you staying at Jenny's again?"

"I don't know. Her place isn't that comfortable. Can you make me some tea too?"

Jacob carefully shifted a pot of water to the stove, balancing it on his spica cast, and dumped in a clump of pasta. He turned to the sink and looked across the island. "Green tea?"

Missy nodded.

He pulled a tin down from the collection atop the refrigerator. "Dwight died today," he nonchalantly told her with just a touch of satisfaction and accomplishment.

She sat up. "Huh?"

"Got hit by a truck."

"A truck? You're joking."

"Swear to God." He laughed. "On Washington."

"Did you see it?"

He nodded and told her the story while making the tea with one hand. He brought the cup over and set it on the coffee table, then showed her the photos he'd taken of the aftermath.

"So you didn't see it actually happen."

"No. I saw it. Dwight kicked my phone down the sewer. This is my old phone." He wanted to point out how smart it'd been that he'd kept it despite her insistence he toss it, but he let that be, and said instead, "Gonna send a note to *The Star Tribune*. Give them the full story of what happened."

"I don't know if they'll care. This is pretty dark. Even for the news."

"They can skip the grizzly bits. Talk about me. I'm a hero."

Missy grabbed her tea, leaned back, and pulled her feet up on the couch, knees to chest. "You are?"

"Yeah. A goddamn American hero," Jacob huffed.

Missy rolled her eyes. "My noodles are probably done if they're the thin ones."

"Yep." Jacob left his phone with her and hurried to the kitchen.

As he ladled the noodles into a bowl, Missy said,

"You got a comment on your last tweet."

"From ten minutes ago? What's it say?"

"That you're a monster and a horrible person."

Jacob laughed as he plopped a bit of butter into the noodles. "What's it *really* say?"

Missy didn't laugh. "That's pretty much what it says. '*Monster. Who brags about getting a man killed? Psycho. Reported.*' That's it, verbatim."

"Reported? That's stupid."

"I could see why someone might get offended."

"Dwight was a drug dealer. Who left the comment?" Jacob sprinkled some salt into the bowl and brought it to Missy.

"You look the user up." Missy set the phone on the couch, took the bowl from Jacob, and dug into the noodles.

Jacob sat beside her and grabbed his phone. After a minute of investigating, he said, "Just some random guy with no life. Professional outrager. All he does is threaten to report people's tweets." Jacob blocked him. "There, doesn't have to look at me anymore. Idiot."

Missy was quiet, munching on her noodles.

Jacob switched to his desk and searched through *The Star Tribune*'s website. He found the email address of the politics and government reporter and sent him a note about his role in that day's events, ending the message with an invitation to reach out for more details.

He sat back and stared at his cast. It looked terribly sterile, so he grabbed a marker and scribbled a message across it. "How's that?" he asked Missy.

She tilted her head and read the upside-down message: "Don't cry because it happened; smile because it's over." She rolled her eyes and went back to her noodles.

X.

No one at *The Star Tribune* replied to Jacob's email. Or the next one. He picked another reporter and emailed him. Nothing. He reached out to the *Pioneer Press*, but by then, a couple of weeks had passed, and even if they would've been interested, he knew he'd missed his window. Dwight's death was old news, and like the student who raises his hand last, he wasn't getting called upon.

Social media had been different, at least. There he'd gotten, and was still getting, plenty of attention. His post had struck a nerve; that first comment had only been the beginning. There were more than eighty comments now, almost none of them good. They ranged from one-word insults to long-winded threats. Nonetheless, Jacob let them remain. He figured he might as well; activity was activity after all. And the comments really fed off one another. Someone posted once, got a reply, and posted again, piling on the Jacob hate. It was a nicely entertaining drama (*People love drama*).

"That dealer was still a person."
"This guy got someone's son, brother, father killed..."
"What white nonsense is this?"
"Go kill yourself."

"Everyone has their demons. Couldn't just help the guy?"
"#HelpDontHarrass."
"You're worse than he was."
"Was he even a dealer? Proof, please."
"#HelpDontHarrass."
"#HelpDontHarrass."
"#HelpDontHarrass."
"Glad you got your arm f'd up."

Jacob did have *one* ally: @pugD3AL3R. Harvey (the guy signed a few of his comments with "Harvey," so Jacob was calling him Harvey) replied to every *#HelpDontHarrass* with *#DontSellDrugs*. Harvey also sent Jacob direct messages with news clips and videos on the drug problems he was seeing in Dallas. The messages got to be a bit much, one after another after another, but Missy told him he was lucky to have such a loyal follower. He was a "hyper," and "hypers" did more for someone's social media account than a hundred basic followers. Considering he didn't even have a hundred followers, he figured he was ahead of the game and made sure to thank Harvey after every message.

In between responding to Harvey and monitoring the Twitter comments, Jacob started work on his drug book, or at least a summary. He'd distilled what'd happened onto a single page. But now, he sat, looking at the second page, wondering where he was supposed to take things. He certainly hadn't collected enough material for a full book. No agent would accept it as it currently was, so he had to come up with a good encore to Dwight getting hit by a truck. He had to raise the stakes. Like in *The Lord of the Rings,* he'd had his battle at Pelennor Fields, but he still needed to cast the ring into Mount Doom. What was *that* going to be?

The newspapers' cold shoulder concerned him. Could any of this actually get attention outside of social media? Would agents respond to this? He had no way of knowing. He could only assume whatever he did next, it had to be spectacular; it had to be so shocking it lit up both social media and traditional media. Then he'd know the story was publishable.

It was a shame Dwight hadn't done the trick, though. Jacob was ready to be done. He was having nightmares about the bits of stringy muscle and bloody bone that'd been strewn across the intersection. Each dream had him right back on Washington, a shovel in hand, frantically scooping up the mess while the police and the crowd watched and waited, tapping their feet. *Faster. Faster! The street needs to get cleaned. The traffic has to get moving!*

When he'd awake, the dreamscape would drift away, of course, but the queasiness associated with all that gore and guts sloshing up the shovel's blade had a vicious tendency to stick around. Every time he bit into anything soft or squishy, he gagged. Fruits were particularly bad. He wasn't going to be able to eat a blueberry for the next year. Or a tomato. The other night, Missy had bit into a cherry tomato and squirted pink juice the length of the kitchen island. He'd nearly lost it.

He was hoping he could capture this revulsion in his book. Not only did he have an obligation to the reader, but he also owed it to himself. Writing was a form of self-therapy. Get it out on paper, and get it out of your head.

As he was trying but struggling to do just that, his phone buzzed: a new message from Harvey, aka @pugD3AL3R. Jacob went for the distraction. It was a link to a new book on the drug crisis. The book blurb said it'd been written by a recovering addict. Jacob reread that bit: a *recovering* addict. Not a *recovered* addict, but a *recovering* addict. *So basically an addict. An addict published a book.* Jacob couldn't help but imagine the addict's book proposal arriving on an agent's desk, scrawled on the back of a fast-food wrapper, and the agent jumping up and down with delight. *Best-seller!*

He kicked the coffee table, and Quincy jumped from the couch in fright. Jacob ignored him, putting his hands behind his head and staring at the ceiling. The pug found something interesting to sniff on the floor, and Jacob fixed on a hairline crack in the plaster, wondering what he had to do to get noticed. His inability to get published was a disgusting embarrassment, like Quincy's cherry eye. He had half a mind to get himself addicted to the Oxy he'd been prescribed. Maybe *that* was the second half of the book. And maybe what poured from his mind and onto the page while in the throes of addiction would be gold. *Forget recovering addict... How about a full-blown addict?* His book proposal wouldn't even be written on a fast-food wrapper. It'd just be a collection of small items his drug-addled mind found captivating, like a dead ladybug with its legs missing or a piece of lint that resembled a cow. And then, once he hit rock bottom, he could turn things around, make a grand recovery, and give readers that feel-good ending they wanted. How could an agent say no?

With his luck, though, an agent would say no—they all would. He didn't have the balls to do it anyway. Even though Missy's "do whatever it takes" mantra commanded such resolute determination, he couldn't go that far.

How far could he go then? *Track down Harvard Hulk? No. Just another dealer like Dwight*. He grabbed a piece of scrap paper from his desk and scribbled, "stash house." That could be good. If he found the *real* 1779 Humboldt, that'd be something. Those houses were chock-full of drugs, weapons, and cash. *That* would make an impact. The newspapers wouldn't ignore that, and no one would shit on him for turning in a stash house. Even if he ran a truck through the front door, no one would take the stash house's side. But there was a problem: he had no idea where a stash house was. *So get to it. Find one!* Harvard Hulk was still out there; he had to have a 1779 somewhere.

Jacob stood and stretched his good arm. Quincy was

at his feet, playing with something on the floor. The dog crouched protectively over his find, trying to keep Jacob from seeing it. "Quincy." Jacob grabbed the dog around his thick chest and lifted him. Quincy grunted in annoyance while Jacob inspected his mouth. Gripped between the dog's tiny front teeth was a wrapped bundle of cellophane. A bit of white powder drifted to the carpet. "Oh, fuck," Jacob screamed. Quincy was eating the teener Dwight had forced him to buy. He'd forgotten he'd wedged it into the leg of the coffee table. "Quincy! Drop it!"

There wasn't much left of the teener by then. Jacob pulled the mangled, wet cellophane from the pug's happy mouth and desperately scraped Quincy's tongue of any residual cocaine. He inspected Quincy's squishy face for ill signs. The cherry eye looked disgustingly, twitchingly unchanged. His pupils were terribly dilated.

Quincy shook his head and wiggled his body, escaping from Jacob's grasp. The pug took off around the coffee table and raced around the room, kicking up blankets and knocking around pillows. He stopped hard near the kitchen and turned back, panting with a crazed look of a million pug thoughts flying through his head.

"Quincy, come."

The dog did as he was told, scampering from the kitchen across the living room and flying onto the couch. He slammed into the back cushion, stopped for a second, scanned the room, then launched himself into the air, taking off again around the apartment.

"Jesus." Jacob chased after him down the hall. Quincy slid across the hardwood floor and thumped into the front door before turning back and sprinting at Jacob, eyes freakishly wide, broad tongue flapping loose from the side of his mouth. Jacob grabbed him as he tried to run by. The pug momentarily struggled, but with a few words—"Quincy, Quincy, it's okay"—Jacob got the dog to settle down.

He carefully cradled the shaking little body in his

arm then carried him into the bathroom. "Stay here," Jacob instructed as he set the pug in the bathtub and grabbed a bottle of MiraLAX from the medicine cabinet. He unscrewed the cap and held the bottle near the pug's mouth. "Quincy, drink." The pug licked at the bottle, and Jacob began to pour, counting the seconds. "One Mississippi..." He had no idea how much to give Quincy, or whether it would even make a difference, but he had to do something to get the cocaine out of him. "Two Mississippi..." If that was even possible. The cocaine could've already been fully absorbed into the pug's bloodstream. If that'd happened, he'd need a full-on blood transfusion. *Is that possible?* "Three Mississippi..." The muscles in Quincy's back shook and twitched under his fur from the stimulant's effects.

Quincy choked and coughed and sprayed the laxative across Jacob's face. *Shit.* Jacob dropped the bottle and rushed to the sink, rinsing and spitting out the tasteless liquid. Behind him, Quincy grumbled and paced around the tub, his nails clicking on the vinyl faster and faster. The dog gave a bark and tried to jump from the tub. He only made it halfway and landed on the rim, balanced like a turtle on a log. Jacob went to push him back, but before he got there, Quincy gave a vicious wiggle and sprayed the tub with diarrhea.

"Holy rip," Jacob yelled. He grabbed the pug and held him steady as the brown flow reduced to a light trickle. The smell hit like a pyroclastic blast. "Oh, my God." Jacob gagged. "Why didn't I take you out? Oh. Fuck. Quincy!" Jacob turned the faucet on full, rinsing away the bubbling shit as fast as he could, and gave Quincy's hind quarters a couple splashes of water. The vividly cold water widened Quincy's eyes.

Once the diarrhea vanished down the drain, Jacob turned off the faucet and helped Quincy settle back into the tub. The two sat in silence, staring at each other. "Is that it?" Jacob asked. "All clear?" Quincy's pupils were still dilated, and he was still shaking some, but he looked better. Jacob wrapped a towel around him and carried him to the couch, where they rested.

Quincy exhaled hard and laid his head on Jacob's thigh. Jacob gave him a pat then grabbed his laptop. He typed into Google: "How much cocaine is too much cocaine for a pug?"

There were no straight answers. A lot of sites offered symptoms to watch for and urged veterinarian care, but none gave any indication as to whether Quincy was in serious trouble. Jacob examined his dog, wrapped up tight like a Chipotle burrito, wondering if a visit to the vet was necessary. He could feel Quincy's heart beating fast and hard. Quincy was also incredibly warm. Jacob removed the towel and set the dog on the floor. "You wanna go outside? Are you hot?"

Quincy strolled around the coffee table. He sniffed a blanket, then a pair of Missy's knee-high, black suede boots. He actually seemed okay. Jacob went back to the search results and read through a site detailing the long-term effects for a dog that had ingested cocaine. Quincy let out a deep gurgle and vomited. Jacob jumped from the couch and raced to the pug, grabbing him and kicking open the door to the balcony. Quincy was finished, though.

Jacob sighed. "Maybe let's go for a walk, Quincy."

Jacob hoped whatever cocaine or diarrhea or vomit that was left in Quincy's system would get worked out as they strolled through Gold Medal Park. It also gave him a chance to stretch his shoulder. There was a deep throb there that would certainly linger if he didn't work it out. Of course, if the stretch didn't do the job, he could always double his Oxy dosage. *The early stages of addiction?* He grinned.

Quincy quickly tired of the walk and veered from

the path, flopping in the grass and rolling over onto his back to take in the sun and expose himself to the birds. His chest rose and fell in steady contentment. Jacob pulled his phone from his pocket and snapped a close-up of Quincy's intoxicated, upside-down mug. He posted it to Twitter with the caption: *Quincy's a fan. #Cocaine #LazySaturday*

Jacob took a seat on the nearby bench and rested his hands in his lap, glancing around the peaceful park. It was a shame Missy was going to San Diego for her conference this time of year. Minneapolis was at its best right now. A trip to beautiful San Diego in January or February, at the height of Minnesota's misery, would've made more sense. But this was no vacation. She hadn't chosen the dates; it was the conference's schedule. She had to go now.

As Jacob enjoyed the summer breeze, glancing around at the world, he realized how strangely empty the park still was. Not of the usual dog walkers, joggers, cyclists, or couples, but of the homeless and addicts. He spun around on the bench, taking in the entirety of the park. The benches were all clear. No raggedy blankets or stuffed plastic bags. No shopping carts filled with weathered belongings. No wandering, strange characters. Not a single one. He'd expected a momentary scattering following Dwight's death, but it'd been several weeks now. Where were they? He took a photo of the serene space, grinning as he imagined his efforts to clean up the park had actually worked. *And it'd only taken the gruesome death of one dealer. Happy un-birthday, Dwight!*

He sent a text to his sister. "*Can you look up a guy who got killed here last month? First name, Dwight. Don't know his last. Was hit by a truck on Washington and 10th.*" Emily had access to everything on everyone. She'd found out his old high school sweetheart was a chronic speeder, his third-grade teacher was a kleptomaniac, and his friend from the gray-and-white Tudor was once accused, but not charged, of rape. She could almost certainly get the dealer's rap sheet.

His book would need it.

A second after sending the text, his phone buzzed, but it wasn't Emily. It was @pugD3AL3R. He'd sent a link to the *Dallas Morning News*. The article said the Dallas PD had arrested three people in connection with manufacturing and distributing meth after receiving an anonymous tip.

"A tip," Jacob grumbled. He grabbed a small stick between his feet and gently tossed it at Quincy. It harmlessly bounced off his pink underbelly. "That's what *I* wanted. Stupid *Tribune*. I just wasn't going to be anonymous."

Quincy rolled himself over and stood, glancing up at the apartment.

"Yeah. Sure, let's go," Jacob said, standing. Quincy led the way back.

Before Jacob even fully opened the door, Missy called to him from the bathroom. "It smells so bad in here. Did you clog the toilet?"

"Had a bad morning," Jacob answered, letting Missy assume that was confirmation of her suspicion. He unclipped Quincy from his leash and peeked into the bathroom. Missy was looking at her complexion in the mirror. The rancid odor of Quincy's emptied bowels was tenacious. Jacob flipped on the bathroom fan, and said, "Toilet's fine if you need to use it."

She looked at him in the reflection. "You okay? Why's the MiraLAX out?"

Jacob stepped across the bathroom and grabbed the bottle. "Yeah. I'm fine." He gave the bottle a shake. It was empty. He dropped it in the garbage. "This stuff is potent. I'll get some more."

"You don't have to. Surprised it worked. Bought it like five years ago." She poked at a small bump on her cheek.

His phone vibrated, and he pulled it from his pocket.

"Dwight Harris: DOB 2/25/1999. Arrested 2016 in Eau Claire. Marijuana possession. Got probation. Can't check Minnesota unless I file a formal request. Why?"

"Thanks. Tipped the cops off to him." Before he could shove the phone back into his pocket, Emily called.

"What do you mean you 'tipped the cops off'?" Emily's voice was low and suspicious.

"I told them about that Dwight guy," Jacob clarified.

"Is that how you broke your arm? Mom told me last night you broke your arm."

He was hoping the word hadn't gotten out. "Hmm, not exactly. But kinda. Before that."

"'But kinda'? What've you been doing?"

He glanced at Missy, who was still inspecting her face. "Long story." *You can read about it in my book.*

Emily gave an exasperated sigh. "What did I tell you about this?"

"I know. That's why I was careful."

"Bullshit. How'd you break your arm? Tell me."

"The guy jumped me," Jacob said, "with a baseball bat."

"I have to look into this guy some more."

"No, you don't. What you gave me was good."

"It's not to satisfy your dumb curiosity, moron. If that guy was a serious distributor or something, and you got him killed... I *told* you not to do this."

"It's fine. No one knows it was me." *Except maybe Harvard Hulk.*

"You need to stop with this."

Jacob's face flushed at the scolding. He wanted to defend himself, argue his point, tell her what he was doing, but he just clenched his teeth. She wouldn't understand anyway. She was doing what she loved and making a difference in the world. She had what she wanted. She'd forgotten what it was like to be on the journey for it, but he kept his mouth shut.

"You'll get yourself killed," Emily chided. "I just arrested a guy for speeding, and he had an AR-15 in the backseat."

"Just an avid deer hunter."

"He was MS-13."

"Oh."

"You don't know who you're dealing with," Emily pressed. "If Dwight was MS-13 or the cartel, you'd already be dead."

"But he wasn't."

"No, he was born in Grove City, Minnesota. But you didn't know that."

He rested on the edge of the tub, bristling with frustration. He *hadn't* known that, but if Dwight had been something different, if he'd been with the cartel, he would've known. It would've been clear after a few interactions. He hadn't just walked up to some random vehicle that'd been speeding. He'd gotten to know the guy. Maybe he hadn't known where Dwight had been born, but he knew he wasn't the cartel or MS-13. He knew. Just like he knew Dwight wasn't even a serious distributor. He was a corner drug dealer. And Emily would've understood if she'd been there. But she hadn't seen what he had. And here she was now, thinking the worst and being the big sister. That was it. That was all. His mind cleared. "Sure. Makes sense," he offered.

"You understand?"

"I get what you're saying, yeah. I'm lucky."

"You *are*. Why were you even doing that? You bored?" Her tone shifted from authoritarian to curious.

"Thinking about writing a book."

"Write a different book. This isn't you."

That hurt. He sighed. He'd been thinking about asking Emily for her help in tracking down the identity of

Harvard Hulk, but that would clearly get a hard "no".

"You can ghost write my memoir if you're so hopped up on crime stories," Emily said.

Missy dropped her hand from her face, grinned, and left the bathroom. A second later, she cried out. "Oh, my God!"

Jacob quickly told Emily he had to go and hurried to Missy's side. She was standing over Quincy, frozen in disgust as the dog lapped up his old, congealed vomit splashed across her black suede boots. "Those were my favorite!"

Jacob remembered the dog having thrown up earlier, but he'd rushed Quincy to the balcony then downstairs to the park. He'd completely forgotten about the mess. He grabbed a blanket, twirled it around itself until it became a thick rope, and snapped it at Quincy, scaring him off into the kitchen.

Missy muttered to herself as she approached the boots. "Ugh. This is disgusting. It smells so bad." She looked at Jacob, gave him the face she knew he couldn't say no to, and asked, "Can you try to clean them? Fast?"

He accepted the punishment and tossed the blanket to the couch. "Sure."

"What'd you eat, Quincy?"

"Yeah, Quincy, what'd you eat?" Jacob parroted as he took the boots to the bathtub and started to rinse away the slimy vomit.

From the doorway, Missy watched. "Is it coming off? Please tell me it's coming off."

He held the dripping black boots up for her to see. "Kind of?"

"Forget it," she whined. "It doesn't matter. I can't wear those. Even if they're clean, I'll be thinking about vomit. I can't. Just throw them out. I'll buy a new pair."

Jacob shook the boots until they stopped dripping then carried them to the tall waste bin in the kitchen.

"Wait. Wait." Missy snuck up behind him. "Let me take a picture." She gently grasped the boots with two fingers, snapped a photo, and handed them back to Jacob.

He watched her swipe furiously at her screen. "We good?" he asked.

She nodded. "Yeah. Go ahead. Chuck 'em."

He released the boots into the bin. "What'd you post?"

"A memorial photo. So sad."

"I need a memorial photo for my literary dreams."

Missy gave him a light slap on his bad shoulder. "Oh, stop it."

Jacob winced. "Careful."

"Really? Still hurts?"

"When you do *that*, yeah."

"Sorry. I'll remember next time."

Jacob retreated to the bathroom and opened the medicine cabinet to check his Oxy. He only had a half dozen of the pale-yellow tablets left. Next to it was a bottle of the children's Tylenol Missy took every morning. He gave it a shake. Sounded half full. *How many children's Tylenol equal an Oxy? Bottles and bottles.*

He hadn't intended on taking the Oxy for long, but he was still hurting. And Children's Tylenol wouldn't cut it. He needed a refill. His arm just didn't feel like it was healing that well. He thought of @pugD3AL3R's message about the recovering addict's book, and he again wondered what it'd be like to get himself addicted to Oxy to write something while in its steely grips. But as before, that wasn't a ledge he wanted to climb out on. It was the stash house he'd settled on. *That* would be a perfectly acceptable way to complete his book, and he wouldn't kill himself in the process. He just had to be careful. Emily might have annoyed him with her warnings and scolding, but she was still right. It was dangerous—but it'd be worth it.

He shut the cabinet door, catching the reflection of

his little shit-eater grin in the mirror. He smiled wider, resplendently confident in the ending he'd come up with for the book. There wouldn't be an agent who'd say no to it. *People love drama.*

And then, once that bona fide hit got published, people would start paying attention to *The Shedding*. No one put a bestselling author's manuscript into the slush pile.

XI.

Vicente got rid of that first set of migrants. He sent them back to the border crossing to wait their turn alongside the throngs of others and brought in an equally eager, but more competent group. It'd been three weeks now, and they were nearly two-thirds of the way there. It was mostly a straight shot except for one section halfway through where they'd had to curl around a cluster of pipes underneath the warehouse across the street. Vicente expected the tunnel to be fully dug out within a couple of weeks. End of the month, July 31st.

El Avispón already was lining people up outside the gates, so to speak. There were agreements in place with several traffickers to start sending people through on day one. *Grand opening. Step right up!*

Vicente still grew uneasy when he thought of their new line of business, but the silver lining was that this would help him remain in El Avispón's good graces while he worked to recover that lost cocaine, which was still buried in the tunnel, next to the body of the migrant woman. It was getting to the point where he might just have to come in from above. He had a reasonable idea where to position some migrants to dig, but it was near the border, and that was such a risk. The Border Patrol would spot the activity, then they'd take the cocaine. Ideally, he just hoped El Avispón would let it go. And given the progress with this tunnel, it was possible. El Avispón was entirely focused on this new venture. Already he was talking about having another one about a mile down the road built; this trafficking business was going to be big money. They'd all get rich.

More important to El Avispón, though, was the subsequent growth of the CJNG. The influx of cash would help recruit new soldiers, buy more police, bribe more politicians, gain more territory, and with a little luck, solidify them as the new kings of the plaza, usurping the Sinaloa Cartel after decades of heavy-handed rule. The CJNG, with El Avispón at the helm, would take the crown and rule over all. It would be a glorious revolution.

Vicente smiled; the recent setbacks appeared almost over.

XII.

Jacob was trying to post on social media as often as possible. Missy had been right. There was a very clear correlation between his activity and that of his followers and their engagement. Activity bred activity. He was also trying to get people to forget that post of Quincy, where he'd said the pug was a fan of cocaine. No one, not even @pugD3AL3R, took kindly to that. If Dwight's death had garnered a shitstorm, Quincy's cocaine had been an absolute firestorm. He'd deleted it a couple of hours after posting it and had been trying to erase the memory of it with numerous posts since then, but it was the internet, and screenshots kept popping up to his annoyance.

He made himself move on, focusing on his growing list of followers instead. He hoped to spot a literary agent among them, but it seemed those people were staying away. Their emails had begun to dry up as well. What'd been a nearly daily arrival was now maybe once every two weeks.

The growing silence wasn't all that unwelcome. The wound of rejection could heal, and he could focus on his drug book. He was now doing a bit of research, reading *Dreamland* by Sam Quinones and *Drug Dealer, MD* by Anna Lembke. The people, the organizations, and the politics behind the scenes were fascinating. He'd even found a website that posted stories about the cartels (Sinaloa, CJNG, Gulf, Juárez, Zetas, Beltran-Leyva) with historical overviews, news clips, reports, everything. He got lost in all the information and loved it, highlighting the most interesting of what he found with tweeted links. *#OpioidCrisis #Sinaloa #BorderlandBeat*

He was posting multiple times an hour—a rate well above Missy's suggestion—and everything was on point. Cocaine, cartels, and calamity. But tweets about Minneapolis were becoming few and far between. The homeless and addicts weren't in Gold Medal Park like before, and it left him without his most convenient, most exclusive material. These recent posts were mostly about events from which he was terribly far removed, and Curly Burly's comment that "if it's not your story to tell, then no one wants to hear it" was constantly playing in his head. He needed to get out and find more personalized material. He needed to find that stash house, but his cast was keeping him grotesquely sedentary. All he could do was put up the same balcony shot of the park in all its homeless-free glory. That, or a shot of his Oxy, which he'd recently gotten refilled. Another fifty tablets at ten milligrams. "*No more*," he'd posted. "*Doctor's orders. Long-term use dramatically increases the likelihood of addiction.*" *#OpioidCrisis* That had garnered some interest. A couple of people commented, calling the claim bullshit and saying most people who took the painkiller didn't develop even a hint of an addiction, but he didn't care. The post was original, personal, and attention grabbing. He even got a direct message asking about the Oxy's "availability", which he later showed Missy.

"No," was her answer.

"Who do you think's asking?" He then added, "For the book."

"Don't you need the pills?"

He did. The cast was coming off in a week, but he still needed the Oxy, so to her relief, he ignored the message. Then came an offer to trade: Oxy for fentanyl.

"What is that even?" Missy asked.

He'd seen a few articles. "It's a synthetic opioid. Really strong. Two milligrams is lethal. That's like five grains of salt."

"Oh, yeah," Missy laughed. "That's what you need."

"Could make for an interesting chapter in the book. Fentanyl and me."

"You've got plenty for your book as is." She leaned over and inspected his laptop, which he tilted so she'd have a better angle. She grimaced. "Ugh, why are you looking at this? That guy's head was really cut off?"

It was an article detailing a recent attack between rival cartels. "It's interesting," he argued. He brought up another article. "There's some stuff about San Diego on here too. San Diego's CJNG land. That guy was a rival cartel. Sinaloa."

"Don't tell me that. I don't need to think about that when I'm there. I'm already freaking out."

"Why are you freaking out?" He studied Missy's thin face for a hint, but there was nothing except for an obsessively clear complexion, bright lip gloss, and sharply drawn eyebrows. She was definitely a number or two above him on the attractive scale.

"Freaking out 'cause I haven't gotten promoted yet."

"So? You will."

"The conference is ten days away. July twenty-sixth."

"You wanted the promotion before then?"

She nodded.

"Did anyone say you'd get promoted before then?"

She shook her head.

"Okay. So don't worry. You'll get promoted when you get promoted." He put an arm over her shoulder.

"I can't be on that panel if I'm still just an executive project manager. Not with Alicia on it too. It's embarrassing." Missy sat up. "What if I'm not getting promoted and Alicia is?"

Anything's possible, Jacob thought. He had no idea what was going on over there at 44th. It was digital marketing. Artificial metrics produced from soft analytics and data that could be manipulated a thousand ways to Sunday to say whatever was desired. *Toll-free phone psychics for the digital age.* He had no way to judge someone's effectiveness in that realm. Nevertheless, he said, "You'll get your promotion. Before Alicia."

Missy gave him a half smile, glanced at the laptop, and asked, "If I don't, can I get the cartel to kill her when I'm down there?" The half-smile turned full.

"Costs extra to cut off her head."

Missy laughed, enjoying the thought immensely. "Oh, that's so mean."

"How about something like this?" He showed her another article.

Oil Drum Found Floating in Chula Vista Bay Contained Body

Authorities recovered the remains of a woman's body sealed within an oil drum Thursday afternoon. The woman has not yet been identified, but it is believed the remains may be that of twenty-four-year-old Jessica Frank, who went missing last month. Frank's abandoned car was found in the long-term parking lot of the San Diego International Airport two days after her reported disappearance, leading some to suspect she had simply left, but traces of blood found in the car suggested otherwise.

These oil drums have sadly become a common occurrence in the bay lately. Concerned citizens have called for more action from the city as cartel- and gang-related violence continue to rise, possibly a result of spillover violence from Tijuana, where the CJNG and CAF cartels continue to battle for control of the city...

Missy drew away from the laptop. "That's horrible."

"It's war down there. The Sinaloa's top guy got extradited to the US, and now all these smaller cartels are taking shots at them." He stopped. Missy was shaking her head. She didn't want to hear any more, so he just quickly added, "That lady was probably connected to the cartels, or related to someone who was. It wasn't just random. Don't worry."

"Easy for you to say. You're not going there."

He sheepishly looked down at his laptop and clicked on another article, which he quietly read to himself.

Massacre in Second Cartel Safe House

For the second time in three weeks, and the fourth in the last four months, a cartel safe house was attacked in the night, leaving two dead on the 48th block of the San Pedro neighborhood. Police say there were no witnesses, but they believe the serial killer known as Castor is responsible. They reiterate that they don't believe Castor is a threat to the public, but they ask everyone to be vigilant.

Castor has been linked to more than thirty murders across the US over the last several years, starting in Atlanta, then New York, Baltimore, Chicago, and now here in San Diego. In every instance to date, the victims have had direct ties with the drug trade...

Jacob bookmarked the page. This Castor figure was intriguing. A vigilante, kind of like him, just with a sadistic, murderous side. Castor was like that character on TV, the serial killer who killed serial killers. Jacob couldn't remember the show's name. Didn't matter. Point was, Castor was getting in the news. People were paying attention to him. *That's the difference between Minneapolis newspapers and San Diego newspapers.* If Dwight had been hit by a truck in San Diego, it would've been covered. *And tonight at six...*

Jacob turned to Missy. "What if I went to San Diego with you?"

"Kind of late for that."

"Flights won't be crazy high yet."

"I'm going there for five days, Tuesday through Saturday. You can't get that off work."

Jacob shrugged. If he couldn't, maybe he'd just quit. The trip might very well be worth it. What could he do in five days? A lot. Especially if he showed no reservations and went full bore into things. His cast would be off, and San Diego's drug underbelly had to be out of control. If he could manage to get results in Minneapolis, a city some 1,400 miles from the border, San Diego would be a bonanza. There'd be so many stash houses scattered around that it'd be hard *not* to find one in five days.

Visiting Minnesotan, a 3M Scientist, Uncovers Stash House: Authorities find largest supply of heroin ever. Tunnel under the house leads to a warehouse in Tijuana with $2 billion worth of drugs.

If that happened, it wouldn't just be a San Diego news story—it would be an international story, an Associated Press story. Jacob suppressed an excited chuckle. Missy and her people would be listening to Google's latest AdWords algorithm adjustment while he'd be making the biggest drug bust in history. *This* was his chance. Make-or-break time. He was certain of it, and he wasn't about to ignore the feeling again.

The last time he'd had such clarity had been back in

Virginia at the FBI Academy right before he'd been kicked out. His SO, sitting at his desk in a dark blue polo adorned with the FBI seal, had told him: "You will be removed from the program if you don't pass the next physical assessment." Jacob had taken things too far. His refusal to put any effort into the physical training wasn't being tolerated. He thought his reasoning had been sound; he was going to be an intelligence analyst, not a field agent, so he'd held back on the physical rigors to focus on the intellectual requirements. But that wasn't how it worked, and his SO was warning him one last time. Jacob gave a nod, apologized, and excused himself from the windowless office to the windowless hall. That was his final warning. Make-or-break time. He got it. But then he didn't change. Maybe it was because of fear or stubbornness or naivety, but as he walked from the SO's office, he became less and less inclined to follow the directive. The physical activity was simply too taxing and distracting. He had gone through the same struggle in both grade school and high school. PE class had been such torture. He couldn't focus the rest of the day. His grades suffered. If he was going to be his best at the FBI, he couldn't be burdened with such strenuous, unnecessary demands. So, as he walked from the building that day into the drizzly fall afternoon, he'd decided he wasn't going to change a thing. If his SO actually went through with dismissing him, then screw it. The FBI wasn't a place he wanted to be then. And a week later, Jacob was out the door, bewildered, angry, dazed.

Now, older and wiser, he recognized he'd lacked the fortitude to do what was necessary to prevent the dismissal. All he'd had to do was play the game, and he would've been fine. Well, so much for that. He'd been booted from the FBI, but he'd learned, and now he was ready to play. He'd go into the war zone and face the cartel. Emily had warned him, and the online articles were terrifying, but this was necessary. He hadn't done enough to get noticed by the newspapers over Dwight, but with a better understanding of the game, he'd go to San Diego and make a splash. This was his shot. Enough was enough; no more pussyfooting around. This was the game; this was the plan. He'd rise up, be better, and execute.

"Let's see what flights cost," he told Missy.

Jacob counted the cash lying on the bed. An even three thousand dollars. All hundreds. This was the investment he was going to make in his San Diego venture. He wasn't going to simply get carte blanche access to the drug world down there. He'd have to buy his way in.

The bills looked utterly obscene resting atop Missy's beloved purple comforter. Truthfully, though, this much cash looked obscene anywhere, even amid a crowd of wealth and luxury, which he'd found out while retrieving it.

The Guthrie Theater had the closest ATM, and while the lobby was normally empty, that evening had been a packed house. Thirty-minutes before the opening night of *Metamorphoses*, a sea of pressed summer suits, flowing dresses, and glittering jewelry canvassed the building in and out. The wealth of the city had shown up in force.

As the ATM spat out hundred after hundred, those nearest in the crowd started giving Jacob sideways glances. He folded the obese bundle in half and jammed it into his basketball shorts. "Damn scalpers," he muttered to an elderly gentleman in a white-and-blue seersucker suit.

"You can have my ticket for half that," the man huffed.

"Sorry. Promised some old lady out front I'd buy from her." Jacob vanished into the crowd, the bulge in his shorts catching several women, and a few men, by curious surprise as he sidled by.

Outside in the humid summer air, the crowd

thinned, and Jacob made his escape. Just as he was about nearly clear, a voice cried out. "J. Hey, J!"

Jacob spotted Charlie frantically waving at him near an art installation resembling an oversized game of pick-up sticks.

"How you doing?" Charlie asked as he came and set his decorated rucksack on the sidewalk. "Haven't seen you since that mess with Dwight. Wanted to say thanks."

Jacob subconsciously grasped the bills in his pocket "Thanks? For what? You stopped him from shooting me. I should say thanks."

"You stepped in first, man."

"Oh, right." He'd forgotten that bit, the recording of it lost in the sewer. "Glad I could help."

"When you getting that off?" Charlie gently touched the spica cast.

"Tomorrow."

"Oh, that's great." As Charlie leaned in close, the strong rubbery odor that claimed territory over the homeless man intensified. "It itch like a bitch?"

Jacob chuckled. "A bit, yeah." The palm of his hand had grown sweaty around the money. "Glad you're doing well," he said, and started to move on.

"Hey, just one thing," Charlie whispered, grabbing the sleeve of Jacob's shirt.

"What's that?"

"Did you try and get Dwight arrested?"

"No," Jacob quickly lied. "Why?"

"Dwight said you did. And thought I was helping you." He released Jacob's shirt. "Don't matter. Just curious. That guy had crazy thoughts in his head."

And then a truck squirted them across the street. World's largest tube of toothpaste.

"Hey, you don't happen to have a dollar or two on you, do you?" Charlie asked.

For a moment, Jacob was tempted to pull out the

stack and hand him one of the hundreds, but while he liked the guy, he didn't *know* the guy. He had no idea how Charlie might react with that wad of cash right there in front of his nose, so Jacob simply shook his head. "Sorry, man."

Charlie smiled and nodded. "No problemo."

Jacob hurried off, making it the rest of the way home without another encounter, then carefully spread the bills atop the soft purple bed. Above the fanned bills was his bottle of Oxy. He hadn't much touched the refill. Maybe there were forty-six, forty-seven tablets left. He figured dealers would exchange information for cash, but addicts would want the tablets. So between the two, he could buy enough trust and clout to gain access to all the players in San Diego. And then those people, he hoped, would lead him to a stash house.

There was a plastic bag on the floor beside the bed, and Jacob grabbed it, scooping the cash and the Oxy inside. He wrapped the contents tightly and tucked the bundle between the box spring and mattress, so Missy wouldn't see it.

He'd tell her about all of this at some point soon, but now wasn't the time, because even if she supported his efforts (the drug book was her idea after all), she was so wound up about her promotion, the panel, and Alicia that he had to keep quiet. He lowered the mattress and pulled the bedspread down. Looked good.

He stretched out his arm, his right arm, for the first time in six weeks.

"Go slow," the nurse, a small, round woman in her fifties, instructed.

Jacob smiled. "Feels good."

"I'm glad. I'll let Dr. Martin know you're ready." She left Jacob alone, shutting the door quietly behind her.

Jacob examined the pale, unwashed lump of meat his arm had become. He poked at it, reintroducing himself to himself. He had healed. He took a photo of his cast-less arm and shoulder, put it up on Twitter, and typed, "*Wouldn't wish this on anyone.*" *#Freedom #SurvivorType*

Someone left a comment within a few seconds. "*I would...on you.*"

They were still going at him. But he shrugged it off, which, he noted, he could do both figuratively and literally now that the cast was gone. He gave his shoulder a gentle rotational test. *Feels good.* Jacob shoved his phone into his pocket as the gray-haired doctor entered.

Dr. Martin smiled, his bushy mustache fluttering, and sat on the stool beside Jacob, hands in his lap. "How's it feel?"

"Good." Jacob gently flapped his arm like a bird.

"Excellent. Did that old spica cast drive you a little nuts?"

"Yeah. Only killed *one* guy," Jacob grinned. "Not too bad."

Dr. Martin gave a polite laugh, not knowing that was actually the truth. "Okay. Hop up on the table, and I'll take a look."

Jacob moved over, the paper crinkling as he positioned himself at the table's edge.

The doctor looked at the arm and shoulder, then said, "I'm going to move this around. Tell me if you feel any pain at any point. Okay?"

Jacob nodded.

"Just let your arm go limp. I'll do all the heavy lifting."

Jacob nodded once more.

Dr. Martin then went about raising and lowering and rotating Jacob's arm. After a couple of minutes, he stopped, and asked, "No pain?"

"Nope. Felt fine. Stiff in some spots, but not

painful."

"That stiffness will diminish after a few days," the doctor assured him. "Let me test your shoulder a bit." He rocked and rolled the joint. "This'll be susceptible to dislocation. Maybe for the rest of your life."

"Ugh, sucks."

"You should be fine with daily chores and regular use. Even some weightlifting."

Jacob smirked at the thought of him in a gym.

"But the shoulder isn't set as securely as before. You could get surgery to fix it, but at this point, I wouldn't say that's necessary. Just be cognizant about it." He placed Jacob's arm at his side and stepped back. "And the X-ray looked good. The breaks have all healed well. I'd say you're all set. Don't participate in any strenuous physical activity for another couple weeks, and no contact sports for at least the rest of the year, but other than that, you can get back to a normal routine."

"Should I come back for a checkup some time?"

"Only if you start feeling pain. You still taking the Oxy?" He looked at Jacob without any accusations or suspicions. Just a genuine question.

Jacob assumed Dr. Martin would be required to report any unused amount to the DEA—they had an entire division, Diversion Control, to monitor inventories and transactions— so he said, "No, it's gone. Flushed it,"

Dr. Martin smiled; his mustache fluttered again. "Did you ask your primary doctor about the low platelets?"

"I did. Saw a hematologist couple weeks ago. All clear."

"Wonderful. You're doing great then. All clear from me here too." The doctor offered his hand, and Jacob shook it. "Hopefully we won't meet again."

When Jacob stepped out of the clinic, free of the cast and his arm at his side, swaying as he walked to his car, he felt weirdly exposed. His shoulder itched, and he gave it a scratch. *Itches love scratches.* He had his freedom again. Everything was in working order. And just in time for San Diego. They were flying there in two days. He was ready for his next adventure.

XIII.

Jacob thought he'd been inconspicuous when he slipped the Air Jordan into his suitcase, but not so.

"What's that?" Missy asked from across the room as she stood over her own, albeit much larger, suitcase.

"A shoe," he dryly told her, hoping she'd lose interest.

"No crap," she huffed and walked around the bed and grabbed it. "It's not yours."

"Why you say that?" He knew what she was getting at, but he refused to make it easy on her. And honestly, he didn't even know why he still had it, or why he was bringing it to San Diego. *Some kind of good luck charm, like a talisman? Or more like a trophy, like a hunter keeping the antlers of a big buck?* That didn't sound right. *Probably sounds even worse out loud.* So he kept quiet, making Missy explain herself instead.

"Well," she said, putting a hand on her hip, "for starters, you've only got two pairs of shoes in the entire closet, and this isn't one of them. And, it's a size fourteen." She turned her eyes down to his bare feet and raised her eyebrows to indicate the obvious.

Jacob took back the sneaker and laid it in the suitcase.

Missy grumbled. “Why do you have that?”

He grabbed a couple of shirts and dropped them atop the sneaker, covering it. “I don’t know. Just a memento or something.”

Missy’s nose crinkled. She tossed the shirts aside and pulled the shoe out, dropping it to the floor like it was a dead bug. “Whose is it?”

“It’s nothing. It’s clean.”

Missy stared worriedly at it as if it might sprout spindly little legs and scurry under the bed. “Whose is it?”

She was really pushing him to say it; he gritted his teeth. “Dwight’s. It slipped off his foot when he was running from the police. I picked it up. I don’t know why.”

“Ew! Why would you pick it up? And why are you packing it?”

She was blowing this way out of proportion. “It’s just a shoe,” he grumbled.

“From a dead guy!”

Jacob rolled his eyes. “Okay. You got me. I’ve got a sick shoe fetish. I was going to have a little sexy time with it while you were at your conference. Can you blame a guy?”

Missy glared at him, unamused. Then she pursed her lips, grabbed the toe of the shoe between her thumb and forefinger, and hurried from the bedroom to the kitchen. The shoe went into the waste bin.

Jacob’s first thought was to fish it out, but he restrained himself. Maybe he could make her feel bad, and she’d do it herself. “Fine,” he mumbled as pathetically as he could. “I was just using it as motivation. Had a plan for San Diego and thought it’d keep me focused on the goal. But whatever.”

She crossed her arms. “What do you think you’re going to do in San Diego?”

“Not to be too dramatic, but find a stash house filled with a billion dollars’ worth of drugs.”

“Come on. I don’t need this. I’m already stressed

about the panel." She repeated, "What are you going to do?"

"That's the truth. I want to find a stash house."

"Yeah, no, that's not going to happen." She dropped her arms and went back to the bedroom.

Jacob looked down at the Jordan. It'd settled amid their morning eggshells and coffee grounds. The side of the sneaker was streaked a dung-like brown. He left the shoe where it was and stormed back to the bedroom. "Why not? What do you care?"

She stared at him, shocked. "Excuse me? Did you *not* just spend the last six weeks in a cast?"

"That's not going to happen again," he huffed.

"Oh, it's not, is it?"

"I know more about what'll happen with this than you do about your promotion."

Missy clenched her jaw, waited a moment, then said in a measured tone, "You're not going. Cancel your ticket."

"Can't. Nonrefundable."

"Then tough. You just wasted three hundred dollars."

"I'm not staying." He crossed his arms and looked at the closet behind Missy as he muttered, "You don't have any idea what publishing my book means to me."

"No idea?" she hollered. "I've been with you every step of the way. How can I not know?"

"It's not just about this book." He turned his eyes to meet hers. "It's everything that's led up to this. I can't tell you how many times I was told how smart I was, how I'd do great things, how much potential I had. And what's happened?"

"A lot," Missy snapped. "Look at what you have." She waved her arm wide.

"What? This apartment? It's an *apartment*. Not a condo. Not our own place. And I hate my job. We barely have any money in the bank. So what do I have?"

"You have me! And Quincy! And your family! And

what about all the trips we go on? All those experiences? Any of that mean anything to you?" She was tearing up. "People would kill to have your life."

Jacob threw his hands in the air and shook his head. "It's not a life. It's just... existing!"

Missy turned her eyes to the ceiling, trying to keep the tears from rolling down her cheeks.

His heart sank. "That came out wrong." He stepped over and embraced her, resting his chin on the top of her soft lily-scented hair. "I'm grateful I have you. Really."

Her body shook as the tears started. "I know you didn't mean it. But you're not happy."

Jacob sighed. "I'm not. But not because of you. It's this book. It's my dream. It's... I don't know... It's just a big part of me that I can't let fail."

"You're crazy," she murmured.

"I know."

She gave a snotty chuckle and sniffed. "Let's think of something else to do for your book. No more drug stuff."

No more? He buried his head in her hair, so he'd take a moment to think before speaking. He tried to convince himself he had enough material to write the drug book without San Diego, but that was a terrible, bold-faced lie. It was half of a book at best.

"Promise," Missy pressed.

He sighed, knowing he was about to say something he didn't want to say. "Promise."

She hugged him tighter. "We'll think of something. Everything will work out."

He wanted to believe that, but the phrase only sounded like the mantra given to a perpetually hopeless man.

"Just relax in San Diego. There's a really nice climbing wall downtown."

"Climbing's your thing, not mine."

"Then go to a baseball game. The stadium's right by

the hotel."

He gave Missy a loving squeeze, and said, "Yeah, maybe," as he eyed the spot between the box spring and the mattress where he'd hidden the cash and Oxy.

Jacob was on the balcony, sitting on the edge of a chair, clutching a glass of bourbon. He and Missy had had their dinner, him mostly in quiet and her chatting about her game plan for the conference. She was now back to packing.

He wasn't a bourbon drinker, not much of a drinker of anything for that matter, but he needed something to take the edge off the sour mood that'd developed while Missy had gone on about her plans, having so recently shot down his. He poured himself an ounce of the first bottle he found in the cupboard and stepped out into the humid evening.

He sipped and stewed, harshly judging the people in the park below. *Too fat. Shouldn't be eating ice cream. She's the reason the healthcare system is going down the shitter.* He scanned to the right. *Can his shorts get any tighter? How don't his balls hurt? Maybe he doesn't have any.* His eyes followed the walking path up the hill. *She's way too pretty for him. Hate their dog too. Stupid-looking ankle biter.*

He took a sip of the bourbon, something Missy's father had bought them last year. Blanton's. Apparently hard to get. It was okay.

Jacob spotted a delicate, pasty-white guy with socks pulled up midcalf giving off a strong pedophilia vibe. The man's dinner-plate glasses and wispy hair hammered home the point. *Creep. Weirdo.* But as Jacob continued to watch him eat his ice cream and read his book, his judgment turned to pity.

Pedo Man was probably a perfectly nice guy. And so was everyone else he'd been criticizing. The bourbon was making quick work of his edginess.

Yet the promise he'd made to Missy still lingered. That hadn't been the right thing to do. He'd end up regretting it. No doubt about it. Maybe not right away, but at some point, on some random day, the thought of it would pop into his head, and a hateful, accusatory acid would start to spread. But Missy was just worried about him. She didn't want him hurt. She loved him. Could he blame her? *Absolutely.* If he flew to San Diego and just went to a baseball game and took a few photos of the ocean, he'd hold it against her. It was just how he worked. He still hadn't forgiven his mom for not letting him play hockey when he was eight. He'd begged her, but she'd said it was too dangerous. And just like Missy now, she'd only been watching out for him. But it hadn't just been about playing a game of hockey. He wanted to hang out with his friends. He wanted to be part of the experience. He wanted to get all the inside jokes. But because of her, he'd missed out on all of that. She ended up putting him in tennis years later, but the damage had already been done. He started tracking those moments when she "protected" him, each instance a LEGO brick, and by the time he turned eighteen, there was a massive, disgustingly colorful wall standing between them. And that wall still existed. He didn't want that happening with Missy.

The door to the neighboring balcony swung open, breaking him from the thought. Curly Burly stepped out, and Jacob lifted his glass slightly and nodded.

"Ugh, Dante's *Inferno*, it's humid," the old man howled as he settled into his lounge chair. He glanced at Jacob. "You have to put a couple ice cubes in that drink there."

"Probably should've," Jacob acknowledged.

"Drinking to celebrate or commiserate?"

"To forget. You want a glass? It's bourbon."

"Oh, sure, if you're offering."

Jacob went and got him a glass, handing the bourbon

(with ice) across the transom.

"Cheers." CB held up his drink.

Jacob extended his own, and they connected the glasses six stories up. "Cheers."

The two sipped the bourbon and watched the treetops sway as an occasional commercial jet drifted across the sky.

"Park seems quieter these days. You ever post that photo on Twitter?" CB asked.

Jacob smirked. "Oh, yeah." He gave him a rundown of what had happened since.

"Great Gatsby. Meant to ask you about that cast. Never would've guessed you'd been beaten like a rented mule." He gave a low, belly laugh that made Jacob laugh. They both took a sip of their bourbon. "Wow," CB muttered. "You got yourself a not-half-bad story there. The *Trib* should've gotten back to you."

Jacob shrugged. "They don't care about that stuff."

"Guess not. If I were you, I'd think about putting pen to paper on that. Needs a little more to it, but that's a good start."

"I think so too. Heading to San Diego tomorrow."

"Oh?" The man's spectacled eyes grew with interest. "My brother worked for the DEA there."

"He still there? Maybe I could talk to him."

"He passed ten years ago unfortunately."

"Oh, sorry."

"It's all right. Death comes for everyone." CB looked up at the underside of the seventh-floor balcony. "Hugh spent twenty years in that office. God, the stories he could tell. Could've filled a dozen books. Wish I could remember what parts of San Diego he talked about."

"I read about some stuff happening in Imperial Beach, Eastlake, and Bonita. Any of those ring a bell?"

"I've heard of them. Can't say any click. My information's outdated anyway. Hugh was there in the eighties and nineties. Go check Imperial Beach. Worst case, you end up on the beach with nothing to do."

Jacob nodded. "I'll just be going to a baseball game or something. Missy has a conference. That's why we're going. Not 'cause I'm researching or anything."

"You should poke around down there."

"Maybe. There's a ton of information online."

CB belly laughed again. "The age of the Internet. Nothing can be a substitute for firsthand experience. Don't forget that. And experiences keep you focused. There's almost too much information available these days, and when you sit down to write, you don't know what to cut and what to keep."

"Maybe you could share some of your brother's stories?" Jacob tensed, sorry he'd made the imposition. "If you want."

CB pressed his lips, giving it a thought. "Could be interesting, if I can remember any well enough."

"I bet you could fill a chapter." Jacob imagined one of Hugh's stories as maybe even the prologue; it could be a nice introduction to his book. He sat up straight as he considered the possibility.

"We'll have to sit down and talk some more when you get back. Maybe I'll have more than just a vague recollection of something insightful."

"I'll take whatever you can remember."

"Be careful. Might all come flooding back." CB finished his bourbon and handed the empty glass back.

"That'd be great. Coauthors then. My story, your story, alternating chapters."

"You can have all the credit. I owe you for the drink." CB stretched his hands high, exposing his generously fuzzy gut. "Time for a little supper, I think. Have a safe flight tomorrow."

"Will do. Be back on Sunday." Jacob watched CB vanish into his apartment, and then he turned his gaze back to the park. CB was right. First-hand experience was everything. Missy would understand. She was always talking about collecting experiences rather than things. But still, he'd keep quiet about this. No sense in upsetting her. She had her conference to think about.

XIV.

Missy showed Jacob the conference brochure. She pointed to her name, clearly annoyed.

It was spelled right. Her picture looked fine. "What're you showing me?" he asked.

"This is exactly what I didn't want happening. I'm still just an executive account manager. It's embarrassing. Kyle couldn't make up his mind." She flipped the small booklet onto an empty chair.

They were in the Starbucks around the corner from their hotel, the Hard Rock. Jacob had wanted to grab a table out on the sidewalk (*It's a sunny morning, mid-seventies, and the breeze smells of the ocean*), but Missy refused. The shops and restaurants of San Diego's Gaslamp Quarter drew too much of a crowd. "I don't need idiots on e-scooters whipping by every thirty seconds," she'd said. Yet it wasn't that much better inside. It was a Starbucks after all. And with today being day one of the conference, the place was alive with bodies vying for space and voices trying to be heard. People were everywhere, waiting for, or sipping on, their morning fuel. *Start your engines.*

Missy went back to her phone, quickly becoming lost in her thoughts, surprisingly unfazed by the venti-mocha-soy-milk crowd standing a breath's width away. He leaned protectively over his cappuccino, claustrophobic and exhausted. It'd been a long flight the previous night. Three and a half hours. Even on Delta, with some of the more comfortable seats of any airline, it was still a butt breaker of a ride. They landed at 8:00 p.m., 10:00 p.m. CST, and then there was the walk through the airport, the gathering of luggage, getting the rental car, and driving to the hotel. It was 9:30 p.m. before they were in their room. Jacob hadn't stayed up much longer.

Missy, on the other hand, had rehearsed her talking points into the early morning hours, finally climbing into bed who knows when. But still, between the two of them, she was the one who now appeared refreshed and ready. She set her coffee on the table and glared hard over Jacob's shoulder toward the shop's entrance, her eyes thinning with hate. *If looks could kill.* He turned around. The line at the counter hadn't diminished in the twenty minutes they'd been there. The baristas were hurrying to keep it moving, but the faces of those in line didn't seem terribly impressed with the effort. One step, wait, wait, one step, wait, wait...

"At least *she* didn't get the promotion," Missy mumbled.

Jacob spotted Alicia near the back of the line. He turned to face Missy. "Why don't we invite her over to sit with us when she's got her coffee?" He grinned and sipped his drink.

"How about you choke on that cappuccino instead?" Missy suggested.

He set the coffee down and gave a long "aaaah," smacking his lips. "Nope, I'm good."

"Such a little bitch," she muttered.

"Me or Alicia?"

"Both."

"Love you too, babe!" He leaned across the table and presented his lips, which she kissed without reservation.

Missy finished the last of her breakfast, a chocolate

cake pop. Jacob was immensely glad to see it disappear. The little cake on a stick reminded him of cupcakes, and cupcakes reminded him of Dwight, and his stomach didn't take kindly to the remembrance of Dwight's head popping in all its squishy, squirty glory. He really needed to put pen to paper and memorialize that bit of history sometime soon, so he could clear it from his head.

Missy set the paper stick on the table. "That wasn't that good. If I had time, I'd talk to the manager. Tasted stale." She stood and grabbed her coffee and tote. "No time, though. Gotta get going."

"When's your panel today?"

"It's tomorrow, the twenty-seventh."

"Not today? You were practicing last night."

She shook her head. "Tomorrow at ten thirty."

"Easy day today then."

"No, it's a full day. Very busy."

He smiled. "Sure. Go."

"See you tonight." Missy spun and hurried through the shop. "Hi, Alicia," she chirped as she passed her in line. Alicia smiled and said "Good morning" in return.

Jacob's day was busy too. He'd explore Point Loma and Coronado in the morning then maybe catch a baseball game in the afternoon. Or maybe he'd drive up to La Jolla and check out the sea lions. He didn't know. He'd make it up. Whatever garnered the fewest questions and kept conversation to a minimum that evening would be perfect. So long as Missy found his day dull, she wouldn't press him for details, and he wouldn't have to fabricate a complicated story, because the truth of the matter was that what he'd actually planned was definitely not Missy-approved.

Jacob plopped into the rental car, a 2017 white Ford Focus. A cherry air freshener was working hard to knock down a cacophony of fast-food oils, sour BO, saltwater, dead fish, and a touch of cigarette smoke (just a touch). Jacob rolled down the windows and got on Interstate 5, heading south. He'd stop just before the border at Imperial Beach, the southernmost city on the West Coast.

As he drove, he stretched and restretched his right shoulder. The flight had aggravated it, and the hotel bed had pressed at it awkwardly throughout the night. A lifetime of shoulder issues, the doctor had said. Jacob recalled his sister had naturally loose shoulder joints. When they were kids, it seemed like she was always dislocating one or the other. Maybe he could ask her how she managed it these days, assuming he remembered. There was going to be a lot more interesting things on his mind and stories to share in five days' time.

He took the Focus through Chula Vista and exited I-5 onto Palm Avenue. He was looking for a small beachside park called Dunes. It was basically just an entry point to the beach from the residential streets. Nothing special. Google Maps showed there to be a few basketball courts, some picnic tables around a water fountain, and a small blue-and-gray restroom where beachgoers rinsed off before hopping into their cars. What he was specifically watching for as he cruised the street, though, was the chic Marriott resort next to it. The eight-story, sparkling white building would give him plenty of advanced notice he was coming up on the city planner's afterthought of a park.

And still, he nearly missed the thin parking lot between the park and the resort, but with a jerk of the wheel, he pulled in and grabbed one of the last remaining spots. He was facing the resort. The sparkling ocean and a scattering of beachgoers collected near the rolling waves was to his right. Jacob turned in his seat, examining the park behind him. It looked decent, except for the massive tent city that'd overrun it. A giant, amorphous beast of fluttering plastic and canvas stretched nearly the entirety of the park, just like the news article had described it.

Along the outer edge was a rough group of men milling about. At first glance, the faces were intimidating. Dirty, mean, dangerous. But the more Jacob watched, the more those faces changed. Pain, fear, hopelessness.

He grabbed his Ziploc bag of Oxy from the center console, jammed it into his back pocket, and stepped from the car.

The sun, just over the top of the single-story buildings to the east, shone down on the already-tanned faces of a half dozen men standing guard near what appeared to be the entrance to their billowing structure. The men were mostly in their twenties and thirties, except for one hunched figure who had to be nearing a roughly lived seventy years.

A thin, dark-haired woman with a pouting face stormed out from the interior and through the men. An even thinner man with a shaved head and bushy beard hurried worriedly after her. The sentries ignored them, continuing a discussion over the ownership of a cigarette.

The old man, his face flat and troll-ish, noticed Jacob first. He stared, swirling and swirling his tongue around the inside of his mouth, his jowls jiggling.

He reminded Jacob of some of the men he'd encountered at the soup kitchen a long time ago. Life had turned against them. They once had families and homes, but over time, by chance or by mistake, they found themselves on the wrong side of the coin, and the losses piled up. Family drifted away. Jobs were lost. Money ran out. Their health failed. And each loss hit harder than the last until one day, they had nothing. It was a terrifying thought, and Jacob sympathized with the man who stared at him from the protection of his more able-bodied comrades.

Jacob didn't approach them right away. He continued on toward the beach where there was a bench that hadn't been engulfed by the tent monster. The breeze came in from the ocean, gentle and fragrant, but there were momentary spurts where it shifted, blowing out into the Pacific, and Jacob became coated in the unclean stench born from within the structure. The third time the wind shifted, Jacob was coaxed into action. *Let's get on with it.* He got up and made his way to the men near the entrance.

The old man lifted and pointed his cane to get the attention of the others. The group grew quiet. Jacob wondered why he'd dressed himself in crisp jeans and a collared Banana Republic shirt. *Is that supposed to make me appear trustworthy?* The men certainly didn't look at ease.

"Get the fuck outta here," a man with a tattoo on his forehead (*A swastika? No, just an unfortunately shaped bruise*) growled.

Jacob stopped, well out of the reach of anyone in the group but close enough to hear the rustling of their clothes as they shifted about. "Yeah. Sure," Jacob said. "But just wondering if you all could help me with something."

The old man, perhaps emboldened by the younger men around him, stepped closer. He smelled of urine and sour vomit. Jacob had an urge to search his pockets for some spare change, but all that was there were keys, a driver's license, a credit card, his cellphone, and the Oxy, so he just smiled at the leathery, wrinkled face.

"Whaddya want?" the old man pressed. Mixed in with the wrinkles that drew down the sides of his face and around his lips were cuts and lumps from too many falls and stumbles.

"Who gives a shit what he wants, Abe?" the man with the bruised forehead said. "Get outta here, dipshit." He waved his hand at Jacob.

"You selling something?" Abe, asked, squinting hard at Jacob. "Out with it. Whaddya got?"

"Oxy," Jacob offered. "But not selling it. A trade. Just want some help."

The men behind Abe pressed forward at the

mention of Oxy.

Abe lifted his cane and waved it at the group with gusto. "Back, you heathens! Back!" When the men settled, Abe looked at Jacob. "Let's see it then."

Jacob nodded and pulled out a tablet. He held it between forefinger and thumb for the group to see.

Abe put his hand out. "Gimme."

Jacob dropped the Oxy into Abe's cracked palm. The man turned toward the sun and inspected the medication.

"Counterfeit." The old man laughed and tossed the tablet into the grass near a patch of pale-blue canvas. A couple of the men scrambled for it, including the man with the bruised forehead. "It's fake, you simpletons," Abe berated. The men paused.

All this sudden commotion attracted the attention of the pouting woman and the thin man who'd left the tents earlier. They watched from the base of a nearby palm tree.

"It's not fake," Jacob argued. "Broke my arm last month. Doctor prescribed."

The man with the bruised forehead found the tablet, snatched it up, and clutched it tightly in his fist. He looked at Jacob.

"Yeah. Keep it," Jacob said. "Enjoy it."

"Eh. What do I care?" Abe muttered. "Can't be worse than the shit meth you bought. Scratch your other nipple off you monkey."

Jacob stared at the group. "Anyone know a dealer I can talk to?" He pulled another tablet from his pocket. "Anyone?"

Abe smashed his cane across Jacob's wrist, knocking the Oxy from his hand. The pain was sharp and piercing. "Fuck!" Jacob held his wrist tightly against his stomach. Abe then drew the cane back, winding up for another swing. Jacob had a flashback of Dwight and his Easton. This time, though, he reacted, jumping away, and Abe's cane swished harmlessly through the air.

One of the men stepped to where Jacob had been and picked up the Oxy. Abe shuffled around the man, aiming to take another swing at Jacob. "I know fakes when I see 'em."

The thin woman near the palm tree was coming over, intrigued by the tablets that were flying free and loose.

Jacob was backpedaling. He jumped when Abe took another swing of his cane and bumped hard into the woman. They both cried out and tumbled to the grass. Jacob's horde of pale-white tablets spilled from his pocket.

"Sorry. Sorry," Jacob mumbled, not noticing the pills. He reached to help the woman, who was on her back beside him. She'd been crying—her cheeks were streaked with mascara—but she wasn't thinking about that grief anymore. She saw the tablets and greedily started to pluck them from the grass. The bearded man saw the bounty as well and joined the fray, grabbing tablets and tufts of grass, trying to get his fair share.

"No!" Jacob cried. He pushed the two to protect what was his, but in mere seconds the others were scrambling over, piling on. Jacob abandoned his stash, rolling from the frenzy. Abe circled the mass and went after Jacob. "Get outta here!" he yelled, his cane in one hand, a box cutter in the other.

"Jesus!" Jacob turned and ran to his car.

He sat inside the Focus, the doors locked, the air on high. No one followed him, but he still turned around in his seat intermittently, scanning Dunes Park for encroaching homeless people.

Abe and his cohort had disappeared into the confines of their structure. There wasn't even a sentry at the entrance anymore. *All inside ferociously crushing and snorting the Oxy.*

He pulled out his phone and took several photos of the tent cluster. On the passenger seat lay his nearly empty Ziploc bag. There was one tablet left.

He hated that old man. Jacob imagined the deep scar near the man's right temple was from a pool cue to the head during a bar fight. The need for a cane was from him getting hit by a truck during a particularly aggressive panhandling session on a traffic median. And the twisted, weakened back was a parting gift from a four-year bout of tuberculosis. *Why couldn't one of those have taken him down?* Instead, the man had survived to be here, swinging his cane and causing trouble.

"Fucker," Jacob mumbled. He glanced at the gap in the tents, hoping to see the man again. He wanted to get a photo of him. He'd wait another five or ten minutes.

Jacob tapped open Twitter. His followers had grown to just over a hundred and fifty. That growth would undoubtedly slow (*And completely stop?*) now that Missy had asked him to quit posting about drugs. If he didn't make something happen in San Diego, all his work would be for nothing. And with half his trade leverage gone, it'd have to be all-cash deals from here on out. He hadn't brought the cash with him, though. He had to go back downtown to get it. *Waste of time.*

On Twitter, Harvey, aka @pugD3AL3R, posted that he'd helped the Dallas police apprehend a major meth distributor.

"What the hell?" Jacob muttered. There was a news link, but he ignored it, going to Harvey's profile page to see his follower numbers instead. They'd ballooned to nearly four hundred. "Fucking hell. I *knew* it," Jacob howled. "I *knew* this would work." He leaned against the headrest and stared through the sunroof at the clear sky.

A tap on his window made him jump. A woman in tight beach shorts and a white shirt stepped back and gave a little wave. He rolled down his window.

"Hi. You okay?" She brushed a strand of dark hair behind her ear. "I saw you get... attacked? I don't know. What was that?" She glanced at the tents.

"I'm fine. Thanks."

The woman studied him.

"Really. I'm okay. I just fell. They didn't touch me."

She smirked. "Didn't look that way."

"They were fighting over themselves for..."

The woman raised her eyebrows, waiting for Jacob to finish the sentence he had no intention of finishing.

"Thanks for checking," he said, and started to roll up the window.

"Hold on. I have to get back to the girls..." She angled her chin towards the sidewalk running along the beach where there were two little girls, each sitting on a pink tricycle, patiently waiting. "But...are you selling...you know?"

Her eyes were wide and hopeful, but Jacob saw a bit of the same desperation in them he'd seen in the eyes of the homeless men. The woman gave a slightly embarrassed, wry grin. *Is she the girls' mom?* She looked too young to have kids. Maybe she was twenty, at most. Jacob looked at her thin hands. She didn't have a wedding ring. Not that that disproved it, but Jacob decided she was the babysitter, not the mother. *Is that any better?*

His hesitation must have given her the assurance she was looking for, and she stepped closer, resting a hand on the car door. She spied the plastic bag on the passenger seat. "Is that Oxy? Ten mils?"

Jacob grabbed the bag and clutched the remaining tablet. "How do you know it's ten?"

"It's white. Forty's yellow. Blue's eighty. Can I buy it? Couple bucks?"

She, like the Uber driver, was lowballing him. *Why do they all do that?* Didn't matter. He told her what he'd told the driver. "I'm not selling."

"Ten bucks? Come on. That's fair." She let out a whine.

Jacob shook his head. "Listen, American Beauty, I'm not selling. I'm looking for someone I can buy wholesale." He held up the bag, and she stared at the remaining tablet. "This is the last of it," he said. "I need more. If you somehow know a dealer, you can have the Oxy. If not, thanks for coming over."

The woman stood up straight, looking over the car to check on the girls waiting on their tricycles. "Just a second, sweeties," she called out. They waved, and the woman waved back. She leaned down to face Jacob again, studying his eyes, then glanced at the Oxy on the seat. "You could probably buy more Oxy from my boyfriend."

"Your boyfriend?"

She nodded and brushed another string of hair behind her ear. "He sold something a few weeks ago. Might've been Oxy. Don't know, but he's got a solid connection in Tijuana. I bet he could get you some."

"He knows a guy?"

She shrugged. "Yeah, some guy. Phil mostly does work on the guy's cars, like for hidden compartments and stuff. You know, so they can get drugs over the border?"

"Okay..."

"But he could get you some Oxy." She brushed the petulant strand of hair aside once more and eyed the tablet in the Ziploc. "Give me your number. I'll give it to Phil."

"This is my last Oxy. You're screwing me over if you're lying."

"I'm not," she assured him.

He recited his number, and she entered it into her phone. He added, "I'm leaving town in a couple days."

She showed him her phone with a text to Phil. "Just have to hit 'send'..." She held out her other hand.

"Who's his source?"

"Don't know. Saw him once at the shop. Kinda freaky looking. Skinny and tall, like a scarecrow. But he left right after I got there. Haven't seen him since."

Jacob pulled the tablet from the bag. "Really hope you're not lying." He rested the Oxy in her palm.

She grasped it tightly. "I'm not." She tapped the screen. "Phil will text you. Promise."

Jacob smiled. "Okay, sure. Thanks. What's your name?"

"Miley. Yours?"

"Jacob."

Miley gave a nod and pushed away from the car. "Don't get yourself killed, Jacob. You seem nice." She pocketed her phone along with the Oxy and rejoined the girls.

Jacob glanced in his rearview mirror. The old man had reemerged. Jacob reversed out of his spot and pulled up beside him. "Hey, bad grandpa," he yelled.

The man gave him a quizzical stare, seemingly already forgetting Jacob's face.

Jacob didn't care. "Fuck you!" he shouted as he snapped a photo of the tanned, crusty man leaning on his cane then sped off.

Jacob stopped at a Subway down the road for lunch. He took his sandwich and strolled the pier, all the while being relentlessly hounded by seagulls crying out for a handout.

"Already gave away plenty this morning," Jacob said as he rested against the wooden railing and stared south along the beach. He was three miles from the border. He couldn't tell if the hazy land on the horizon was the beginning of Mexico or the last of the US. He tried to find the border fence, but if it was there, his eyes weren't good enough to spot it.

Jacob repeated Miley's warning: "Don't get yourself killed." A man of lesser fortitude might abandon his efforts under such an omen, but not him. He was going full speed ahead.

His phone chimed with a text message. The text was from a 619 area code, San Diego. "*U want Oxy?*"

Jacob quickly responded. "*Yeah. How much?*"

"*UABC cafeteria. 1 hour. k?*"

Jacob typed "UABC" into Google. It was a state university in Mexico. He had an enhanced driver's license, so he could cross the border without delay, but he texted, "*I'm in San Diego. Let's meet here.*"

"*UABC or nothing.*"

The guy was trying to get him to Tijuana to prove he wasn't a cop. *That's fair.* He checked the travel time to UABC. Thirty minutes. He texted, "*UABC works.*"

"*Send me ur pic.*"

Jacob took a selfie, cropped it, and sent it. There was no response. "*We all set?*"

A thumbs-up emoji came back.

Jacob considered asking for a selfie as well, but he'd already gotten his meeting, so he didn't press his luck. Who knew how touchy this guy might be anyway?

Jacob sensed something to his right and turned, coming face-to-face with a seagull the size of Quincy. It gave a very un-doglike squawk, and flapped its wings in his face, a feather grazing his cheek. As he stumbled back, the garbage bird hopped closer, grabbed the sub he'd set on the rail in its massive maw, and took flight. A dozen smaller seagulls circling above immediately went trailing after their successful brother.

Jacob slammed a fist onto the rail. First the Oxy, now his lunch. What was wrong with San Diego? Had he brought along the cash, he'd probably have lost it by now too. But that did bring up an interesting point: should he go back to the hotel for the cash? He checked his phone. Even if he wanted to, he didn't have the time. He'd just have to see what he could do with his good looks and charm. Grabbing the sandwich wrapper, he walked back down the pier. Off to Tijuana.

XV.

Jacob was early by about twenty minutes. He sat by himself in the center of UABC's cafeteria, where he'd be easily seen. Overhead, exposed ventilation and iron support beams lined the ceiling. Several thick columns came down and landed among the gray and cream-colored tables and booths arranged neatly throughout the space.

Jacob was eyeing a man and a woman to his left. They were leaning close so as to hear each other over the chorus of cafeteria chatter. Between them, there was a plate of sausage and eggs. Jacob's stomach rumbled. He gazed at the far wall where there were six food vendors, their sweet, spicy aromas tempting and tormenting him. He couldn't resist.

He went to Ricardo's Express and ordered a plate of huevos con chorizo in the shittiest Spanish Ricardo had probably ever heard. But Jacob got his food, and with no thieving seagulls around, he went back to his table to eat it in peace. Unfortunately, his centrally-located table had been taken. There was a booth along the side wall, not particularly visible, but now his best option, so he grabbed it.

The sight lines weren't very good. The entrance was even partially blocked by one of the columns. He positioned himself at the booth's edge, making himself as visible as possible to Phil when he walked in.

Between bites of the chorizo, he checked his phone, making sure he hadn't missed a text. He was also loading up on photos. He'd been snapping pictures ever since he'd reached the border. He wasn't looking for anything in particular; he just wanted to get as many snapshots as possible. He'd create a cohesive story later. Perhaps he'd even string together a series of posts that spoke to a greater theme; that would be good. That'd look better than what @pugD3AL3R was doing.

Jacob was all about being better than @pugD3AL3R now. The news about the meth distributor's arrest had unleashed his competitive side. Harvey was no longer a "hyper". He was his adversary, and if he didn't step things up and get his act on the road, Harvey would swoop in with another bust or two, and then...then he'd rip his heart out and announce the new @pugD3AL3R book deal.

So it was a good thing he was now sitting in Tijuana. Phil sounded promising. Maybe the guy would even share a story or two about the car modifications he'd done for the cartel. Those could be interesting. Car mods were an art form. It wasn't just about finding empty space to shove the drugs into, but *creating* space where there was none, and doing so in precise areas where the smells could fool the drug-sniffing dogs, like the gas tank or engine. Jacob was sure Phil had some great stories, but first and foremost, the Oxy. How much could he get? Did Phil have anything else? If so, where'd he keep it? Could he see it? Jacob was really hoping Phil had a stash house. That'd be the home run he was looking for, but even if he didn't, Jacob was telling himself it'd be fine. He could just keep moving up the chain. Miley had said Phil had a source in Tijuana, the scarecrow-looking guy. Perhaps Phil would make an introduction. It wasn't a stash house, but he'd take it. He smirked thinking about Miley's apparent fear of the guy.

Should've seen Harvard Hulk.

Jacob checked his phone again. It'd been nearly an hour since Phil had texted him. He scanned the room, studying the faces, trying to find a set of eyes gazing back, but no one was paying him any attention. Just a mix of people talking among themselves, picking at their food, watching one of the many TVs mounted to the columns, or lost in thought, looking at nothing in particular.

He settled on a man standing near the door checking his phone. He didn't look particularly nice. A little beefy, a little unkempt. If anyone in the cafeteria was going to be Phil, he'd put money on him.

And he would've lost his money. At that moment, a skinny, fashionably unshaven man in a clean T-shirt and black jeans slid in on the other side of the booth. He crossed his arms, raised his head slightly, and looked down the bridge of his nose at Jacob.

Jacob examined the man's tattooed forearms, which were littered with scars. He could only imagine the sick cartel torture technique he'd been forced to endure. *They wrapped his arms in razor wire.*

"What's up, Ed Sheeran?" the man asked.

Jacob stopped staring at the mangled tattoos. "Ed Sheeran?"

The man uncrossed his arms and leaned close, inspecting Jacob's face. "I don't know. You look like him." He sat back in the booth. "Maybe it's your eyes." He turned to a couple of girls sitting at the table next to them. "Hey. He look like Ed Sheeran?"

The girls glanced at the man, at Jacob, then back at the man. "Yeah," they said in unison.

"No, I don't," Jacob argued.

The man winked at the girls. "Thanks." Then he turned to Jacob. "So what do you need, Ed?"

Two can play this game. Jacob said, "Looking for someone I can trust, Pedro."

The man rolled his eyes. "Oh, that's racist."

"Come on," Jacob huffed. "You look like Pedro from *Napoleon Dynamite*."

"Racist." The man slowly shook his head. "Wow."

Jacob met his stare for a moment then broke away. "Fine. Phil."

"Not Phil either. Phil's my mechanic."

Jacob was confused. *This is Phil's Tijuana source?* The man didn't look anything like a scarecrow. What'd Miley been smoking? *Oxy.*

"Name's Vicente. How you know Phil?"

Jacob didn't know what the right answer to that question was, so he told the truth. "I honestly don't. Met his girlfriend this morning, and she made the introduction."

"You move fast." Vicente crossed his arms again, revealing an old burn mark in the shape of a hornet on his left biceps.

He's known as the "Killer Bee." Jacob filed that note away for later. He'd be sure to reference Vicente that way in his book. *Phil's source, whom I came to call Killer Bee, wasn't so much catatonic as he was plagiaristic.* Jacob had no idea what that meant, but it sounded cool and writerly.

"Where you from?" Vicente asked.

"You know Minnesota?"

Vicente nodded. "Where exactly?"

"Minneapolis?"

"You telling me, or asking me?"

"Telling."

"We don't ship up there, don'tcha know?"

Jacob ignored the bad impression, focusing on the "we" instead. Who was "we"? Did "we" mean the cartel? Was he talking to someone from the cartel? *Please, please, please...*

"That's Sinaloa's territory," Vicente explained.

Not the Sinaloa cartel then. "I know. I bought from them," Jacob lied. "But Guzman's in prison, and Sinaloa's going to shit. I'm done with them." As Vicente nodded slightly, Jacob added, "I need another supplier."

"So here you are talking to the CJNG?"

Shit, Jacob thought, *I am talking to the cartel*. He kept his composure. "Here I am."

Vicente studied him from across the booth. "Let me see your driver's license."

"My license?" A bead of sweat trickled down Jacob's spine before catching the bottom of his shirt and soaking in. Panic rose from his stomach and collected in the back of his throat. He regretted coming here. He should've turned around at the border. He'd been sitting in line there thinking about it. He could've just poked around San Diego some more. He didn't have his Oxy, but he had his cash. He could've found something in San Diego. So why was he in Mexico sitting down with the cartel? *The fucking cartel. Because I thought I was meeting some mechanic*. Jacob carefully peeked at his phone. It was only half past one. He could go back right now and still have a few hours to search the city before he had to meet Missy for dinner. That sounded like a safe plan. He just needed to get out of this little encounter.

"Let me see it." Vicente placed a hand, palm down, on the table.

"If you don't trust me, I can go."

"I don't trust anyone." Vicente tapped the table with a finger.

"Okay." Jacob didn't want to, but he was compelled to follow the directive. This was the cartel after all, so he retrieved the license from his pocket and held it out for Vicente to inspect.

Vicente took it and studied it intently for thirty long seconds. Then he finally muttered, "How much you want?"

The question took Jacob by surprise. "How much?" He scratched his head. "I've got three grand back in San Diego."

Vicente grimaced and handed the license back.

"That's not a lot. Kinda wasting my time. Fucking Phil," he murmured.

Jacob sensed the opportunity slipping away, failure looming large. He couldn't let that happen again. "I've got more," he quickly reassured Vicente. "Just not in cash. I can withdraw more." He pocketed his license and smiled.

"Phil said you wanted Oxy. I don't have Oxy. Got a modified version. M-30. It's close."

"I'll take it." Not that that mattered. Just like with Dwight, he had no intention of taking anything. He only needed to know what Vicente had and where, and then he'd call the police. *Or the DEA!* He wrung his hands in excitement. He was going to help the DEA bust the CJNG. This was going to be big.

"How much?" Vicente asked.

That too didn't matter, but he wanted to sound serious, so he said, "Couple thousand tablets, to start."

"To start, you pay up front," Vicente warned. "Twenty thousand dollars."

"Fine. Where're the tablets? Here or San Diego?" Jacob leaned in, elbows on the table. If he pulled this off, he'd have a best-seller.

"Both."

"I'll pick it up in San Diego then."

Vicente shook his head. "You can pick it up in Minneapolis."

"You said you don't ship there."

"Now we do."

No, no, no, that won't do. Jacob couldn't have anything sent to Minneapolis. What was he supposed to do there? Turn himself into the police? *No.* He said, "You don't want to deal with transporting it all the way there."

"You spend twenty grand, you get free delivery." Vicente grinned.

Remembering the bump Dwight had made him take, Jacob exclaimed, "I need to check its quality. If I'm spending twenty grand *up front,* I need to know it's okay."

"That's fair." Vicente dug into his pocket and slid a blue M-30 tablet across the table.

Jacob quickly covered it with a napkin and pushed the M-30 back with conviction. "I want to see what's actually being shipped. Not your pocket candy."

Vicente took a long breath, held it, seemingly counting to ten, then exhaled. The air whistled slightly as it passed through his nostrils. "Fine. Got a house in Nueva Tijuana with some ready to go soon. Come take a look. You can check it, mark it with your initials or whatever, and we'll send you that."

"Nothing's in San Diego?" Jacob pressed, thinking he wouldn't get half the media attention for a bust in Tijuana as he would in San Diego.

Vicente snickered. "You're not getting to see anything in San Diego. First-time buyer buys here."

"If you've got the M-30 already over the border in San Diego, just let me take that."

"Don't worry. We'll get your stuff across. Going through a brand new tunnel. First class right to Otay Mesa."

Jacob's heart skipped a beat. *Holy shit.* "You've got a tunnel?"

"Course we do."

Jacob was about ready to piss himself with excitement. A stash house in Tijuana, a stash house in Otay Mesa, and a tunnel connecting them. *Yatta!* He had to calm himself and mute the burst of hungry ambition rising in his chest, so he muttered, "A tunnel. How safe is that?"

"Best one we've built."

"Can I check it out?"

"I don't care." Vicente glanced at his phone. "I have to get going. Meet me here tomorrow morning. At ten. In the west parking lot."

"Okay. At ten," Jacob repeated, extending his hand.

Vicente gave it a hearty shake, making Jacob

grimace. "What?"

"Just the shoulder. Hurt it last month." Jacob gave it a rub. "It's fine."

Vicente rolled his eyes and slid from the booth. "You bring the cash tomorrow."

Jacob nodded.

Vicente stepped away, disappearing around a column and out the door.

As Jacob continued to rub his shoulder, a grin spread across his face.

"I want to go to Fashion Valley before we leave," Missy announced.

"What's Fashion Valley?" Jacob asked.

"A luxe shopping center," Alicia said from across the table. "I was telling Missy about it earlier."

Missy clutched Jacob's hand and grinned. "LV, Prada, Gucci, Burberry. I want to buy your mom a Burberry scarf. She doesn't have one, does she?" Missy was talking in her fake networking voice.

"I wouldn't know," Jacob said, forcing back a smile. With his free hand, he grabbed his nearly empty beer glass and drained it.

Alicia had asked Missy to dinner within earshot of some other industry professionals back at the convention, and in the spirit of good corporate appearances, Missy hadn't been able to say no.

"I had no idea LVMH was behind Google's last algo adjustment," Alicia chirped. "Did you?"

Missy let go of Jacob's hand and pulled a nacho from the shared plate. "I actually had a feeling it was something like that."

"Yeah? Surprised me." Alicia also took a chip.

Jacob glanced around the restaurant, looking for

their waitress, hoping it wouldn't take more than another few beers to reach the point of non-sobriety where their discussion about which social media engagement metrics showed them how to best manipulate consumers would become interesting. Until then, the conversation was driving him mad with boredom, especially since he couldn't help but juxtapose it against his afternoon discovery of two stash houses and a border tunnel. *That* was earth-shattering news. He'd hit the jackpot. He was still a little shaky from the adrenaline rush he'd gotten from being down there—from the discussion with Vicente, but also from what had happened afterwards.

Once Vicente had left, he'd gotten up and driven over to Nueva Tijuana, cruising the main boulevard, snapping photos. *Let's see Harvey compete with this.* He turned down a side street and found low-slung, windowless warehouses full of docking bays.

As his Ford rental got bullied by semi-trucks and cargo vans rumbling in and out of the lots, he channeled his inner Ansel Adams and gave more attention to his phone's camera than where he was. Venturing deeper into the neighborhood, he turned down a street where the industrial buildings fell away, stubby stucco homes drew near, and a spider web of electrical wires crossed overhead with knotted-together shoes hanging from them like caught insects. He swung his phone side to side, captivated with the colorful, sharp graffiti. The homes pressed hard against the street, no gaps between them, forming a low-walled canyon that guided him onward.

He knew Vicente's tunnel was in one of these houses on one of these streets. A woman stood near an open door. He took her photo and tried to peek into the home, but it was shrouded in darkness. She fixed on him with suspicious gray eyes, and he gave the car some gas. Up ahead was a cluster of boys kicking a soccer ball in the street. They gave him room to pass but eyed the Ford with annoyance; he took their picture. A couple of guys standing on the corner refused to cross in front of him when he stopped. They waved him through then stood and stared. Everyone, he realized, was watching him. He should've listened to Missy and taken the rental that had the tinted windows.

At a T-intersection devoid of any watchful eyes, he sat, thinking. He'd made one too many random turns and now had no idea where he was or even what direction he was facing. *Left or right?* A Dodge Charger was coming from the left. Feeling like it was safer to go where someone was headed than where they'd been, he pulled out ahead of the car. He should've let it pass.

As he peered down cross streets, watching for signs of the main boulevard, the Charger crept closer. Jacob turned; the Charger turned. He turned again, and so did the Charger. Jacob dropped his phone on the seat and tried to focus on his driving, telling himself the Charger wasn't following him. The turns were coincidental. Except the longer it continued, the less he believed it.

Was he going to end up like those Canadian tourists? He'd read about a honeymooning couple who'd ventured out for an authentic meal away from the tourist traps. Their cab drove them into the hills of Tijuana, where a group of men had pulled the husband from the car, slit his throat, and vanished with his wife. Three days later her body had been found, raped and beaten, in the desert.

He was watching his rearview mirror when a dog wandered into the street. He slammed the brakes so hard the Charger only just barely missed rear-ending him. "Fuck," Jacob said as the mutt obliviously ambled off behind a collection of rusted oil drums/trash cans. He shifted in his seat, his pants clinging to his legs with sweat. Popping his shirt, giving himself a puff of air, he hurried on ahead. And the Charger did the same.

Jacob stepped on the gas, hurrying through the

neighborhood, not bothering to look behind him anymore, eyes focused on the road. Another stray appeared ahead. He swerved and pressed on. The Charger was forced to stop and wait for the animal as it crossed.

Jacob widened the gap, crested a small hill, and cheered with glee when the main boulevard reappeared. He made a quick turn and was greeted by an overhead sign indicating the upcoming Otay Mesa Port of Entry. That wasn't the crossing he'd come through earlier, but he didn't care. A crossing was a crossing.

Half an hour later, as he made his way back to San Diego, he was still tightly clutching the steering wheel and wiping sweat from his brow, thinking about that Charger (*that damn Charger*), wondering what would've happened had he hit the stray dog. Would he have stopped? *No. Screw the dog. But what if the car was messed up? What if a terrible grating, grinding had started? What if the car had begun to shake?* He would've had no choice but to pull over. And then the Charger would've stopped. They (whoever *they* was) would've been grabbing AR-15s or AK-47s from the backseat. Then bullets piercing glass and metal would've rang through the neighborhood.

"Jacob? Babe?"

He turned to Missy. She was looking at him with an "are you deaf?" glare. He acknowledged her with a quick "Hmm?"

"Did you get any nice pictures today?" she repeated.

"Erik, my boyfriend, went up to La Jolla," Alicia told Jacob. "Hiked up the hills there. *Really* cool pics." She handed him her phone.

He glanced at the blue-and-green panoramic vistas of the coastal town, smirking as he thought about the dusty hills of Tijuana and their metal shanties dully shining in the sun. "Looks nice." Jacob reached across the table to give Alicia her phone.

"Where'd you go?" Missy pressed.

"Just around," Jacob said, trying to reach Alicia's outstretched fingers.

Missy grabbed Jacob's phone lying near his empty beer glass.

The photos of the cafeteria, Nuevo Tijuana, and the border crossing flashed through his head. Distracted, he missed the handoff with Alicia, and her phone fell into the nachos. "Ah, shit," he said, quickly picking it out of the sticky mess and shoving it into her hand.

"Gross," she mumbled.

Jacob ignored her and went to protect his phone.

Missy pulled it away. "I just want to look." She punched in his security code and opened the photo album. Her face grew serious. There were no pictures of the La Jolla coast or of a Padres baseball game. "Where *is* this?"

"Just south of here. By the border." She didn't need to know it'd been from the southern side of the border.

"Were you trying to find drugs?" Her voice grew in volume and pitch like it did when she caught Quincy rummaging through the trash.

"Drugs?" Alicia said.

"No," he sputtered.

Missy glared at him. "You were. Don't lie!"

Alicia nervously dropped her head, focusing on the cheese and sauce that coated her phone.

"I didn't know where I was going. Just went out driving," Jacob insisted.

"And you just happened to stop and wander into this place?" She pointed at the picture of the food vendors in the cafeteria.

"I don't know. Yeah," he muttered. "Got hungry. Looked okay."

Missy shook her head and stared out the window at Sixth Street and a truck with a color that matched the flush of her face. "You promised..."

"I know. But I talked to CB and—"

She cut him off. "And he convinced you to break your promise?" She spun around and stared at him with eyes that could cut steel.

Jacob looked at Alicia, who was still picking at her phone, pretending not to notice their discussion. He turned back to Missy. He didn't regret what he'd done. *Two stash houses.* He shrugged.

Missy gave a disgusted sigh then threw Jacob's phone into his lap. "You promised."

"Look." Jacob swiped a hand over his chest. "I'm fine. Nothing happened."

Missy didn't say a word.

Exactly. Jacob triumphantly set his phone back on the table. He, Missy, and Alicia sat in silence before Missy decided to reveal her secret.

"You know who pug dealer is? On Twitter?" she asked Jacob.

Jacob nodded.

"How many followers does he have?"

"A lot. Why?" Harvey's followers had rocketed past his. *Where is she going with this?*

She picked up her phone and tapped the screen. "He helped with a couple drug busts, didn't he?"

"In Dallas. Yeah."

"He's doing pretty well, huh?"

"What's your point? Trying to make me feel bad? I'm not so special? Anyone can do this?"

"I'm telling you that you don't have to actually do anything to do something."

"I don't get it."

"That's me, you idiot," she huffed. "I'm pug dealer." She held up her phone showing @pugD3AL3R's tweets.

Jacob had seen all these in own his feed before. There was nothing new. "I don't get it." He looked at Missy. "What?"

She furiously swiped at the screen for ten seconds,

then looked back at Jacob with a let's-see-what-you-think-of-this look.

His phone buzzed, and he glanced at it. A Twitter notification.

"Check it," Missy insisted.

He did. It was a direct message from @pugD3AL3R.

I'm Missy, you idiot.

"I'm a digital marketing genius," Missy proclaimed. "It's not that hard. You don't have to get yourself killed over this. So stop!"

An anxious, frustrated wave of heat flushed through Jacob from head to toe. *Missy is Harvey? @pugD3AL3R isn't real?* He bounced his leg, twitchy and fast, trying to release the angry energy building within.

Alicia leaned forward. "What *did* you do? Can I see?"

Missy ignored her. "I told you not to do this stuff. But you wouldn't listen."

"If that's you, then you were encouraging me," Jacob argued. "You were standing up for me in all those comments."

"*Before*, yeah. You needed a buddy. You were getting depressed. The point *now* is you can stop. Just stop. I'll make you a star."

"So it's all fake? All Harvey's busts and shit? Fake?"

"Yeah." She sighed. "I mean, the busts actually happened. I just framed them in a way so you'd believe he'd done it."

Jacob clenched his jaw. "How's that supposed to lead to a book? If it's fake, you can't write a book about it."

"Yeah, you can. Inspired by a true story or something. It'll be fiction. Like your other one."

"My other one can't even get published," he yelled. "Why would another novel be any different?"

"'Cause you'll have a platform now," she shouted back. "'Cause you can tell an agent you've got all these followers ready to buy it."

"No, I don't. Not if they all think it's real and then I say 'Oh, just kidding! Made it all up. But buy this book anyway. It's inspired by it.' Jesus, Missy." Jacob's other leg began to bounce; his blood was running hard and fast through his veins.

"Oh, my God." Missy threw her hands in the air and sat back in her chair. "I can't deal with you right now. You have no idea how the world works." She looked at Alicia for the first time in five minutes. "Alicia, can you believe him?"

Alicia was picking at her cuticles. She lifted her eyes and looked from Missy to Jacob and back. "I'm not comfortable getting involved with this."

"You're in the business. You know I'm right, though, right?"

Alicia grimaced. "I don't know. He kinda has a point."

"Oh, please," Missy huffed. She grabbed her hard lemonade and took a long sip, swiping away the condensation that rolled off the glass and collected on the table.

"Who was that guy who wrote *A Million Little Pieces*?" Alicia asked. "Years ago, remember?"

Jacob knew who she was talking about, but the author's name had slipped his mind as well. The point was valid, though. The guy fabricated a story about his life, passed it off as nonfiction, and become a best-selling author. Oprah even endorsed the book. And then it all unraveled. The truth came out. He was a fraud. "Yeah. Is that what you want to happen?" Jacob asked. "I'd never publish a thing ever again."

"You're such a green-tea bitch, Alicia." Missy slammed the lemonade down, grabbed her phone, and stormed from the table and out the door.

Jacob looked at Alicia. She quickly wiped the

beginnings of a tear and gave a half smile. There was an uncomfortable acceptance in the grin. She'd known where she stood with Missy all along, but she'd always hoped, and pretended, it wasn't true. "You're such a green-tea bitch, Alicia" made things obviously clear.

"She didn't mean that," Jacob offered with as much fake inflection as he could muster.

"It's okay." Alicia looked at her lap then grabbed her water and took a sip.

Jacob stared at the half-eaten plate of nachos. "I should probably go."

"Erik's coming soon. I'll wait for him."

"Okay." He stood. "Good luck with your panel tomorrow."

"Thanks." Alicia glanced outside. "Hope she isn't too upset."

"She'll be okay." A smirk drew across Jacob's face. "I'll sleep on the couch tonight, but she'll be okay. Don't worry."

Alicia frowned. "Okay. Sorry."

Jacob stepped from the table and left the restaurant, following in Missy's path.

XVI.

Vicente stood next to Bravo in the front of the house in Nueva Tijuana. A girl of about six, maybe seven, sat quietly watching cartoons on TV. They were looking at her, but she wasn't of immediate concern.

"California plates?" Vicente asked.

"White Ford Focus, California plates," Bravo reiterated.

Vicente scratched his ear, contemplating whether Bravo's encounter could have just been coincidence. A California license plate wasn't all that unusual, particularly on this street lined with warehouses and factories that had vehicles coming and going at all hours of the day. In fact, the hustle and bustle of international commerce was precisely why they liked this spot. It made it difficult, if not impossible, for the authorities, and neighbors who couldn't keep their eyes to themselves, to separate the illegal from the legal. He and Bravo came and went from the house along Sor Juana Inés de la Cruz as often as they pleased, disappearing among the constant flow of trucks transporting goods and employees arriving for work. The key was to slip into the crowd and get on your way. No one simply cruised the neighborhood, gawking at the scenery. There was no scenery to gawk at. So, Vicente wondered, what had that

Focus been doing?

Bravo had gotten a decent look at the driver, and Vicente thought it sounded a lot like that Sheeran look-alike he'd met. He'd already been suspicious of the guy. He wasn't buying his "lost puppy" act. And now it appeared as though he was staking out the area. He had an agenda.

"This guy you met today," Bravo mused, mirroring Vicente's thoughts, "would know better, unless..."

"Unless he's not really looking to buy," Vicente finished.

"Castor?"

Vicente shook his head. "He's not as innocent as he tries to look, but he's not Castor."

"Helping Castor?"

"Don't know." Vicente initially wanted to meet Jacob, because Phil had made him sound like a major buyer. It was also a nice opportunity to make himself look good in front of El Avispón. Even if the boss wasn't holding his feet to the fire about the cocaine, and the progress with the tunnel was excellent, Vicente didn't want to pass up an opportunity to build some goodwill with the man. So he'd gone into that meeting hoping to sell Jacob all the M-30 he could afford, but not anymore. "We'll get what we can out of him, and then that's it."

Bravo nodded. He understood. "And her?" He gazed at the little girl.

"She can stay for a bit longer."

"She should've gone with the others."

Vicente agreed. They'd sent a couple of girls earlier that morning through a tunnel on Canon Otay. That tunnel hadn't been constructed for people, though. It was similar to the tunnel where he'd lost the cocaine. No one should be going down it, but El Avispón was demanding they start moving people, especially the little ones who wouldn't have any trouble getting through anyway, so Vicente had carefully ushered them into the space below the floor, persuading each with an encouraging word and a slight nudge. The last girl probably would've gone down had he forced her, but he couldn't bring himself to do that. She had shook so much the yellow ribbon in her hair had come loose.

"She'll go soon," he told Bravo.

XVII.

Missy didn't even want to let him in. She had his suitcase by the door and told him to get another room.

"On a different floor," she added, standing in the entryway.

He squeezed through the half open door. "What are you talking about?"

She shook her head. "I can't. You're obsessed. It's crazy. You're crazy." She was near tears.

He thought about hugging her, but the fat little suitcase between them made it awkward, so he stood, doing nothing, unsure what to even remark upon. He could readily admit there was plenty wrong (and dangerous) about his efforts, but he was being careful, and he had good reason for doing it. Where to start? Would she even listen? *Maybe it has nothing to do with me.* Was she just overwhelmed? Was the conference fraying her nerves? *Maybe that's it.* "How about I don't do anything tomorrow? You can focus on your panel. No need to worry."

"You won't do anything *tomorrow*?" She let out a fake sigh. "Oh, so relieved you'll do something stupid on Saturday instead."

"I didn't mean that. I'm—"

"I don't care how you meant it."

"I'll stay here in the room. It's fine."

"Great. So I'm just some bitch who drags you here then makes you stay inside the whole time?"

Jacob managed to get around the suitcase and wrap his arms around her. "No. I love you. You're not a bitch. It's my choice." He squeezed her tight. He couldn't keep putting her through this. "I'll go up to La Jolla or something in the afternoon. How about that?" *Is that it then?* His literary dream began to fade like the Cheshire Cat. A wave, a flick of the tail, then vanishing until only the pearly white smile remained.

Missy was quiet, but she hugged him back.

"Come on," he said, shuffling his feet, leading them from the entryway. They sat on the hard-but-so-very-chic sofa and stared at the blank TV.

"Turn on your phone's GPS tracking," Missy mumbled.

"You don't trust me?"

"I trust you. I just don't trust you today. And it'll just make me feel so much better." She leaned her head against his shoulder.

Jacob was hurt, but he pulled out his phone. After searching through the settings for a minute, he said, "I don't think that function is here."

"It's part of maps or something. Or download an app."

"This phone's so old."

Missy sighed and lifted her hand. "Give it to me."

He did and watched her go through everything he had just tried. "See?" he mumbled.

"No. It worked. I just turned it on." Missy dropped the phone in his lap. "Take a lot of photos. Make sure you get some nice ones." She then stood with a jolt, and said, "I have to practice," and went into the bedroom and closed the door before Jacob could say another word.

"Okay. Bye. Love you," he said, imagining the

Cheshire Cat's toothy grin now vanishing, leaving nothing but the Tulgey Woods to keep him company.

His stomach growled. The three nachos and one beer weren't anything close to a proper supper. Missy was likely to skip her dinner entirely, but he couldn't, so he headed downstairs to the bar where the television was silently showing a Padres game and the speakers played alternative rock. He ordered a short rib grilled cheese, then pulled out his phone and scrolled through the photos of Tijuana. They were a far departure from the photos Alicia's boyfriend had taken of La Jolla. People took those same shots in those same La Jolla locations every day. There were thousands of them online. *#Blessed Who cares?*

Several years back, he and Missy had gone to the Grand Canyon. It'd been unexpectedly awe-inspiring, and Jacob found himself staring out at the expanse, ogling the rock formations, the exposed layers of history, the plummeting rock face—it made his knees weak. Admittedly the experience wasn't any different than those of the countless others who'd come before him. They all saw the same thing. They all felt the same way. It was unforgettable. Yet Missy had only wanted to experience it through her phone's camera. She turned her back to the view and snapped selfie after selfie. Then she buried her head in her phone, inspecting and cropping and filtering.

"You can do that later," he'd complained.

"No. I have to make sure I got a good one."

He let her be and gazed out at the canyon. A hawk was circling near a ridge where the Colorado River made a winding curl. He didn't bother pointing it out to her. She wouldn't have looked anyway.

When they'd left and were driving south on Highway 64, she finally put her phone away, satisfied with her pointless posts. Just like the lattes and desserts and shoes and skirts that were posted in the billions, its contribution to the world would be infinitesimal. It wasn't even worth the time it took to share really. He couldn't grasp the purpose of it. And now she wanted him driving up to La Jolla tomorrow to collect a bunch of those same photos.

His sandwich arrived, neatly cross cut and carefully stacked on the rectangular plate. A tiny but aesthetically pleasing dollop of chipotle mayo was in the corner. He dug into the dish with anger, the bartender appearing slightly surprised, as if he'd expected a picture to be taken. Jacob shoved a few fries into his mouth. There'd be no photo. The bartender left.

Jacob had half a mind to go up to La Jolla and not take a single picture. She could track his location, but she wouldn't see what he saw. He'd just enjoy the views and the sun...while Vicente sat in the UABC parking lot waiting for him to show.

He leaned back from the bar. Had he really gone through everything he'd gone through to abandon his plan now? He'd somehow managed to get someone with the cartel—a CJNG drug smuggler with two stash houses and a border tunnel—to agree to meet him tomorrow and show him everything, and he was going to abandon it now?

And on top of that, if he got through this last bit, his book was going to be done. Did Missy realize that? *Of course not.* If she did, she wouldn't tell him to quit now. Her "do whatever it takes" motto didn't align with abandoning something in its final step. If she *really* knew how close he was, she'd tell him to keep at it. She would. And then that'd be the last of it. She wouldn't have to worry again. He'd just stay inside and write his book.

He let out a quiet chuckle, imagining himself being so foolish as to head to La Jolla tomorrow. Vicente would be waiting for him in Tijuana. He shook his head in amazement. Missy had almost gotten him. He leaned into his plate to finish his meal. *Forget La Jolla.*

• • •

The next morning, Missy and Jacob were at Starbucks again. She with her coffee and cake pop ("Hope it's better this time," she'd muttered to the cashier), and him with his cappuccino, light foam. It was nine o'clock. He had an hour before he was supposed to meet Vicente, but he was cutting it close. At this time of day, sixty minutes to get out of downtown, reach the border, cross the border, then zip over to the university was optimistic. But as far as Missy was concerned, he had nowhere to be, so he sat there, internally screaming at her to *just fucking leave already.*

She nibbled at her cake pop, first pulling off a bit of the frosting and eating that, then taking a bite of the vanilla cake inside and eating that, then having a sip of coffee. Rinse and repeat. She did this as she scrolled through a series of tweets with the hashtag *MotivationalMonday*. Not that it was Monday. Far from it. But she needed the boost, or so she said.

Jacob watched her quietly read the phrases to herself: "The distance between your dreams and reality is called action... Believe in yourself... Hard work beats talent when talent doesn't work hard... A positive mental attitude is determined by you, not others." She smiled at that last one and took another bite of the cake pop.

He'd been relegated to sleeping on the marble slab the hotel called a couch, and his shoulder was killing him. He sat, ingesting his caffeine, rubbing his shoulder, and glaring at Missy to *just fucking leave already.*

Perhaps finally sensing the enormous amount of malice he was throwing her way, she looked up. "So you're going to La Jolla?"

It was the third time she'd asked since they'd sat down. "Yeah." He nodded. "Right after we're done."

"Send me some pictures. Alicia got some really nice ones from Erik."

Not happening. He'd already turned off the GPS. "Sure thing." He half grinned behind the coffee cup, thinking of the pictures he'd downloaded to his phone to present as his own over dinner. She wouldn't know the difference. *Might not even matter by then.* If the day went as planned, he'd be on his way to hero status. His book's ending would be complete. He could just come clean and admit he hadn't gone to La Jolla. Then again, maybe it was best to wait until they were back in Minneapolis. No reason to piss her off right before a three-hour flight. Still grinning, he set his cup down. "Nice weather today."

Missy took a deep breath.

"All set?" Jacob asked.

She exhaled and clenched her fists. "I'm ready." She stood.

He quickly got up and saw her out the door. "Good luck." He blew her a kiss.

She went marching up the street toward the convention center.

Jacob dropped his half-finished cappuccino in the trash and ran to the parking garage under the hotel. It was 9:15. Maybe there wouldn't be traffic. But it was Southern California. Of course there was traffic.

When Jacob pulled into the university's parking lot outside the cafeteria, it was 10:10. He cruised the lot, looking for Vicente. There was no sign of him. Jacob grabbed an open space near the exit and waited, snapping a couple of photos. *There aren't thousands of people posting pictures of this. Should get a quick video too.* He turned the camera on himself.

"Sitting at the University of..." He paused and scanned the area. "I forget the name. There's a sign right there, but it's facing the wrong way. Anyway, sitting here waiting for a guy who's with the cartel, the CJNG, and he's going to take me to his stash house, and there's a tunnel there that goes under the border to another stash house in

Otay Mesa. Holy shit, right? So the next time you see me, I'll be on the news with the DEA standing next to piles of drugs and cash." He stopped the recording and pocketed the phone.

And not a moment too soon. Vicente tapped on the window and crossed his mangled, tattooed arms.

Jacob smiled, quickly grabbed the paper bag on the passenger seat, and got out. "Hey. Sorry I'm late. Traffic." He opened the crumpled bag. Inside were the thirty $100 bills he'd brought from Minneapolis and another 170 strips of printer paper he'd swiped from the hotel's business room. Naturally only the actual cash was visible. "Twenty k."

Vicente was dressed in black Nikes, slim fit dark jeans that still looked large on his frame, and a white Real Madrid T-shirt. He briefly glanced in the bag then started walking. "Come on."

Jacob scooted after. "So this M-30," he said when he'd caught up, "is all ready to go?"

Vicente nodded.

"Okay, cool." Jacob tried to feign a sense of relief, playing the part of a buyer ready to get a deal done. "What else you have? Any cocaine?"

"You'll see in ten minutes," Vicente muttered as he stepped up to a white Dodge Charger.

It took a moment before Jacob realized it was the car that'd followed him yesterday. *Or is it? Was the other a darker shade*? He couldn't quite remember. It might've been darker.

Vicente got into the car and unlocked the doors.

No. It wasn't darker. This was it. Jacob quickly convinced himself it didn't matter, though. So what if Vicente had seen him? He'd just been scoping out the neighborhood like any diligent buyer would. Going to Nueva Tijuana indicated nothing of a nefarious nature. He was actually glad he'd been seen. It showed his seriousness. He climbed in. Missy, he imagined, was taking a seat herself right then. Her panel was about to begin. *Worlds apart.*

"Turn off your phone," Vicente instructed.

"Don't trust me? GPS is off," Jacob told him, sniffing the air, trying to determine the source of some weirdly sour smell. *Probably some bad marijuana he'd transported recently.*

"I want the entire phone *off*," Vicente insisted.

Jacob did as he was told, flashed the blank screen to Vicente, and shoved it in his pocket. "Your car kinda smells."

"Vomit. Can't get it out of your seat."

"Ew. Gross." Jacob lifted his butt and scanned the cushion. There was a stain, but it was dry.

"Sit down. It's old." Vicente tossed a pair of swimming goggles in Jacob's lap. The lenses were painted black. "Put them on," he said. "And then these." He flipped a pair of large sunglasses atop the goggles.

"Hope we don't have to go through this every time I'm down here."

"It's just going to be this once," Vicente promised.

Jacob struggled to slip the goggles over his eyes. "They're tight as hell."

"Tough shit."

Jacob loosened the straps, and the pressure lessened some, but it still felt like he'd have his own cherry eye when he pulled them off. *Pop!* Maybe, he thought, he and Quincy could then get a two-for-one surgery discount. "Are these kids' goggles?"

"They are."

"Really? You got a kid?"

"Yeah, she loves swimming around in goggles you can't see shit in. It's hilarious watching her smash her face into the side of the pool," Vicente mocked. "Put the sunglasses on. You look like a mental defective with those."

Jacob blindly grabbed the sunglasses and rested them over the goggles as the car began to move. *And away we go.* The car turned from the lot (a right turn) then accelerated. Nueva Tijuana was to the east of the university. *So far, so good.*

Jacob vaguely remembered there'd been a stoplight soon thereafter. And upon thinking it, the car slowed to a stop. *Perfect.* He closed his eyes. That was better. Calmer. At least, he could trick his mind into thinking the darkness was of his own volition and not the directive of the cartel. Yesterday, the trip to Nuevo Tijuana had taken four minutes. If this went longer, he was taking the goggles off and...*and what?* He didn't know what, but he'd do something. Right now, though, he needed to start tracking the seconds, two hundred forty seconds; he began to count. *One Mississippi, two Mississippi, three Mississippi...*

Vicente cleared his throat. "You and your girl got a kid?"

"No. Just me and her." Had he mentioned Missy when they'd talked yesterday? He couldn't remember. *Five Mississippi, six...*

"She come down here with you?"

"She did. She's got a digital media conference."

"Convenient."

Six Mississippi... "Worked out well. She's a marketing exec. Has these conferences a lot."

"An exec. That's pretty good money, isn't it?"

"I guess. I make more at 3M." Jacob lost track of the seconds. He had to be around eleven. *Twelve Mississippi...*

"What do your parents do?"

"My mom's retired. My dad passed. Was a lawyer."

"Brothers? Sisters?"

"Got a sister." Jacob almost said she was a cop. Almost. "Accountant."

"You didn't grow up poor then, did you?"

"No. Why?" He nearly lost count again. "What's with all the questions?"

"Good to know my buyers. Good to know who they

are, where they come from, what they stand to lose."

"That's ominous," Jacob muttered.

"That's how it's intended."

Jacob had completely lost track of the seconds. Emily's warnings were flashing. The car made a sharp left turn, and he tipped against the door.

"Buckle your seatbelt," Vicente mumbled.

Jacob straightened himself and strapped in. He imagined they were getting close to the highway, Highway 2. That meant they were maybe sixty seconds into the trip now. *Sixty-one Mississippi...* There should be a gradual loop ahead, a straight section, then an exit right onto that main boulevard. He forgot the name of it. (He needed to get better at that. The book needed specifics.) But the important thing was that after they reached the boulevard, it'd only be a left turn then some side streets before the house. That would be it. *Seventy Mississippi...* There was the gradual loop.

The two sat in silence, the air conditioner blowing gently. Outside, someone honked. Vicente tapped the brakes then continued on. *One hundred Mississippi...*

Missy was starting her panel now. He wished her well. Her discussion about Google Analytics or engagement metrics or whatever it was should be easy enough. She'd practiced for hours. In the end, the panel would probably be more awkward than anything. She and Alicia, seated right next to one another, might be able to hide the tension from the audience, but the two of them would be thinking about it plenty, and like a nasty little dog that gets shut in the bedroom when guests come over, "you're such a green-tea bitch" would have to be let out at some point lest it start tearing apart the bed and pissing on the carpet. They still had to work together after all. *One hundred fifty Mississippi...*

The goggles were starting to itch. Jacob went for a scratch.

"Get your hand away from your face," Vicente instructed.

"Itches."

"Just keep still. We're almost there."

They'd reached the main boulevard. *One hundred seventy Mississippi...* The car slowed and turned left. They were on the side streets. *One hundred eighty Mississippi...*

"Who'd you buy from before? Beltran-Leyva?" Vicente asked.

With no facial cues to misinterpret or distract him, Jacob easily caught the tone in Vicente's voice that betrayed the fact he remembered what he'd been told yesterday. Vicente was testing him, trying to catch him in a lie. "Sinaloa," Jacob corrected. *One hundred eighty-five Mississippi...*

"Oh, that's right. What'd you buy from them besides Oxy?"

"Cocaine mostly. Cocaine and Oxy sell really well in Minneapolis." *One hundred ninety Mississippi...*

"We've got cocaine. Heroin's the money maker, though."

"Heroin's some real nasty shit," Jacob said, thinking of the needles in Gold Medal Park.

"Maybe, but ours is the best. The poppies in Veracruz are excellent. People love it. You want some, I'll get you some."

"Sure. Okay." Jacob didn't care. He'd agree to whatever, because once he claimed Vicente's M-30 wasn't up to snuff, he'd be gone, back to San Diego, and Vicente would never see him again, except maybe in the courtroom during the trial.

Another turn. This time the car went right. *Two hundred Mississippi...*

"How much cocaine you been buying from Sinaloa?" Vicente slowed the car.

Jacob had no idea what a plausible answer to that would be, so he said, "It's up and down. Depends on the season. How much you think I could get from you?"

Vicente stopped the car. "Depends how much you can afford."

"No issue there."

"Good."

There was a long pause. Jacob sensed Vicente watching him. "We there?" he asked. *Two hundred fifteen Mississippi...*

"Yeah. We're here."

Two hundred and fifteen. Less than he'd expected. He hadn't started counting right away, though, so it was close enough.

"Stay put," Vicente said, getting out of the car. "I'll come around."

When the passenger door opened, Jacob was careful, testing the ground with a gentle tapping of his feet. He'd counted the seconds. He'd tracked the turns. But still, for a moment, he worried he'd made a gross miscalculation. He imagined Vicente had driven him to the coast. They were standing atop a seaside cliff, and the edge was very near. There were no waves crashing into rocks or seagulls cawing overhead, though. They were in a quiet neighborhood. The rumble of a truck rose up then faded. A car passed. This was Nueva Tijuana. He climbed out.

Vicente put his hand on Jacob's back and gave him a slight push. "This way," he said.

The ground was soft, sandy. It wasn't a long walk, only several yards or so to reach the stash house, but there was no pathway, and Jacob kept tripping. Vicente basically dragged him the last few steps, then placed a firm hand on his shoulder to stop. Jacob grimaced at the dull pain that pulsed down his arm from a nerve that hadn't yet gotten used to being without the protection of the cast.

With a soft squeak and rattle, a metal gate swung away, and then the door to the house opened. The hair on Jacob's neck fluttered as a rush of air was sucked inside. *An invitation? Or a desperately needed breath from a suffocating beast?* A sudden urge to rip the goggles off and run overtook him. He'd made a terrible mistake. What was he doing off in who-knows-where Tijuana, holding a bag of cash and printer paper, about to step into a house run by the cartel? Who does that?

Do whatever it takes.

Fuck that, he thought. But just as quickly as the fear had risen up inside his chest, it drew back, replaced by the image of words on paper, his adventure in print, a book deal.

"There's a lip," Vicente said. "Watch it." He guided Jacob over the threshold.

The warmth of the sun vanished. The air grew still and pregnant with strangely aged aromas. *Fermented fruit. Bleach. Heavy rust.* "Need a little Pledge in here," Jacob said in the general direction where he imagined Vicente to be. "Pungent."

"All I smell is your Axe body spray, bro." Vicente shut the door and snapped the lock in place.

"It's Old Spice."

"Whatever. Take off the goggles."

"Old Spice is classier." Jacob took off the sunglasses and pulled the goggles from his face. "God, those hurt. My eyes were getting sucked out of their sockets." He handed the accessories to Vicente, who quickly tossed them onto a nearby couch where they settled on crisscross-patterned cushions wrinkled and deflated with use and neglect. Sitting quietly against the far armrest was a little girl. Her feet just barely hung off the edge, bouncing slightly as she watched *The Powerpuff Girls* on a TV across the small room. The volume was turned down, so the cartoon was barely audible, but the girl seemed content. She adjusted a dirty yellow ribbon in her hair then carefully returned her hands to her lap.

The rest of the space was empty. No chairs. No side tables. No toys. Nothing. "Your kid?" Jacob asked.

"Hey, Bravo," Vicente called out, ignoring the

question.

"Yeah?" a voice replied from the back of the house.

Jacob peered down a corridor of unpainted, yellowed drywall to what looked to be a kitchen based on the off-kilter cupboards that were visible. *Probably the kitchen.* At least that was how he'd describe it in his book.

"Get out here. Ed Sheeran's in the house," Vicente mocked.

"Oh. No shit?" came the voice.

Jacob scowled at Vicente. "Pedro," he murmured under his breath. Behind Vicente, above the couch, was a window covered with a black sheet, dismally blocking out most of the day's light. The upper-right corner had slipped from the duct tape holding it to the frame. There was a touch of blue sky and the top of a white building.

Down the hall, the man Vicente had been calling rounded the corner.

"Jesus," Jacob said, catching sight of the tall, spindly spectacle. It took Bravo just four steps to reach the front room. He was all arms and legs. *Like a scarecrow or a spider.* Jacob grinned at the stoic giant staring down at him. He thought about making a "need to eat a hamburger" joke but kept his mouth shut. While the guy was even thinner than he was, Bravo had a massive wingspan and could very well pop him in the nose from halfway across the room. Jacob shifted back to Vicente. "Can I see the M-30?"

Vicente ignored him and asked Bravo, "Morena eat today?"

"Not yet. Said she wasn't hungry," Bravo replied.

"Get her something to eat after this. A churro or something. She'll eat that." Vicente turned to Jacob. "You and your girlfriend having a good time in San Diego?"

Jacob thought of Missy storming out of the restaurant the night before and how he'd slept on the couch. He thought of those ravenous homeless people attacking him. But then he thought of where he was, getting through the last segment of his book, and said, "Yeah, been good."

"Nice city." Vicente gave him an unconvincing smile.

Hearing a door open in the back of the house, Jacob looked down the hall. Another giant spider emerged. Four long-legged steps and he was beside Bravo. They were identical. "Twin towers," Jacob nervously laughed.

The twins didn't crack a smile. In fact, Bravo's brother couldn't manage much of a smile even if he wanted to. It appeared as though he had Bell's palsy, the left side of his face drooping in a permanently tired frown. It was the only real difference between the men.

Jacob let out a final sad chuckle before shuffling his feet and readjusting his arms, crossing them over his chest. A silence drew over them, save for the soft chirpy noises from the cartoon the girl was watching. Jacob looked at her. *Whose kid is she?* For some reason, even though he was surrounded by the cartel who looked ready to jump him, he found himself more interested in the girl. She didn't resemble any of these men in the slightest. Fair features, delicate hair, large eyes, elfish ears. Jacob glanced at the twins then Vicente. No resemblance. And yet, there she sat, amid the comings and goings of the cartel shipping drugs north. Perhaps, Jacob thought, he could get some details from the police once he led them to the house.

Unfortunately, to get to that point, he first had to know where he was, and that was proving difficult. So far, all he could say was that the house was in Nueva Tijuana and it was across from a white building and it had its front window covered with a black sheet. *Good luck with that.* The sheet probably wasn't even visible from the street. Just another darkened window. *So what else?* The house wasn't very wide. Seven or eight paces if the room he was standing in was any indication. *One story?* Yes, no staircase anywhere. He turned around to look at the front door. It was a dark brown PVC plastic. And outside, he remembered, was just a short lip, no steps. And sand. There was a short strip of sand out front. Feeling pretty good with that assessment, Jacob looked at the group. "The M-30?" he asked.

"It's in the back." Vicente gestured down the hall.

The twins stepped aside, clearing the path.

"After you," Vicente told Jacob.

Two exposed bulbs lit the hallway with a dull glow. Jacob got a flush of goose bumps. Excitement, anxiousness. *Terror? Maybe a touch.* But this was mostly exciting. He hoped he could adequately capture this in words later. He stepped past the twins.

A large hand grasped his right shoulder with such force that he dropped the paper bag filled with money and scraps. Wincing, he looked back to see Bravo staring down on him. "What?" Jacob said, the hair on his neck standing at attention. *This isn't right.* Vicente told him to go down the hall, but now Bravo wasn't letting him proceed. *What game is this?*

Bravo then grabbed Jacob's wrists, pulling them behind his back as if he were placing him under arrest.

"What the fuck? What're you doing?" Jacob hollered. He tugged away, but Bravo held firm. "Let go." He jerked harder, and his shoulder flared with such an ache it nearly buckled his knees.

Bravo might have noticed this, or he might have simply wanted to put a stop to Jacob's resisting, because he swiftly wrapped a leg in front of Jacob's and shoved him in the back, sending him toppling face first to the concrete. Jacob caught his chin hard on the floor, splitting it open. Through it all, Bravo maintained his hold on Jacob's wrists with a single spindly hand.

Jacob didn't move. He couldn't think fast enough; he wasn't sure what to do. But also, deep down, a part of him thought he should let it happen. It hadn't been too long ago he'd read about the kidnapping victim who'd gotten a book deal.

Out of eyesight, someone cranked a long strip of duct tape from a roll and bound his wrists. Bravo let go and stood.

Jacob turned from the floor, blood dribbling down his chin and neck.

"Get him up," Vicente said, grabbing the paper bag.

Two sets of hands, one on each bicep, gripped him hard. "My shoulder. My shoulder!" he cried, but the twins didn't pause. They pulled him to his feet. "Ah, fuck!" He caught sight of the yellow-ribboned girl sitting on the deflated couch. She wasn't paying them any attention, her eyes calmly fixed on the cartoon.

The twins spun him around and marched him halfway down the hall and through an open door on the right. With his eyes tearing up from the expanding fiery pain in his shoulder, he blinked several times to take in the new space. He imagined the room would be filled with the cartel's favorite torture devices: meat cleavers and machetes and pliers and ice picks. The room would glisten from these hanging from the walls. And there'd be a table in the corner with neatly arrayed metal rods and a single car battery. The rods would be for anal probings and the battery for shocking the balls. His genitalia puckered and withdrew at the thought. *But holy shit, what a great story!* A rod up the ass might even be worth it if it guaranteed that book deal. Unless, of course, they heated the rod in the oven before using it. *Oh, shit. No.* He'd never have a proper dump the rest of his life.

All of these images flashed through his mind in a fraction of a second, and then they were replaced by what he saw: a bare mattress on a metal frame, a window covered with cardboard, and a naked fluorescent light.

The twins pushed Jacob to the bed, where the coils were soft and the fabric was peppered with tiny black spots. *Dried blood.*

Bravo patted Jacob's pants pocket, finding his keys and pulling them out. "Sleepy, check the other pocket."

Bravo's brother, called Sleepy apparently, leaned in close and searched the pocket. Jacob stared at the large, blackhead-filled pores across his drooping left cheek, and for a split second, he had the bizarre urge to jerk forward, open his mouth, and chomp down on the porey gob of skin like Hannibal Lecter. *Wouldn't that shock them all?* It'd serve no purpose of course. He wouldn't be able to escape, nor would they let him go, but it'd shock the hell out of them. And then he'd get *two* hot metal rods up the ass. So Jacob decided to let Sleepy pull his phone and wallet from the pocket unmolested.

Vicente came into the room carrying the paper bag.

"If you weren't ready to show me the M-30, you could've just said so," Jacob chided.

Vicente dug his hand into the bag. A sly smile crossed his face. "If you weren't ready to buy the M-30, *you* could've just said so." He flashed the blank paper strips to the brothers.

"You weren't supposed to see that," Jacob said dryly.

"At least not until you'd left, right?" Vicente dumped the bag's contents onto the floor and kicked at the pile, evening it out. "Still working for Sinaloa? That's the game, isn't it? They send guys like you to find where we are, and then the house gets hit tomorrow?"

"No." Jacob cried emphatically. "I swear."

Vicente asked to see Jacob's phone; Sleepy tossed it over. "I looked you up, Mr. 3M Scientist. Your apartment looks nice. Right by the river like that."

"How do you know that?"

"You showed me your license yesterday, didn't you?"

Jacob got another rush of goose bumps. If he got out of this, he and Missy were moving, out of state. And they'd get married; he'd take her surname. Jacob Chan. That'd work.

"Who you working for?" Vicente repeated as he leaned against the far wall shared with the front room.

Jacob remembered the little girl on the couch watching the Powerpuff Girls and desperately wished he had some superpowers of his own. Or that Jason Bourne Jeet Kune Do would do just fine if it wanted to reveal itself right about then.

"You afraid of what they'll do to you if you rat on them?" Vicente crossed his arms and nonchalantly scanned the peeling paint behind Jacob, as if he weren't terribly interested in this portion of the interrogation.

He wants to get straight to the torture. Jacob imagined the glowing metal rod, but now it had a fish hook affixed to its base, because Sleepy, the mute sadist, was always coming up with sick, new techniques. The hook caught and grabbed at the soft tissue of people's anuses. *Or maybe he'd tape the rod full of razor blades...* Sleepy was capable of anything, Jacob decided.

"Whoever you're working for isn't the one who has you sitting on a mattress with your wrists tied," Vicente said. "You owe us the truth. Deal with them later. You should be worried about us right now." Vicente glanced at the twins.

Jacob considered lying. They wouldn't know. He could just throw a name out there and see how they reacted. *Except for Sleepy. His Bell's palsy gives him an incredible poker face.* Maybe he could give them Dwight? Throw him under the bus, or more appropriately, under the truck. *That had better symmetry for the book.* But no. Giving them a name admitted his involvement in whatever plot the named had been scheming. "I don't work for anyone," Jacob assured them.

Vicente sighed and stared at his shoes. He casually bent down and brushed a bit of dust from one, letting the accusatory silence hang around for a bit longer.

Jacob covertly tested the strength of his bonds. His shoulder flared, and he relaxed. The tape wasn't giving at all. The other option, bouncing up from the bed and running, making a beeline to the front door and escaping into the street, had occurred to him, but even though the street was right outside the door, he doubted he'd even get out of the room before one of the twins laid him out with a casual stretch of his lanky arm. Jacob looked at Vicente leaning against the wall, playing with his phone.

"Call Missy," Jacob announced with excitement. "Yeah. Call her. She'll tell you."

"Your girl? Wouldn't trust her any more than I trust you," Vicente said, but he then asked, "You got the GPS off?"

"Yeah."

Vicente powered up the phone. "Your pass code?"

"1234."

Vicente shook his head and unlocked the phone. He tapped and scrolled.

Oh, shit. Jacob remembered the photos he'd taken of the city, the cafeteria, San Diego, the homeless people, but more importantly, everything back home. And all his Twitter posts. The app was right there. Vicente only had to...

"#OpioidCrisis? #DrugDealer? #DontSellDrugs? #CleaningThingsUp?" Vicente flashed the phone at Jacob, so he could see the posts. "What's this?"

Jacob puckered his asshole tight. "It was a joke."

Vicente continued his scrolling. "What'd you do to this guy in the street? Jesus."

"I didn't do anything," Jacob swore. "He ran. Got hit."

"Ran from what?" Vicente pushed himself from the wall and walked to the twins, showing them the full breadth of Jacob's activity. When they reached the end, Vicente looked up. "You trying to rat on us? The cops here don't care. We *own* them."

"Please don't fuck up my asshole," Jacob pleaded. "Please."

Bravo laughed. Sleepy half laughed.

A drop of sweat rolled down the side of Jacob's temple; his whole body was covered in a slick layer of perspiration. "I don't know anything. Seriously. I don't know you. I don't know this house. Or this neighborhood. Nothing. I'll go back to San Diego; Missy and I will fly home tomorrow. Done. Nothing happened. Really. I promise."

Vicente shook his head and said, "No." He drew the word out long and slow. "You have to pay for this."

"Oh, God," Jacob mewled.

Vicente tossed the phone onto the mattress and stepped to the side of the bed and grabbed Jacob's wrists.

"Please. Please. I promise," Jacob whined.

Vicente fumbled with the duct tape for a moment, found the end, then began to unravel it.

"Please. What're you doing?" The tape loosened. He knew Vicente wasn't letting him go. There was no chance, so why remove the tape? Were they going to make him sodomize himself? He should've never read that article; the thoughts would've been unimaginable otherwise. *Ignorance is bliss.* But he *had* read the article, and the thoughts were there.

Vicente flicked the last section of tape away. "Call your girl."

Jacob couldn't comprehend the simple request. "Who?"

"Your girl," Vicente repeated. "You said she was in San Diego?"

Missy! "Oh, yeah, right. I can call her." Jacob grabbed his phone from the soiled mattress. "Why should I call her?"

"Tell her to get the cash in your bank account. All of it."

Jacob figured there was only about $5,000 there. Much less than what he'd tried to lead Vicente to believe there was, but he'd deal with that later. *First things first.* He dialed Missy. "It's ringing...still ringing..." He then lowered the phone to his lap. "Went to voicemail."

"Call again," Vicente instructed.

Jacob nodded. "Ringing..." *Pick up.* He wiped the sweat from the palm of his free hand across his thigh. The phone went to voicemail again. He looked at Vicente and shook his head.

"Again," Vicente demanded.

Bravo and Sleepy smirked at each other.

Jacob called Missy a third time. *Pick up the phone!* And she finally did. "Missy! Missy, listen. I need you to do something, okay?"

"I'm at the conference," Missy told him. "Stop calling. I'm busy."

"No, it's important—"

She cut him off. "My panel just finished. I'm talking to some people about an opportunity." Her voice became hushed but rose in pitch. "At Google!"

"Missy, listen—"

"I have to go. We can talk tonight."

"Missy—"

She hung up.

"Fuck," Jacob whined. "Missy! Jesus Christ." He called her back, but it went straight to voicemail. "Gotta be kidding me," he said. "She turned off her phone."

Vicente chuckled and took the phone from Jacob. "You're a lucky guy to have a girl like that."

"She'll call back," Jacob insisted, but he truly didn't know. He was only hoping.

As if sensing Jacob's trepidation, Vicente said, "I'll text her," and scrolled through Jacob's texts. "There's no

'Missy' here."

"She's 'Princess Peach.'"

"Are you Mario?" Bravo laughed.

"Yes," Jacob muttered.

Bravo laughed even harder. "Toadstool your dog?"

"Screw you, Earthworm Jim," Jacob said.

Sleepy placed a hand on Jacob's chest and pushed him flat on his back.

Jacob lay where he landed, face to the cracked ceiling.

"No name-calling," Vicente warned Jacob. He stepped away from the bed and told the twins, "Tape Ed up. We'll have to wait until the princess calls back."

The bedroom had no door. Every so often, Vicente or one of the twins would peek in on Jacob, making sure he was still securely taped to the metal headboard. They needn't have worried. He had no intention of trying to escape. At least not yet. Jacob was still deciding what made for a better story: bolting for freedom or letting things play out. He sat on the crusty mattress, legs splayed out before him, twiddling his thumbs and thinking.

Time was moving at an odd pace. With the window covered, there was no natural light to monitor, nor shadows to track. And Jacob's mind wandered...to his book, to his adventures, to Missy, to some random childhood memory of a tennis session he'd been forced to attend. His thoughts were all over the place, and any internal barometer for the passing of time he may have had was getting wildly skewed.

Through the far wall, Jacob could just barely hear the low notes of a cartoon, maybe still *The Powerpuff Girls*. Curiously, he hadn't heard a peep from the girl with the yellow ribbon. She hadn't even laughed once. She was quieter than he'd ever been at a 44th Parallel company outing. And it spooked him. She'd probably make for a great writer someday.

His phone lay at the other end of the bed, out of reach. Vicente had set it there, its ringtone turned up high, so they'd hear it if (*not if*, Jacob told himself, *but when*) Missy called. Jacob had also promised to give a shout if it rang, but Vicente had told him it wouldn't be necessary. He assured Jacob they'd hear.

He was avoiding eye contact with the old Samsung lying there next to a blood stain that bizarrely resembled a pug. If he didn't look at it, he didn't get angry. *Why isn't Missy calling back? Ring. Ring. Ring, you stupid piece of shit.* But it only sat there, mute.

For the fourth time in who knew how long, Vicente passed by the room. Bravo and Sleepy followed. Each one took a cursory glance at Jacob who gave a pathetic smile and a thumbs-up. He figured he might as well do what he could to garner some pity points. If things went south later (as if they already hadn't), he could try to cash those points in. *Could they really torture such a pitiful creature? Probably.* They most assuredly did it all the time. But still, he kept that smile until they'd all gone by.

The front door opened with a protracted screech, and for a moment he thought they might be leaving. He started to scheme: how to loosen the tape, how to pull himself free, where to go. Should he grab something for defense? His left leg had fallen asleep; he shuffled and wiggled atop the mattress to get the feeling back.

But it was unnecessary. Vicente and the twins weren't opening the door to leave; they were letting someone in. Lots of someones. A parade of pattering and shuffling awakened the house. No voices, though. The someones said nothing, and Jacob's imagination identified the unidentified as CJNG members crowding in, assembling to...*make a tunnel run...come to inspect their hostage...discuss the best method of torture?* Jacob squeezed his ass cheeks, testing how well he could protect his vulnerable innards from molestation. Of course, the group at the front door would assuredly have other torture methods if they couldn't get in his back door. There'd be a cornucopia of techniques to try. The cartel was notorious for their resourcefulness and brutality. Glass shards took chunks of flesh away. Gas rags were lit, tossed on backs, then ripped away, again and again. Hydrofluoric acid dissolved bodies. He'd even come across a video of one guy pleading for mercy while his heart had been pulled barehanded from his chest.

Vicente finally spoke. "All right. Good."

"This way," Bravo instructed.

Jacob pushed the thoughts of torture to the back of his mind. He was an American. The cartel wouldn't do *that* to an American. Even if Missy never called, Vicente wouldn't kill him. He'd scar him for life in some way, no doubt, but Jacob was still pretty sure he'd be let go no matter what.

A multitude of footsteps approached. Bravo and his elongated frame went by the room without so much as a glance. Jacob held his breath, hoping whoever was behind him would do the same. *Let me be. Let me be. Let me be...*

While it wasn't a torture squad that appeared, Jacob still sat up straight with a terrible fear when he saw the new arrivals. Three little girls, roughly the same age as Yellow Ribbon, trailed Bravo, all walking with a tired, vacant urgency; their heads were bowed, loose greasy strands of hair dangled over their eyes, and their bony-kneed legs hurried to keep pace with Bravo's long gait. Sleepy followed the procession, and then they were gone.

"Yeah, it's fine," Vicente said to someone in the front room. "The rest on Tuesday?"

"Tuesday," a male voice answered.

There was a sharp slap of skin (*a firm handshake?*), then the man left.

"Keep watching your cartoons, Morena," Vicente

said in a softer voice. He came down the hall, passing Jacob's room with a sideways scowl, and continued on to attend to the business of the girls.

Jacob didn't need it spelled out for him. He knew what was happening. He hoped he was wrong; he hoped the girls were part of a migrant family who'd grown desperate at the border and sent their girls on an alternate route, but the dark pit that'd opened in his heart told him they weren't part of any family who'd made the tough decision to split up. These girls were being trafficked.

A sad, opportunistic thought came alive in his mind. *I'm a horrible person. That's terrible.* But the truth of the matter was that a part of him was happy to see the girls in this situation. For all they'd been through, whatever trauma they'd endured, he was kind of glad they were here. Because, if he could find out where he was, where this house was, his story—the story that'd begun with addicts and drug dealers—could end with the rescue of trafficking victims.

Jacob held his breath, listening to the group, which was now somewhere in the back of the house. A door opened then closed. A muffled voice (Vicente's) sounded through the wall behind him. Jacob strained his head closer to the wall, but the tape held firm, and he couldn't draw any nearer. Vicente was talking, then one of the twins. The words were inaudible, but Jacob could guess the tunnel was in the room behind his. It had to be. They were leading the girls into the tunnel. In a few minutes, they'd be crossing the border.

His heart sank. By the time he alerted the authorities, the girls would've reached the other side and vanished.

But there was still Yellow Ribbon. Vicente seemed to have some sort of fondness for her, but there was no justifiable reason for her to be here. She was in danger, and he could still save her. And all the others who'd come after. Those three girls surely weren't the last to be run through the tunnel. Vicente had referenced "the rest" on Tuesday. He'd save them. He just had to figure out how to save himself first.

Jacob spent what felt like another few hours just sitting and listening. There were some promising sounds and mutterings through the wall. The three girls hadn't been escorted down the tunnel; they were still in the room. Vicente and the twins apparently weren't in any rush to get them north. Jacob knew this could change at any moment, but for the time being, his imagined best-seller still included these girls.

As he continued to listen and entertain various book titles other than *A Vigilante Tale* (*Whatever it Takes,* or maybe *Hashtag,* or how about *An Opioid Story?*), his phone came to life, first the vibration and then the ringtone. This being his old phone, he'd completely forgotten the ringtone he'd purchased nearly ten years earlier for ninety-nine cents. He'd been watching a lot of *SpongeBob SquarePants* then.

"Are you ready, kids?"

"Aye, aye, Captain!"

"I can't hear you!"

"Vicente," Jacob called out. "Missy's calling!"

"Aye, aye, Captain!"

"Oh...who lives in a pineapple..."

"Vicente!" Jacob reached out his foot, trying to drag the phone over, but it was at the very end of the mattress. He wasn't even close to it. He gave the mattress a series of small thumps with his heel to get the phone to bounce closer, but it only took a couple little hops closer to the edge of the bed, and he quickly stopped before it toppled over and smashed on the concrete.

The ringtone continued its fifteen-second loop of SpongeBob. A small round face poked around the edge of the doorframe.

"Hey," Jacob said with all the sweetness he could muster. He tried to think of her name. *What had Vicente called her...? Morena!* "Hey, Morena."

The girl glanced at him with large brown eyes that were mixed with curiosity and hesitancy.

He asked her, "Can you give me my phone?"

She took one step in, a hand still on the frame.

"Hurry. Before Missy hangs up." He rose the pitch of his voice, trying not to alarm her but still convey urgency.

The girl didn't move. She found something of interest near her finger on the frame and picked at it while giving a couple of glances into the room.

The theme song cut off in mid "Captain." Jacob sighed. The house was quiet.

Morena dropped her hand from the frame and decided it was safe to take a couple more steps into the room. Her elfish ears were pierced. Cubic zirconia crystals took what little light there was from the fluorescent bulb overhead and reflected it in tiny beams.

"Your earrings are pretty," Jacob said, still hoping she might hand him the phone.

The girl gave one earring a brief touch as she stepped up to the bed, inspecting the phone. She carefully laid a hand on the Samsung. Her thin wrist was marked with ugly bruises and slashes of red where rope had rubbed off a layer of skin.

His phone beeped. A *voicemail.* The girl lifted the phone and picked at its side buttons. She unconsciously stepped back from the bed.

"No, no," Jacob uttered. "Leave that here."

She paused and lifted her eyes, staring at him in an oddly distant, half-gone way.

"Can I see it? Here. Give it to me."

Her eyes flicked across his face, then to the tape

across his chest and wrists.

"Here." He lifted his hand.

She took one slow step backward.

Jacob changed tactics. "Where'd you get your ribbon?"

She took another step back.

No, no, no. "Is yellow your favorite color?"

She gave a barely perceptible nod.

"It's a very pretty color."

Another step back.

"Can you do something for me?"

Another small nod.

"Can you help me with this tape?" Jacob glanced at his chest. "I got stuck." He gave a sheepish laugh.

She quickly shook her head and looked back toward the hall.

"It's okay. Vicente won't care," Jacob promised. Mentioning Vicente's name was a mistake, though. The girl's demeanor changed. She scanned the room, checking the corners for previously unseen dangers.

"Leave the phone," Jacob called out. "Leave my phone. Please."

The girl scurried away.

"Don't go."

Clutching the phone against her chest, she rounded the corner into the hall, and was gone, a dirty bare sole the last of her to disappear. She pattered back to the front room.

"Princess Peach left you a voicemail," Vicente announced as he stepped into the room holding Jacob's phone. He played the message.

Missy's voice chirped. "Hey, babe. What's going on? Call me back."

Vicente handed Jacob the phone. "Go ahead. Call

her back."

Jacob nodded.

"Put it on speaker."

"Sure." The phone was undamaged. Morena hadn't done a thing to it. *Thank God.* He dialed Missy and stared at the screen while Vicente stared at him.

Missy quickly answered. "Babe."

Jacob smiled. "Hey."

"Where are you? Saw your text. What do you mean you're not coming back tonight?"

Vicente held up a hand to silence Jacob. "Where are you, Missy? Right now, where are you?"

"Huh? Am I on speaker? Who's that, Jacob?"

"Where *are* you?" Vicente pressed.

Missy was quiet, thinking, then said, "Like where at the conference center? I'm by the Starbucks in the lobby. Why? Who—"

"Listen," Vicente cut her off. "Jacob got himself into a little situation here in Tijuana, and you need to help him get things settled. Okay?"

"Tijuana?" she cried. "Jacob, you're in Tijuana?"

"Missy, Missy," Jacob hushed her. "Just listen. I need your help."

"Did you get arrested?"

Jacob took a breath. "It's the cartel, Missy."

"That's not funny."

Vicente groaned. He took the phone, stepped back from the bed, and snapped a picture.

When Missy received the photo, her voice broke. "Oh, my God. Jacob."

"He'll be fine," Vicente told her. "He *is* fine. Not a scratch on him, you see?"

"Ah-huh," Missy said, and sniffled.

"Don't let this go bad. Jacob says you have money in your bank account. Ten grand buys his freedom."

"But we don't have that," Missy said.

Vicente glared at Jacob.

"There's like five maybe," Jacob admitted.

Vicente rolled his eyes then spoke into the phone. "It'll take you about forty minutes to get here, so I'll give you an hour and a half. Meet us at the north end of the Alameda Otay parking lot with five grand."

"I don't have a car," Missy argued.

"That's your excuse? Get one," Vicente directed.

"You want me to get a car, go to the bank, then drive to Tijuana in ninety minutes?" Missy whined.

"Jesus," Vicente groaned. "Don't then. I don't care. Jacob just won't go home with all his fingers."

Jacob examined his hands. *Cleaver? Razor? Scissors? Quick or slow? Any major veins? Will I pass out?* "Missy! Do it. Please!"

"You asshole," she hissed. "How could you do this to me?"

"If this is too much trouble," Vicente huffed, "forget it. But it's a pretty simple ask. Five grand for your boyfriend? That's a good deal. We've asked for much, much more before."

There was a long pause.

"Where do you want me to go?" Missy finally spoke. "Ala what?"

"Alameda Otay. It's a shopping center. We'll be at the north end of the parking lot."

"I'm going to have my GPS on," Missy warned. "Don't try anything."

"Don't plan to. But," Vicente warned, lowering his voice to a growl, "if you want to see what we're capable of, Google CJNG. Don't *you* try anything either."

Jacob doubted Missy needed the additional motivation, but the gruesome images he'd seen online would certainly get her moving. Mutilated bodies hanging from overpasses. Severed heads lying lopsided on the ceramic tiles of a restaurant. A young couple shot dead, their five-month-old baby caught in the crossfire. He almost hoped she *wouldn't* look. She could very well become frozen with fear.

Out of the corner of his eye, he caught sight of Morena standing at the threshold of the room, staring at Vicente. "I'm hungry," she said in a nearly imperceptible voice.

Vicente looked over his shoulder. "You're hungry, Morena?"

The girl nodded.

"Okay." Vicente turned back to the phone. "Missy, we'll be there at four. You two can be back at your hotel in time for dinner."

"Just don't do anything if I'm a little late."

"Just don't be late." Vicente ended the call.

Jacob let out a long sigh. He still needed to get the precise location of the house, but things were moving in the right direction. By the time the evening rolled around, he'd be the center of attention at the DEA's office up in San Diego. He'd be spilling all the dirt on the CJNG's operations. He glanced up at Vicente. *Enjoy your last few hours of freedom.*

Vicente laid Jacob's phone near the end of the bed.

"Where you disappear to?" Jacob asked, trying to get some more detail for the DEA (and the book). "Haven't seen you for some time."

Vicente didn't answer.

"Playing in your tunnel?" Jacob pressed. "Bet it's pretty cool."

Vicente smirked and turned to Morena. "What do you want to eat?"

"Who are the kids?" Jacob interrupted. "Where'd they come from?"

Vicente walked toward Morena. "Some cereal?"

"Who's *she*? Morena? Where'd she come from?"

"Let's go," Vicente told the girl.

A rush of disgust and frustration overwhelmed

Jacob. "How can you do this? They're kids," he yelled.

Vicente paused. "Yeah. They are kids. And it's you people who buy them, you sick fucks."

XVIII.

Jacob listened to the pat of Morena's bare feet as she followed Vicente down the hall to the kitchen. Then there was the sound of a fridge being opened, a spoon dropping into a bowl, and the sprinkling of cereal.

"Fucker," Jacob mumbled. Did Vicente really think he got a pass because he was the supplier? *Well, he isn't going to be the supplier for much longer.* He was going to shut Vicente down, him and his freaky spider twins. These guys were probably the area's primary suppliers, too. They were in charge of everything from Tijuana to Tucson. This was going to be a bust for the ages. He was going to get them all thrown in prison for life; he was going to rescue Yellow Ribbon and the girls in the back room; and he was going to put it all up on social media and in his book. He would shine a spotlight so bright on the despicable practice that the world would gasp at what they saw. Social workers would rush in. Governments would establish joint oversight committees. Anyone with a heart, anywhere in the world, would donate to the cause. And he would too. He'd donate a dollar for every book he sold to keep the momentum going after the story was published.

The clinking of the spoon against the bowl stopped; Morena ran by the doorway back to the couch and the cartoons. As she passed, it sounded like she was muttering SpongeBob's theme song: "Aye, aye, Captain..." He grinned then waited for Vicente. He had a witty comeback prepared and was ready to hurl it from the room once Vicente appeared, but Morena was the only one to pass. *Vicente went in the tunnel.* Jacob slumped in the bed as much as the tape would allow and became distracted with thoughts of SpongeBob and a multi-city book tour.

An hour passed before Vicente showed his face again, but by then, Jacob's wit and wisdom had been forgotten. Jacob stared up at Vicente with only a blank stupid look.

Vicente said, "Time to go."

Bravo and Sleepy were waiting in the doorway, and with those words, Bravo came over, standing opposite Vicente, and helped him unwind the long strips of tape around Jacob's chest. When they'd finished, Bravo flipped the wadded ball of tape to his brother, who caught it and tossed it down the hall.

Jacob arched his back and took a deep breath.

"Put these back on," Vicente instructed, handing Jacob the blackened goggles.

"You know," Jacob said, taking the goggles, "I'm not giving you anything above two stars on TripAdvisor. Would've been one star, but the car service is nice. Still won't recommend you to my friends." He pulled the goggles in place.

"Get up," Vicente groaned, grabbing Jacob under the arm and pulling him from the bed.

"Yep, up we go." Jacob swung his hands out for some momentum and stood. He smiled around the room for all to see. He couldn't see shit with the goggles, but he imagined no one smiled back. *Not the smiling types.* "Can I have my phone and wallet and keys?" He held up his hand.

"When we're done," Vicente said. He gave Jacob a shove, and the four of them made their way through the house. "Keep watching your cartoons, Morena. We'll be right back," Vicente said as he opened the front door. A gust of warm air, smelling of dust and exhaust, poured in.

Jacob regretted leaving the girl. It was a shame he hadn't been more clever and thought of a way to escape. He could've taken her straight to safety. They would've gotten a grand reception. *Missed opportunity.*

Vicente led him out of the house with the twins following.

Now focus. Jacob strained his eyes up and around, left and right, trying to find a gap in the goggles where he might catch a glimpse of the house or the street, anything that would give him a chance to identify the place, but the goggles mercilessly hugged his face and kept the world black.

The car door opened. "Get in," Vicente grumbled.

Jacob flopped in the seat. The old sour vomit smell confirmed he was back in the Dodge Charger. Maybe this was their only car. The DEA could look for it parked outside the house. The twins climbed into the back.

"Why're they coming along? Think Missy's going to be too much to handle?" Jacob mocked.

"Put these on," Vicente said, pushing the sunglasses into his hands.

Jacob slipped the glasses over the goggles. "It's good they're coming. She's a real firecracker. Zing. Pow!"

Vicente started the Charger without a word.

Like before, once the car began to move, Jacob started counting the seconds. He'd be absolutely silent this time. No distractions. He imagined himself standing in front of a blackboard, like in grade school, with a piece of chalk, and he started to draw, left to right. Four seconds passed, then Vicente took a right. The chalk changed course toward the bottom of the board. Ten seconds, then another right. The chalk went left. The car picked up its pace, so Jacob moved the chalk along with a little more urgency. The twins were muttering between themselves in the back, and Jacob was tempted to eavesdrop, but he had to keep his focus; he went on counting and drawing.

Vicente didn't deviate from the path for a long time. This was the main boulevard. The chalk continued left for nearly 250 seconds. Then came another turn, this one more gradual, wider, as if two major multi-lane roads were intersecting. Vicente accelerated. *Side streets to main boulevard to highway*, Jacob thought. He counted 120 seconds before Vicente started to slow. The car curled around a bend, coasted for a moment, then came to a stop.

Vicente shifted into park. "Get out." He gave Jacob a light backhanded slap across the chest.

Jacob examined his blackboard. He had the path now. *Just don't forget it.* He fumbled for the door handle, found it, and stepped from the car.

The warmth of the sun made him instinctively squint even though the world remained in pitch darkness. It was an oddly discomforting sensation, so when Bravo emerged from the car and told him he could take off his eyewear, Jacob ripped them away. "Damn it's bright," he cried.

"No shit," Bravo snarled.

Jacob stared at the blacktop for a couple seconds until his eyes adjusted. He then turned and tossed the goggles and sunglasses into the car before having a look around to gather more details.

They were in a vast parking lot, the Alameda Otay Mall's parking lot according to all the signs. Most of the vehicles were bunched together off in the distance near the mall's entrance. For privacy, Vicente had parked the Charger close to the end of the lot near the employees' section.

Bravo and Sleepy escorted Jacob toward the very edge of the lot.

"Vicente coming?" Jacob asked, pretending to

genuinely care. He only wanted an excuse to turn around and get one last good look at the Charger. *What's the license plate?* It was a bad angle. *BF something... 33...something something*.

Vicente followed the group. "Eyes forward," he muttered.

Jacob had the chalk drawing of the route, a description of the car, and some crude details on the house. That was all he'd get. It'd have to be enough.

As they proceeded to a patch of grass along the lot's outer edge, the sight of the twins started to weigh on Jacob. Why *had* they come along? As escorts? Did Vicente really think he and Missy were going to try something? Or was it the other way around? Were the twins and Vicente planning something? They seemed on edge, heads up, quietly scanning the lot.

"What's she look like?" Vicente grumbled.

"Thin, short, black hair. Sometimes it's curled," Jacob answered. "She's not here. I don't see her." A part of him almost hoped she wouldn't show. Having her arrive, pay Vicente, then drive off with him safely in the car was terribly anticlimactic. He'd then call the DEA, and they'd go rescue Morena and the other girls, and that would be it. The End. He wrinkled his nose. That didn't sound as amazing as it had while he'd been tied to the bed.

The four of them stopped near a Ford F-150 and a Subaru Impreza. Vicente settled against the truck's bumper. "It's four o'clock," he warned.

Jacob searched the lot for an approaching vehicle, but the only movement was near the mall's main doors.

Bravo smirked. "Give any thought to which fingers you'd be willing to lose?"

"This one maybe?" Jacob grinned and flipped him the bird.

Sleepy gave Jacob a sharp punch to the kidney.

Jacob buckled over.

"Dumbass," Vicente muttered.

The group grew quiet, standing in the sun, sweating and waiting.

Five minutes later, as Jacob continued to rub his side, he said, "You really got me."

Sleepy didn't pay him any attention. He was watching a car approach.

The white Honda Civic slowed, and Jacob peered in at the driver. It was Missy. Her eyes widened in a confused mixture of delight and fear and relief. She stopped the car in the middle of the aisle and jumped out.

Vicente placed a hand on Jacob's shoulder, holding him steady, making Missy come to them.

She did, without hesitation. She smiled and let out a single sob, throwing her arms around Jacob, giving him a kiss, pushing him back and slapping him on the chest, then hugging him tightly again, burying her face in his shirt.

He kissed the top of her head, the lily scent of her shampoo rising up to greet him. Whatever desire he'd had about her not showing vanished. "Thanks, babe."

"What'd you bring us?" Vicente pressed.

Missy continued to clutch Jacob, then finally let him go, dug into her LV tote, and pulled out the cash. She handed it to Vicente without looking at him.

Vicente flipped through the bills. "Thanks, Princess. You saved Mario."

Gingerly, Missy touched the coagulated cut on Jacob's chin, then gripped his hand tightly and pulled him toward the Honda. Jacob glanced at the twins as he passed, wishing he'd never have to look at their beady heads and spindly limbs again. They *really* looked like spiders, spiders that'd taken human form, and it absolutely freaked him out. He knew he'd see them all again, though. Across a courtroom as he gave his testimony.

"Hope you learned your lesson," Vicente said. He walked away down the aisle with the twins trailing behind.

"Oh, you betcha," Jacob mocked.

"Stick to your music, Sheeran," Vicente called out. "This doesn't suit you."

Missy pushed Jacob behind the wheel of the Honda before scampering around to the passenger side. She hopped in. "Let's go."

Jacob quickly put the car in gear and drove them from the lot.

"I don't even want to know what you were trying to do. Ever. Okay?"

"You won't be able to read my book then," Jacob said. He went left, unsure how precisely to get back to UABC, but he'd figure it out. For the moment, just getting some distance between them and Vicente seemed appropriate.

"Nope. Won't read it," Missy huffed.

He smirked. She'd read it. When it was on the best-seller list, she'd read it. He continued down the road for a couple hundred yards, watching the rearview mirror, trying to see if the Charger was trailing them. It wasn't; he pulled into a Fiesta Inn.

Missy looked around the hotel's parking lot. "Where's the Focus?"

"On UABC's campus."

"What's here then?"

He was inspecting his blackboard line drawing. *How's this supposed to lead anyone anywhere?* And the rest of his descriptors were equally pathetic. "I don't think we can go back to San Diego."

Missy scrunched her face in bewilderment. "Huh?"

"Those guys...they're trafficking kids. They've got four girls, all younger than ten, in the house I was just in. They need help."

"Yeah. For sure. Let's call the cops." Missy pulled out her phone. "What's the emergency number here? 911?"

"I don't know where I was."

"Just tell them what you do know."

"Except I don't know anything. The house is over in Nueva Tijuana somewhere, but they blindfolded me."

"Tell them that then."

"Missy. You're not listening to me. They won't know where to go. I've got some vague idea, but not enough to get anyone there. They won't find it. We have to go find it ourselves." *Because I'm the hero of this story.*

She erupted in a fit. "*We*? We don't *have* to do anything. This isn't our problem."

"They're trafficking kids. You can't ignore that."

"I'm not! I'm calling the police."

"They won't be able to do anything!"

"Get out. I'm driving." She furiously unbuckled her seat belt.

"Jesus, Missy, how can you be so heartless?"

"*I'm* heartless? You're only doing this for a stupid book deal. I know you, and that's sick! *You're* sick!"

Jacob had no retort. She was mostly right. But then he perked up, and said, "So? Who cares? I'm still *helping* them. We're getting them out of that shit."

"Oh, is that right? How exactly is *that* supposed to happen? Go back to that house and kick everyone's ass? You're Liam Neeson? Got a special set of skills?"

Jacob sighed. *No, I was thinking more like Jason Bourne.*

Missy lowered her voice. "There's nothing you can do. And that's okay. Just call the police and tell them what you know."

"They blindfolded me. I've got nothing. I was trying to track the turns in my head, but it's a mess. Can't we just try to backtrack real quick?" Jacob watched as the thought rolled around in Missy's head. "And we know what their car looks like. If we see it, we'll call 911. And that'll be it. Then we go," he promised. "I just can't drive back to San Diego right now. Not with the chance of actually finding the house. We find the house; we save those little girls," he argued, his voice breaking.

A shimmer formed in Missy's eyes.

"You know it's the right thing to do." He squeezed her hand.

"Alicia got the promotion," Missy told him. "And Google wants to talk to me some more tomorrow. A mini interview, so...no... I can't be doing this. We have to go back."

Jacob stared at Missy, his mouth slightly agape.

Missy wiped her eyes. "It's crazy she got it, I know, but now here's Google. I can't screw it up. Let's go back."

Jacob sighed. If Missy was forcing him to do this, then so be it. He said, "All right. We'll go get the Focus and head back."

Missy leaned over and gave him a kiss on his cheek. "Call the police when we're back. Tell them everything you saw. Let them do their job."

"Yeah. Sure." He looped the car around the hotel's drop-off circle and turned right, heading away from UABC. They passed the Alameda Otay Mall, and Jacob started counting the seconds.

"Where's UABC exactly?" Missy asked after they'd driven for five minutes.

"Just up here," Jacob mumbled as he followed his chalk line. There were only a few more seconds to go before the next turn. Vicente had made it relatively easy on him, sticking to primary roads and taking no unnecessary turns. Assuming his own counting had been consistent and the speed relatively similar, he'd need to turn left at the next set of lights. Then a straight shot for ten seconds. It'd be right around the corner.

Jacob reached the lights and turned.

Missy sat up in her seat ever so slightly, gazing at the crumbling collection of one- and two-story stucco buildings crowding the street. "This is a college campus?"

Jacob figured she knew what he was really doing, but he said cryptically, "Doesn't look like one, does it?" The unspoken truth was there, though. He'd become an addict. He couldn't help himself. He needed this. He needed to be a part of every aspect of the story. He needed to see his plan play out in its entirety, and despite what anyone else said (*Just call 911*), despite what good, common sense said (*You're no hero*), he was looking at the line of cocaine and picking up the rolled-up bill once again.

He glanced sideways at Missy, expecting to see her wide eyed and twitchy, breathing in rapid little bursts like a mouse caught in a corner, but she sat motionless, hands folded in her lap, staring intently at the glove box, her emotions seemingly so wound up she didn't know what to say.

Up ahead, the street came to a T-intersection. A warehouse at the top of the T welcomed their approach. The stash house would be around the corner to the left, if he had somehow gotten his blind measurements correct, which suddenly didn't seem all that likely.

There was a corner store. Too many people were milling about. A food cart was set up on the sidewalk. The owner was frantically assembling containers of a specialty Jacob couldn't quite see.

The intersection appeared too active. He hadn't heard any of this before. And didn't the cartel want privacy? There was no way he'd gotten this right. He reached the end of the street in roughly the ten seconds he'd expected, though, so he made the final turn.

His eyes scanned the parked cars, looking for the white Charger. No, no, no, but then there it was. He cried out with excitement and pointed. He pulled over, parking between a cargo van and a sedan, and pointed again. "That's it."

"I see it," Missy muttered, coming out of her Zen-like trance.

"Which house is it?" Jacob asked himself as he leaned over the steering wheel, shifting and craning his neck to examine the buildings near the Charger. Several homes were set back from the road and protected with thick, aggressive front gates topped with razor wire. *Not those.* He turned left, gazing at the houses directly across the street, then back to the corner store. The third house from the store was an intriguing subject. It was only fifteen, maybe twenty, feet wide with a sandy front strip between the house and the street. He'd tripped on that shifting sand when he'd arrived, hadn't he? And there was a little ledge at the base of the front door. To the right of that was a large window shrouded in darkness (*the black sheet*?). "That's it. It has to be. Right there." Jacob stabbed the air, pointing at the single-story, pale-brown stucco building sandwiched between its neighbors like a middle airline seat.

Missy pulled out her phone, tapped the screen, then placed it against her ear. "What's the address?" she asked.

He scanned the exterior of the house for a number. "I don't know. Can't see it."

"Doesn't matter," Missy said, then spoke into her phone, "Yes, do you speak English? Okay. I'd like to report a kidnapping. The street?" Missy looked at Jacob.

"I don't know. I didn't see a sign. Somewhere in Nueva Tijuana. I know it's off Bellas Artes. I saw that sign. That's the main road."

Missy relayed the information and looked around. "There's an OXXO and a warehouse. It's white with a blue stripe on top." She listened for a moment. "No idea. I'm terrible with those." She asked Jacob, "Are we north of Bellas Artes?"

Jacob nodded as he watched the house for movement. "Yeah. North." *This is a waste of time.* He imagined the girls being escorted by the spider twins right under their car at that very moment. In a few seconds, they'd cross under the warehouse, then under the sandy dead space that flanked the border walls, and finally, as the bustle of freight zipped into the US on the frontal roads, they'd emerge into a house that was the CJNG's distribution point.

Missy's voice faded to a dull percussion as he focused on the black sheet hanging in the window. If the girls happened to still be in the house, Morena would be sitting just under that window. *She's so close to the door*. He'd barely have to step in to get her and escape. At least that would guarantee the safety of one of them. It would be on the police to save the others. He was no Jason Bourne (or Liam Neeson).

Missy was still chatting when Jacob opened the door and made his way across the street. He ran to a rusty pickup and crouched against it. Missy frantically waved at him to return. He shook his head. She gave him one glorious death stare, realized he was about to do something either terribly stupid or terribly heroic, and abandoned her call. She pointed her phone out the window.

Smiling for the camera, Jacob poked his head around the truck's half-cocked rear bumper. The house looked a little larger, a little more imposing now that he was on the precipice of action. The top corner of the window's black shroud hung loose. There was no doubt this was the house.

A man near the corner store let out a heavy belch, and even at such distance, it made Jacob jump. But it also broke his semi paralysis, and he duckwalked around the truck, up the short stretch of sand that fronted the house, and pushed himself against the stucco just underneath the window, the rough surface scratching his back.

To his left was a cinder-block wall pressed against the side of the house, cutting a harsh line between it and its neighbor. The same thing existed with the other neighbor.

No trying the back door.

Jacob turned, facing the window, and carefully stuck his hand between the rust-covered bars and tapped the dusty glass softly. Hopefully Morena was there. Hopefully she was alone. There was no response. Jacob tapped the glass again, fast and firm—*tpp tpp tpp tpp. That was loud.* His nerves broke, and he sprinted from the window back to the pickup, where he lay flat on the sun-drenched street, ignoring the burn of the asphalt on his belly. He gazed under the truck, watching the house. The sheet fluttered. Someone was grasping at it, but then it fell still.

The sheet, Jacob remembered, had been taped to the wall. Whoever had tried to move it didn't want to pull it loose (*or couldn't pull it loose*). That someone was surely Morena. Vicente or Bravo or Sleepy wouldn't have bothered grabbing the sheet. They would've just gone to the door. *Right?* Jacob hoped so, because he was up and moving to the house again.

He reached through the window's bars and tapped an inconsistent, unnatural pattern for several seconds. The sheet fluttered, harder than before, but still remained taped in place.

"Go to the door," he whispered. "The door..." The image of Bravo and Sleepy standing next to the couch, each with a hand on the girl's shoulders, flashed in his head. Jacob turned to Missy. She was still recording. *This is stupid.* What'd he really think was going to happen? That...

The front door creaked, and he spun his head around so fast he pulled a muscle. Morena was standing there, a hand on the door, the other on the frame. Her eyes searched around. Jacob scrambled to his feet, slamming his head on the underside of the window's security bars. "Fuckin' A."

Morena glanced over.

Jacob straightened up and gave a little wave. "Hi."

She didn't move.

He took a half step, as if he were approaching a

rabbit in the wild. "Do you remember me?" Another half step. Closer and closer, everything fine. *But the rabbit could suddenly take off into the brush, never to be seen again.* He couldn't let that happen. *Just be slow. Don't scare her.* He took another step. "Hi. Where's your mom and dad?"

She blinked twice, a concerned, confused expression across her face.

He suddenly felt like *he* was the sexual predator trying to lure this girl from her home. "Let's go find your mom and dad." He took a step. He was within arm's reach of the door. "Do you want to find your parents?"

She shook her head.

"Why not?"

"They died," she mumbled.

Jacob took a breath. "Oh. Let's just get you out of here then." He reached for her hand.

From the street, Missy blared the horn.

XIX.

"What the fuck? Missy!" Jacob turned. Vicente stood behind him, rage in his eyes, ready to pounce, ready to drag him into the house and feed him to the spiders. Jacob stumbled away, tripping as his feet sunk into the sand, and fell to the ground.

Vicente launched himself at Jacob with a guttural cry. Jacob half turned, instinctively protecting his vital organs, as the man landed with a hefty thud on his right side. Jacob screamed, feeling his shoulder pop then slide back into place. Vicente's hands grabbed his neck and clamped down, fingernails digging deep. Jacob sobbed and gasped, his eyes going wide. The edge of his vision swelled with a white glow.

A plastic bag packed with items from the corner store lay in the sand near Morena. Jacob tried to grab something, anything from the bag that could serve as a weapon, but he couldn't reach it. He kicked and struggled under Vicente's weight, trying to move closer, but the sand only shifted under him, and he sunk deeper. The white glow at the edge of his vision turned gray then misty black. The dark fog began to expand, its tendrils crawling, covering the entirety of his sight. He was terribly lightheaded. The sound of Missy blaring the horn grew dim.

Then the pressure around his throat suddenly fell away. Vicente dropped like a ragdoll to his side.

Coughing and gasping for air, Jacob rolled away. The color returned to his face, and his senses fired back up. The fog cleared. He sat up on his knees and took a steady breath.

Vicente groaned, his face half buried in the sand as he carefully touched a bloody spot on the back of his head.

Beside him, Morena stared, mouth wide with terror, clutching the can of Campbell's soup with which she'd hit Vicente.

"Fuck," Vicente hissed, and turned on his back, eyes gazing up at the sky without focus.

Morena dropped the can and backed away toward the house.

"No," Jacob yelled in a dry rasp. His throat burned, the crushing hatred of Vicente's hands still very present. Jacob swallowed hard, said "No" more firmly, and pushed himself to his feet. He grabbed Morena's hand. "Come on." He gave a tug, trying to lead her away from the house, but she wouldn't move.

Missy was still sounding the horn, and Jacob waved a frantic hand at her to stop. He knelt face-to-face with Morena. Her eyes were terribly pained, raw, tired, distant. The last time he'd seen such a hopeless stare had been in his father's eyes after he'd battled his cancer for three hellish years. Everything had been taken, and even when his father had given what was supposed to be a final comforting smile, Jacob had only seen those defeated eyes. He saw that same stare in the girl. "Hey, we're going to get you out of here. Take you somewhere safe."

Behind the girl, through the open door, something moved in the hallway. A spider was coming up its webbed funnel with silent grace; Bravo was approaching.

Jacob quickly wrapped his arms around Morena. His shoulder exploded with pain, but he ignored it.

Bravo abandoned his creeping steps and broke into a run.

A shot of adrenaline hit Jacob. He tightened his hold on Morena and sprinted across the sand into the street.

Bravo reached out with two lanky arms, grasped the doorframe, and burst from the house as Vicente wobbled to his feet. Vicente didn't see Bravo, and Bravo only saw him at the last second; the two collided. Vicente went twirling, crumpling in a heap. Bravo stumbled wildly on shaky legs, caught himself, and lurched ahead. His clothes, hanging loose, rippled across his spindly frame, knees and elbows poking sharply under the fabric, as he went to catch Jacob and Morena.

With Morena clutched to his chest, Jacob flung the car's back door open and dove inside.

Missy was ready. Having shifted to the driver's seat, she hit the gas.

Bravo reached out.

The car zipped from the curb.

The giant's fingers grazed the back door as it slammed shut.

"Where am I going? Where am I going?" Missy cried as she tore down the center of the street, barely missing a truck pulling out of a warehouse lot.

"Anywhere. Just get away." Jacob pushed himself up in the seat, peering out the back window. Bravo was racing toward the Charger. "Turn," he instructed Missy.

"Where?" she screamed.

"Anywhere. Lose them." Jacob tried to set Morena on the seat next to him, but she clutched him like a security blanket and wouldn't budge. She was humming the SpongeBob theme song. Jacob let her be and peered around her at the street ahead.

Warehouses and factories continued up the right side for as far as he could see. Each property was surrounded by security fences and closed gates. They might have been able to ram through a gate to seek help inside, but at this time of day late on a Friday, there was no guarantee anyone would be there. More than likely, they'd only be trapping themselves. Bravo would catch up, pull out a gun, and shoot them as they stood outside some locked door. And that was assuming they could even smash through the gate. This wasn't the movies; gates didn't simply fly off their supports. They were built to withstand punishment. It'd be like hitting a brick wall. They'd kill themselves before Bravo had a chance to do so himself, so Jacob instructed Missy to "turn left here."

She did, sideswiping a parked van in the process. The street narrowed and became lined with squat stucco homes. The next block up, a group of boys (*The same ones from yesterday?*) were playing soccer in the middle of the street. Missy blared the horn. The boys stopped and stared. "Move!" Curious more than frightened, they didn't, so Missy turned right, onto an even narrower street. "They wouldn't move," Missy cried as she slowed in the cramped space.

"It's okay. This is okay. Keep zigzagging," Jacob encouraged. Morena squeezed him tightly as Missy made another turn.

"I have no idea where I'm going," Missy said.

"That's okay. Don't let the Charger find us. We'll figure out where we need to go later."

"Are you ready kids?"

Jacob jumped at the sound of the ringtone. He yanked the phone from his pocket. Caller ID showed "UNKNOWN 526647818447." He knew who it was. He hit "ignore" and set the phone on the seat, imagining Vicente standing outside the house, one hand pressed gently against the Campbell's-induced lump, the other holding his phone, ready to give Jacob an ultimatum.

Jacob looked behind them. No Charger. Missy slowed and turned right again.

"Oh, shit," she muttered, bringing the car to a crawl.

"What?" Jacob spun around.

"It's a market or something."

The street was crowded with colorful tarps and canopies and people wandering about, inspecting fruits and vegetables and used clothes hanging from strained dowels. Boxes of random odds and ends spilled into the street. Morena loosened her grip and peered around at the activity.

Missy stopped the car as an elderly woman and her grown daughter crossed. "We're safe here," Missy exclaimed, turning to Jacob with a wide grin. "All the people. This is okay, right?"

Jacob shook his head. "It's the cartel, Missy. No one here can help us." Jacob looked behind them. Through the crowd, he saw the Charger. "Shit. We have to go. He's right there."

Missy's eyes shifted to the rearview mirror; an agonized grimace formed when she spotted the white car. "Shit," she repeated. Missy honked, and the elderly woman jumped a mile. As the woman's daughter furiously gestured at them, Missy swerved around and pressed ahead, giving anyone who seemed to be thinking of crossing in front of the Honda a near-death experience.

Jacob continued to eye the Charger. Bravo was easily gaining on them, his path having been cleared by Missy.

"Okay. Finally," Missy sighed, reaching a cross street. The market continued down the next block, but Missy turned from the crowd, jerking the wheel left and zipping away. One short block later, she turned right, onto a wider street, where the buildings stood a little farther back from the road, giving them room to breathe. An even wider, sunnier street arrived, and Missy turned onto it.

"This is good," Jacob told her.

Up ahead, there were traffic lights, the first set they'd seen since rushing from the house. Missy raced ahead to make the green light. Jacob eyed the road behind them, watching for the Charger, but it didn't appear.

Missy yanked the car into a quick, hard turn, and they were out of the closed quarters of the side streets and onto the six-lane main boulevard. The Civic dissolved into the heavy traffic of sedans, buses, and semis. Jacob slumped in the seat and sighed. Morena, sensing the situation had changed for the better, let go, squirmed to the seat beside him, and rested as well.

As Missy continued down the road, "*Are you ready kids?*" chimed from Jacob's phone again. It was the same number as before. Morena bopped her head to the song, so Jacob let it play a few loops before he sent it to voicemail. He turned to the window the girl was gazing out, and they watched the shops pass in an endless stream of gray and white stucco draped with colorful signs, logos, and posters.

"It's like SpongeBob," Morena said, pointing at a yellow building.

"Yeah." Jacob smiled. "You like SpongeBob?"

She nodded and watched the building disappear behind them.

Jacob glanced over his shoulder, out the back window, and scanned the vehicles. No Charger.

"Where am I going?" Missy asked. "I don't know where I'm going."

"Keep driving. There'll be signs for the border." His mind registered there were hills on the horizon, undulating hazy hills, and if they were driving west toward the crossing (and by extension, the ocean), there wouldn't be hills on the horizon, but the realization didn't have a chance to stick. SpongeBob began again, and the hills faded to an afterthought. He grabbed the phone, rejected the call again, then fumbled through the settings, trying to remember how to silence the phone.

A text popped up: "*ANSWER.*"

The phone rang again.

"Are you ready kids?"

Jacob stared at it. There was no reason to answer. But with the Charger nowhere in sight and them cruising on out of Tijuana, he thought, *What the hell? Why not?* He might as well get one last parting comment from the CJNG for the book. He lifted the phone to his ear.

"Bring her back. Now," Vicente bristled.

"That's a hard no from me, chief," Jacob answered. Tiny tufted palm trees lined the center median, and he watched them rush by in a mesmerizing blur.

"Where you think you're running to? This is Tijuana."

"Maybe *you're* in Tijuana. We're back in San Diego." The collection of shops lining the road gave way to long, homogeneous warehouses. The sidewalks were becoming empty. Fewer sedans and more semis crowded around the Honda.

"Bullshit. No fucking way," Vicente said. "You're sitting at the border. And I've got guys walking the lines. They'll find you before you get through."

"We're already through."

"You and your bitch are dead."

Jacob chuckled. "That comment just put you down to one star on TripAdvisor."

"You think I'm joking?"

"Can you recommend someone else I can get my M-30 from?" The palm trees ended, and Jacob was left staring at a bare, dusty median. The warehouses also thinned out as the road sloped upward. Jacob glanced ahead. The hills, which were once dull and distant, were rising up, rushing to greet them. There was no ocean. There was no border crossing. *Where the fuck has Missy taken us?*

"You think I'm joking?" Vicente repeated, louder.

"I've gotta go," Jacob told him. "We're stopping at In-N-Out."

"When we find you—"

Jacob pulled the phone from his ear and ended the call. He turned and glanced out the window beside Morena at a landscape that was covered with tiny, packed homes running for miles toward a lone mountain in the distance. The shadows were all wrong. They were angled right to left; the sun was behind the car.

"Missy, we're going east," Jacob warned.

"I don't know," she answered.

"No, I'm *telling* you. We're going east. We need to go *west*. You're taking us into the desert." The road morphed into a highway. A concrete barrier split the opposing lanes and a sharp drop-off to their right prevented them from pulling over.

Missy hit the brakes. The semi behind them blared its horn.

"What're you doing?"

"You drive. I'm done."

"Don't stop in the middle of the road."

"What do you want me to do?" Missy yelled, taking her foot off the brake.

The eighteen-wheeler jerked around the Honda, just missing its back bumper, and sped by with a long wail of the horn.

The highway was climbing the side of a hill, rising up and up. There was nothing for them to do but continue heading east, so he told her, "Get through this pass. Keep going."

"You said it's the wrong way!" She tapped the brake again.

"We don't have a choice!" The highway dug into the hillside; rock walls rose up around them.

"You drive. You drive," Missy said, veering the car toward the wall. "There's no one behind us."

There wasn't anyone, but they'd reached the hill's peak, and just twenty yards back, the highway dropped out of sight. A truck was likely to come barreling up over the crest, and there'd be no way it could stop in time. Jacob squeezed Missy's shoulder. "Don't stop. Keep going. We'll switch soon. We'll switch at the bottom of the hill. Get to the bottom of the hill."

Missy didn't accelerate, but she didn't depress the brake any either. The car coasted to the edge of the peak and began to descend, picking up speed as the stone walls shrank back and the highway realigned with the hill's natural slope.

Jacob gave her another reassuring squeeze. "There. You see? Where that car crossed down there? Go there." At the base of the hill, a dusty side road intersected with the highway.

She nodded and hurried down the highway. "What's that?" She pointed to a cluster of buildings near the intersection. "That a police station? No? Is it?"

Jacob saw it. A small white structure with a large gold star splashed across the front.

As they drew closer, Missy shouted, "It says 'Police.'"

Jacob grimaced. "Missy. I don't know. The police aren't—"

"It's the police," she repeated, and brought the car to a crawl as it approached the turn.

This isn't right. Vicente said the CJNG owned the police. *These police?* Maybe they were too far outside the city for the CJNG to pay this particular station any attention. *Possible.* He really wanted to just turn around, though, head west, and get help at the border. Vicente's voice sounded in his mind: "*I've got guys walking the lines. They'll find you...*" Maybe the border wasn't any safer.

Missy turned from the highway, curled onto the side road, pulled into the station's gravel lot, and parked near a faded blue door. A cracked layer of blue paint ran away from the door in both directions along the base of the wall. Jacob imagined the paint circling to the back of the station...*where the dead are buried.*

Missy cut the engine and turned around in her seat. She smiled at Morena. "Come on, sweetie. We're going inside. Talk to the policeman." Missy glanced at Jacob. "Help her get out."

"This is risky," he warned.

"It's the *police*," she hissed, then smiled sweetly at Morena.

The station's heavy metal door was somewhat reassuring as Jacob pushed it open. If a station was under the CJNG's control, he assumed they wouldn't need to invest in such a security measure. This door, a couple inches of solid iron, had been put up to stop bullets, he told himself as he held it open for Missy and Morena.

Inside, to the left, natural light, filtering through a small west-facing window, splashed the concrete floor at the edge of a four-by-eight holding cell. To the right of the cell, and directly before the three of them, was a large oak desk with a uniformed officer, whose girth was almost as wide as the desk. He was staring at a scattering of loose papers but looked up to examine his guests.

"Hi there," Missy said. She took Morena's hand and led her across the room to the desk. Morena could barely see over the top of it. "We need your help. This little girl was kidnapped."

"And there's more girls. They're being trafficked," Jacob clarified. He stepped forward and stood behind Missy. "I found them. There's a house with a tunnel under the border. In Nueva Tijuana."

The plump officer, Officer Juanqui according to the gold placard on the desk, shifted his eyes from Missy to Morena to Jacob. He seemed to have a pug-like breathing problem. "That so?"

"It's near the border. By an OXXO," Missy added.

Officer Juanqui turned to Missy, focusing on her legs more than anything. "What's the street?"

"We didn't see," Jacob admitted. "But I can get back there. It's just off Bellas Artes."

The officer scribbled something on the back of a sheet of paper. "That's a ways. Nueva Tijuana," Juanqui said, setting his pen down.

"We got turned around," Jacob said.

Juanqui gave Jacob a smile, exposing round little teeth. "You sure did, didn't you?"

"Police might already be at the house," Missy added. "I called them when we got there. But we had to leave."

"This CJNG guy attacked me, and I grabbed her"—Jacob nodded toward Morena—"and we ran."

"Brave of you." The officer took a raspy breath and sighed. "All right. Well, great. Let me have a look at the little one." He waved for Missy to bring Morena around the side of his desk.

"She seems okay," Missy offered.

"Uh-huh." Juanqui gave Morena a cursory glance, turned her in a circle, then let her go. "Yeah. She's fine, aren't you?"

The girl didn't respond. They all stared at one another, the only sound coming from the stream of air squeezing through Juanqui's fat-pinched nasal cavities.

Jacob scanned the room, memorizing the space for his book. Against the right wall stood a row of faded file cabinets bursting with paperwork. *Like the innards of a sloppily disemboweled cartel victim.* Dozens of cardboard boxes were stacked and scattered in the corner. They pressed hard against a neglected break area cluttered with soiled paper plates, a half-eaten loaf of white bread, and several crumpled bags of chips. A matte-black weapons safe with a half empty pot of coffee resting atop it stood behind Juanqui. The holding cell, a bare concrete space with a wooden bench, finished the room. The station was a depressing display of indifference.

"I'll handle this," Juanqui informed them. "Unless you got something else to report, I don't need you."

Jacob pursed his lips. He'd expected a little more gratitude or recognition for what he'd accomplished. He'd personally rescued a trafficking victim. *And more to follow.*

"The cartel was chasing us," Missy warned. "Is it safe to just leave?"

"I'll call Tijuana. Get you an escort. You come down Padilla?"

"Don't know." Missy pointed. "Came from that way."

"Padilla," Juanqui affirmed. "You go. I'll call and have an escort waiting just over the hill."

"Great," Missy chirped. She patted Morena on the head and spun away.

Jacob blinked. *That's it?* Unsure what else he could possibly do, he gave Morena a smile. She gave a shy wave. It was an unremarkable series of events. He turned and followed Missy as she marched from the station and approached the car.

With the sun glaring down on them, Jacob said, "That wasn't how I expected it'd go."

"Don't talk to me," Missy spat.

Jacob stopped walking.

"Don't pout," she groaned. "Let's go. You're driving."

But Jacob wasn't pouting. Something was wrong. The situation hadn't been resolved. And it wouldn't get resolved by climbing into the car and heading to San Diego. He turned toward the station...

"Jacob!" Missy called out.

...and went back inside.

Officer Juanqui was talking on the phone and abruptly ended the call at Jacob's reappearance. "Yes?"

Morena stood at the side of the oak desk, fidgeting

with her hands.

"What's going to happen to her now?" Jacob asked, approaching the desk.

"We'll figure out who she is. Give her back to her family...of course."

"She said her parents were dead."

Juanqui shrugged. "I'm sure she's got more family than just her parents. Someone will claim her."

"What if no one does?"

"You just head back to San Diego. It's fine," Juanqui said.

Jacob glanced back at the door where Missy now stood, arms folded. He turned to Juanqui. "What makes you think we're from San Diego?"

"That's obvious, isn't it?" Juanqui eyed him up and down. "You didn't come from anywhere south of here, did you?"

"Maybe we should stay, make sure you can find the house?" Jacob offered. Yes, he thought, that was the right thing to do. "I can even go with you to find it."

"I know where the house is," Juanqui assured him.

This was Jacob's final out, his final chance to head back to San Diego if he wanted to take it, but he passed. "Just to be safe, we should stay." He looked around for a place to sit. There was a short wooden bench in the left front corner of the room piled high with paperwork and trash. Jacob walked to it and shuffled the mess aside so he could sit.

"Do you mind?" Juanqui interjected. "Just sit on the other one." He gestured to the bench in the cell.

"It's okay," Jacob argued. "I can slide some of this stuff over."

"No," Juanqui barked. "I've got it organized. I know what's where. Don't mess with it."

Jacob kept his hand atop the pile, thinking.

"Leave it." Juanqui forced a smile, baring his beady

teeth. "Here, why don't you sit with the girl? Keep her company." Juanqui lifted himself from the desk with tremendous effort and waddled to Morena. He put a hand on her back and nudged her toward the holding cell. "Have a seat." He pushed the metal door open until it clacked against the side bars. "Go. Sit," he directed her.

Morena stepped in and took a seat, scooting all the way back against the wall, her feet dangling. "Good girl." Juanqui returned to his chair and plopped down, straining the supports. He smiled at Jacob and waved at the cell. "Or fine, stand if you want. Doesn't matter. Might not hear back about your house for another thirty minutes." He glanced at his phone.

"I'm not standing for half an hour." Missy marched to the cell and took a seat beside Morena, setting her LV tote on the floor.

Juanqui kept his eyes on Missy for a touch longer than modesty should allow, then leaned back in his chair and folded his hands atop his gut, staring down his nose at Jacob beside the trash-heaped bench.

Jacob crossed his arms and leaned against the wall.

Juanqui scratched the side of his belly, glanced over his shoulder at Missy then back at Jacob. His eyes narrowed, growing flinty and serious. "Sure you wanna stick around? If I get a call saying there's no such house, or the officers found nothing wrong there, it might be best if you weren't here."

"What's that mean?"

Juanqui checked his phone, tapped the screen a few times, then looked back at Jacob. "I mean, if there's nothing there, you two become my prime suspects."

"That's ridiculous," Missy said. "We brought her here."

"Maybe after you had a change of heart? I don't know. Tourists take cute kids off the streets here plenty. Claim they're being humanitarians." He gave a huff.

"They're just trying to fast track their adoption plans. Your little guy there not working? Shooting a smoothie with no nutritional value?" Juanqui shifted his eyes to Jacob's crotch. Then he turned to Missy. "You want me to see what I can do for you? Or is it you who's all mangled up like a steer fresh through the slaughterhouse?"

Missy drew a sharp, shocked breath, her eyes doubling in size.

"Jesus," Jacob hissed. He went to the holding cell and placed a hand on Missy's shoulder. He gave her a couple of gentle squeezes, staring at Juanqui, uncertain what to say to the uniformed vulgarity sitting comfortably in his chair.

The hostility fell from Juanqui's eyes. "You want some coffee?"

Jacob glared at him.

"Well, I think I'll get myself a cup." Juanqui groaned as he rose from the chair.

"What an asshole," Jacob whispered to Missy.

Juanqui grabbed a mug from the sink in the back corner, gave it a rinse, and filled it with the oily liquid from the pot atop the safe. He then waddled back to his large oak desk, smiling at Jacob. Juanqui rested the mug on some paperwork and let his hand fall gently to the desk's edge. He paused then turned to the cell. "Does she want anything? Maybe water?" The officer strolled to the open cell and peered in, staring at Morena.

The girl's head was down as she examined her knees and swung her feet, back and forth, back and forth.

Juanqui leaned into the cell, grabbed the door, and pulled it shut.

XX.

Jacob rushed across the holding cell and kicked out his foot, trying to slip it between the door and the metal frame before the lock engaged, but he was too late. His foot struck the bars and twisted at a painfully sharp angle and sent him stumbling to the floor.

Juanqui lost sight of Jacob. Anything that lay in a four-foot circumference around his feet, he couldn't see given his bulbous waist, so he took a step back. Juanqui then grinned. "Give me your cell phones. Both of you."

Missy whimpered.

"You piece of shit," Jacob spat.

"Come on." Juanqui held out his palm and wiggled his knobby fingers. "Give them."

"It's in the car," Jacob told him.

"Is it?"

Jacob pulled his pockets inside out. There was no phone.

"You," Juanqui called to Missy. "Cell phone!"

Missy jumped. She pulled her phone from her tote and hurried across the cell with an outstretched hand.

"No." Jacob scampered to his feet, his ankle bursting with sharp pain under the weight. He wanted that phone, though, so he ignored his twisted ankle and swiped the phone from Missy's hand before she could give it to Juanqui. Clutching the phone tightly at his side, he demanded, "Let us go."

"Oh, boy," Juanqui mocked. He fumbled around at his utility belt before snapping something loose. He gave the item a quick inspection, then pointed the Taser at Jacob and fired it point blank into his chest. The barbed probes stuck him hard, one above his left nipple and the other smack center into his bony sternum.

For a moment, Jacob sensed nothing but the two sharp pricks, but then the Taser's generator awakened and sent a high-voltage electrical pulse down the insulated wire dangling between the men. Fifty thousand volts took wild control of his central nervous system, and his body spasmed with violent contractions.

Missy jumped back with a pitchy scream. Morena jerked her knees to her chest, eyes wide as her face turned red, and the tears burst forth. The phone fell from Jacob's hand and cracked against the concrete.

Juanqui kept the electricity flowing as he carefully took a knee, reached his free hand through the bars, and grabbed the broken phone lying amid the confetti-like ID tags that'd popped from the Taser. Juanqui struggled back to his feet, and only when he'd stabilized himself did he finally stop the Taser.

Jacob's legs gave way, and he crumpled into the bars. "Oh, God," he muttered, catching his breath.

Juanqui ejected the Taser's cartridge, and it clattered to the floor. The officer cleared his throat, teeter-tottered back to his desk, and set Missy's phone next to his own.

Jacob gingerly touched the probes sticking from his body, giving them a wiggle. He felt nothing. His nerves were temporarily in disarray. He pinched the probes, breathed deep, holding the air in his lungs, and yanked them out. There was a slight resistance as the barbs hooked into his skin, but the thin layer of tissue tore, and the probes came out. He tossed them aside. A trickle of blood seeped from the tiny holes in his chest, and he pressed a hand against his shirt to stop the flow.

Missy lightly touched his shoulder as if she thought he might hold an electric current. “Are you okay?” she asked, straining to remain calm.

He nodded and leaned his head back, staring at the ceiling. “You motherfucker,” he called out to Juanqui.

The officer didn’t answer.

Morena’s fitful sobs and sniffling broke to the forefront of his conscious mind. He went to the bench and sat. The girl scooted over and leaned against him. Jacob wrapped an arm around her and squeezed tightly. “Missy.” He gingerly tapped the bench to his right, and she joined them. He put his arm around her as well. “What a fucking story,” he mumbled as a drop of blood trickled down to his stomach.

XXI.

By the time Vicente reached the little shed of a police station in Pontevedra, the sun had set below the Pacific. The desert glowed gently in twilight's blue hour as the last bit of light bounced and scattered in the upper atmosphere. Just down the road, a couple hundred yards away, he saw the cluster of leafy vegetation that grew around the Tijuana River. The greenery wouldn't follow the river downstream for much longer. Closer to Tijuana, it would get crowded out by concrete, metal, and stucco, and the water would become polluted by the flow of garbage and waste channeled into it. By the time the river hit the Pacific, it would be mostly sewage.

And speaking of change, Vicente thought, Juanqui, that fat slug, had somehow managed to catch the son of a bitch from Minneapolis who thought he could be a hero. As Vicente pulled up to the station, he hadn't yet decided which pieces of Jacob he'd cut off and which he'd burn beyond recognition, but the guy was going to see some changes too. Vicente parked next to the white Civic and walked inside.

Two fluorescent tubes, one hanging over Juanqui's desk, the other just outside the cell in the back, glowed brightly. Jacob, Missy, and Morena were huddled on the bench in the cell. Juanqui "Don't Call Me Sluggo" was at his desk, sipping a cup of coffee. He saw Vicente, took one more sip, then set the cup down. "These them?"

Vicente nodded as he stepped across the room. "That's them."

Juanqui stood. "All right. You two kids," he muttered, looking at Jacob and Missy, "step up over here, your backs to the bars."

Jacob began to dejectedly rise from the bench, but he was held back. Morena didn't want him to go. She grasped at his shirt. He gave her a gentle pat on the head and pulled away. "Come on," Jacob told Missy, helping her to her feet. They shuffled to where Juanqui was waiting.

"Hands behind your backs." Juanqui jangled two sets of cuffs, then looked at Vicente. "I'll want these back when you're done."

Vicente nodded. "Sure."

When Jacob backed up close enough, Juanqui reached through the bars and grabbed him by his forearm, snapping the cuffs in place.

"Please," Missy begged, standing with her back to Juanqui.

"Nasty business you stuck your nose in." Juanqui licked his lips, grabbed Missy's wrists, and locked the other set of cuffs tightly with a sharp, metallic *snick, snick*.

Missy groaned at the sound.

Juanqui waddled to the cell door, unlocked it, and waved his hand for Vicente to proceed.

Vicente walked over to Morena first. He crouched on a knee and looked her in the eyes. "You want to get away from this stinky, fat man?" He glanced over his shoulder at Juanqui. "He's so icky."

Juanqui shook his head.

Vicente helped Morena from the bench and walked her out of the cell and across the station. "You hungry?"

She didn't answer as they walked out the door and

into the coming night.

Vicente put Morena in the front seat of the Charger and told her he'd be right back, before returning to the station.

Missy was arguing with Juanqui, telling him he was going to hell, guaranteeing his heart attack was going to be excruciating. "But first you're going to prison for this. You're going to be someone's bitch!"

Vicente rolled his eyes as he stepped into the cell. He grabbed Jacob by his cuffs and tried to lead him out, but Jacob quickly shook him loose. Vicente grabbed the cuffs again and tugged hard. Jacob cried out in pain then planted his feet like a stubborn mule, refusing to move.

Juanqui stepped in to offer a hand, but Missy joined in the resistance and kicked at Juanqui, aiming for his groin. He stopped, more annoyed than anything, grabbed her by the shoulder, and shoved her aside, sending her crashing against the back wall where she collapsed in a dazed heap.

"Missy!" Jacob broke free of Vicente and hurried to her side.

Juanqui wrapped his fat hands around Jacob's neck and threw him from the cell like a spare tire.

Jacob went rolling across the concrete floor.

"Should've reloaded the Taser," Juanqui muttered. He and Vicente picked Jacob up and led him toward the door.

"Missy! Missy!" Jacob yelled, twisting and turning and fighting.

Missy didn't respond; she just cowered against the back wall.

Vicente kicked open the metal door, and Jacob went limp. He nearly slipped from his grasp, but with Juanqui's help, he regained his hold, and they continued dragging the little prick from the station. At the Charger, Jacob changed tactics again and straightened up, flexing and straining.

"You know what? Fuck this," Vicente said. He

shoved Jacob into Juanqui's arms and pulled a pistol, hammering the butt of the gun against the top of Jacob's head with a crack.

Jacob's eyes fluttered, and he settled into a quiet stupor.

"Dumbass." Vicente went to the back of the Charger and opened the trunk. He and Juanqui pushed Jacob in, head first, then slammed it shut.

Juanqui wiped a layer of sweat from his brow. "And his girlfriend? You want that pill too?"

Vicente saw a hopeful glimmer in Juanqui's small pig eyes, like that of a child trying to convince his friend he didn't want the toy he himself wanted. Not that any convincing was necessary. Vicente didn't want to deal with her. "She's all yours, Sluggo."

Juanqui grimaced at the nickname, but for the reward he smiled, flashing his creepy baked-bean teeth.

XXII.

The Charger's engine started, and the car went into motion, reversing for a second then speeding forward. Gravel pinged against the underside of the car, echoing around the trunk, making Jacob's head throb.

He was on his side, curled like a fetus, and with each dip and bump, he was jerked and tossed around. Up he'd go, and his head would strike the underside of the trunk precisely where Vicente had hit him with the pistol. Down he'd crash, and he'd press harshly on his shoulder, making the joint scream for mercy.

He tried to roll to his back, but his knees met the top of the trunk after only an inch of movement. He gave his spine a twist, lessening the pressure some, but it mostly just shifted the pain from his shoulder to his back. *A precursor to all the pain to come.*

The gravel eventually turned to asphalt, and the car became calmer. The steady rolling hum of the tires also helped clear the fog swirling in his head. He imagined Missy sitting in the backseat just a foot in front of him. Somehow they'd get out of this. He still didn't believe he'd gotten them killed. That wasn't how these things worked.

• • •

The trunk opened. Vicente was pointing his pistol at Jacob's head. The twins stood at his side. "Out," Vicente grunted.

Jacob tried and wiggled around like a helpless turtle, but he was stuck and needed help. The twins reached in, grabbed him by the armpits, and lifted.

"Ah, God," Jacob groaned as the pain in his shoulder flared.

The twins held him aloft until he'd planted his feet on the earth.

Morena stood behind Vicente. She smiled at Jacob when he looked at her. Vicente put a hand on the girl's back and gave her a slight nudge toward the house. *And we're back.* Apparently the police hadn't raided the house after Missy's call.

Jacob turned to examine the Charger's interior. "Where's Missy?"

Vicente led Morena across the sand and into the house.

"What did you do to her? Where *is* she?" Jacob hissed, chasing after Vicente as visions of the Canadian tourist's raped and beaten body flashed in his mind. Then his panicked mind showed him severed heads and hands being pitched out of moving cars before finally producing Missy's headless corpse. He whined at the idea of an emaciated coyote finding her head in a roadside ditch, clamping its teeth into a tuft of her hair, and taking it home to gnaw on, her head dully swinging from the coyote's jowls as it trotted away into the desert. The thought was terribly, vividly clear, like a memory more than a conjured thought. A wave of bile rose from his stomach and touched the back of his throat. He swallowed hard. "Where *is* she?"

Vicente told Morena to sit on the couch while he turned on the TV. Then, with a matter-of-fact shrug, he went to Jacob, said, "Sluggo wanted her," and grabbed him by the elbow.

Jacob yanked his arm back. "Who the fuck's that?"

"Your fat cop friend. Now come on." Vicente took Jacob's elbow again, tighter, and pulled. The twins, waiting to get inside, pushed.

The coyote trotting around with Missy's head morphed into Juanqui's bloated. Jacob cursed himself. He should've known. He *had* known. He just hadn't let the concern materialize and take hold. He'd been too busy angling for recognition and reward. *Bravo, good sir! You saved this little girl! And countless others! The CJNG is in shambles. Bravo!* Jacob's chest tightened; his heart raced; and he began to hyperventilate. By the time Vicente and the twins brought him back to the soiled mattress, his face was shining with sweat.

The twins taped Jacob to the bed frame again, wrapping his chest.

"I can't breathe," Jacob groaned.

"Least of your problems," Vicente grumbled.

And he was right. Jacob's mind was starting to slip. It was trying to process the situation but the inputs were too horrible, too hideous to accept, and his thoughts were becoming erratically disjointed. Childhood moments popped in—birthday parties, weekends at the lake, presents piled under the tree, family dinners—but then there were thoughts of torture, the cartel, Missy and the coyote, Sluggo, trafficking victims. These thoughts flashed like an automatic weapon in the dark of the night. His body twitched and shook.

Vicente, standing at the foot of the bed, spoke, but to Jacob his voice was distant. He was telling the twins to "go see what we've got at Doc's. Just bring a bag of shit. Let's see how long Sheeran can handle it."

Jacob stared across the room in a state of shock. For the first time in any of his drug adventures, he regretted, truly regretted, what he'd done. The book wasn't worth this. The story that could be written, the book being published, the life goal being achieved...it wasn't worth it. He should've stopped when Missy had told him to. Or when Dwight had died. Or when he'd taken that beating. He should've stopped when that homeless couple had chased him. He should've stopped when Emily had warned him... But he never had. The book had been so damn important. And *why?* For the accomplishment? Something worth pursuing? Something to contribute? Something that made life seem a little less pointless? Something to break up the incessant, inconsequential monotony? *Why couldn't you have just been happy with things? Because it wasn't worth being happy over, Mom! It's depressing, Missy!* Everyone just goes about their day, consuming garbage, producing garbage, refusing to lift their heads, to look beyond their own noses, and do something of consequence. And there were 7.7 billion of them scurrying about the ant hill. He couldn't stand the thought. It put him teetering on the edge of depression, wallowing in self-pity and apathy. He desperately wanted his 1 out of 7.7 billion to be meaningful. *That* was why he hadn't stopped. And *that* was why he certainly couldn't stop now.

Jacob held his breath and listened to the house. A cartoon was on in the front room; Morena was watching it. The door to the fridge opened down the hall; Vicente was in the kitchen. The twins had left. Even in his daze, he'd noticed them scurry from the room at Vicente's directive. They'd be back, but for the moment only Morena, Jacob, and Vicente were in the house. *And hopefully those three other girls.*

He twisted and puffed his chest under the tape's grip. The twins had wrapped him with at least a dozen layers. It would be impossible to wiggle out from its lung-crushing embrace. There was some leeway with his hands, though; the cuffs weren't terribly tight. They actually seemed rather loose as he rotated his wrists around. *Maybe...* He shook and fidgeted, coating the cuffs in sweat as the metal lifted and moved around his wrists.

He raised an arm and lowered the other, tugging at the restraints. He had the cuffs at a favorable angle. If he could keep jamming and squeezing and cramming...little by little...

The restraint started to slip over his hand. Harder and harder he pulled, but wait... He had to stop for a moment. His fingers were painfully wedged. The bones were being crushed. *If that's what it takes, break them.* It really felt like he was almost free. He had to keep going. He took a breath. Held it. Counted one...two...and then pulled. With everything he had, he pulled.

The cuff barely moved, but he refused to give in. Pulling, straining, pulling. *Come on!* The metal dug into his skin. *Keep going!* He was getting lightheaded. His bones ground against one another. The cuff slowly slid, scraping away the skin as it went. He was flaying himself. The muscle lining his thumb was slowly becoming exposed. But he wasn't about to stop. *Fuck that. Doesn't matter!*

Jacob grunted and jerked his arm. His shoulder popped loose, and then his thumb dislocated. The pain was excruciating, but the cuff fell away. He went limp and bit his lip, struggling to keep from crying out.

After a moment, the sharp shock of it all retreated to a deep ache. He couldn't move his right arm. It hung, free of the cuff, behind his back. He wiggled his left arm out from beneath the tape and rested his hand in his lap. The empty cuff hung loose, glaring at him. There was a strip of skin stuck to the edge in an accordioned clump. He flicked the skin away then grabbed the cuff to keep it from rattling as he went to work removing the tape from around his chest.

His right arm was useless. The shoulder hadn't popped back into place; he couldn't really move it. Painstakingly, he pulled at the tape with one hand, peeling it halfway around his back, bringing the good hand around, grabbing the tape, and pulling it again. This was repeated a dozen times.

It took far too long to reach the final pass. He couldn't hear Vicente in the kitchen. For all he knew, the man was heading down the hall to check on him. And the twins were walking up to the front door. They'd converge on him just as he was about to climb from the bed. And then it'd be over. He was going to get himself killed.

But Vicente didn't appear, and the twins didn't step through the front door. Jacob pulled the last segment of tape from his chest and tossed it aside. He swung his legs from the bed, resting his feet on the floor. His shoulder burned. His arm was still dangling oddly behind his back. He grabbed it and gingerly brought it around to his lap. The hand was mangled and broken, the thumb bloody and stripped of its skin. Gingerly, he grasped his shoulder, clenched his teeth, and shifted the shoulder around, trying to get the ball to find the socket. The sting of a thousand bone-deep needles brought tears to his eyes. He gave up. *No time.* He wrapped the bottom of his shirt around his broken hand for support and hurried to the doorway.

"Hey," Vicente spoke from the kitchen.

Jacob's heart jumped to his throat.

"Yeah. Yeah. Ice picks," Vicente said. "Whatever Doc's got like that. Whatever you two want to carry back. I don't care."

Jacob peeked down the hall. Vicente was on the phone, his back to him. Tucked in his pants was his pistol, an ugly-looking silver and black thing. And Jacob wanted it. *So move your ass.*

He sprinted from the bedroom like a pug on cocaine and was in the kitchen before Vicente had a chance to register what the approaching noise was, let alone turn around. Jacob grabbed the pistol and jumped back, aiming the heavier-than-expected gun at Vicente's back.

Vicente froze for a moment then finished his call. "Yeah. Just get back here. Fast. I *really* want to jab a pick straight through this motherfucker's eye." Slowly he placed the phone on the chipped counter and turned to face Jacob. "Really?" Vicente's eyes were filled with exasperation more than anything.

"You're not doing this." The pistol wavered in Jacob's hand; the dangling handcuff shook.

Vicente rubbed his scarred arms. "We've already been doing this."

Jacob scanned the room, unsure of his next move. The lime-colored countertop, broken up by a sink, a greasy stovetop, and a dented fridge, ran the length of the back wall. In the corner was a closed door. *The room with the girls.* A plastic folding table with a set of car keys bearing the Dodge logo was set against the wall to his right. Jacob wriggled his messed-up arm from his shirt and flopped his hand over the keys.

"You're not even getting out the door before Bravo and Sleepy get back," Vicente told him.

Jacob knew Vicente was probably right. He imagined the twins sprinting with those long spindly legs back to the house that very minute. They'd be here in no time. But he had to try. He clutched the keys as tightly as he could manage. "Don't fucking move."

Vicente clearly didn't believe the warning was genuine. He leapt across the small room. And Jacob shot him.

In the front of the house, Morena cried out in surprise.

Vicente winced and clutched his stomach. Shock and pain streaked across his face. His left eye gave a funny twitch, and he stumbled back into the counter and collapsed to the floor. He didn't move, and the house was silent once again.

Then came crying. But it wasn't Morena. It was

from behind the closed door. Jacob sidled around the table, maintaining an unflinching eye on the crumpled Vicente, and pushed on the door. *Locked.* He put an ear against the faux wood composite, and the crying became clearer, magnified in the hollow of the door. He could kick it in. *Just one swift boot.* He took a step back. "Get away from the door."

He picked a spot just beside the doorknob and smashed the heel of his sneaker against it. The door gave way like Styrofoam, and his leg went sailing straight through. Unprepared for the door's absolute flimsiness, Jacob fell forward and smashed his face against the significantly more solid door frame. His nose split open, and a rush of blood poured over his lips and down his chin. No time to bother inspecting the damage, he just turned his head, gave a quick snort, filling the back of his throat with blood, and spat, speckling the table with dark-red globules. "Almost gotcha," he mumbled to the girls. "Almost there." He spat again then pulled his leg from the hole and peered in, wide eyed and bloody. In the far corner was a large hole in the floor with a ladder poking up from the darkness. *The tunnel.* Beside it sat the three girls who'd been marched into the house earlier. Jacob pulled away, reached through the door, unlocked the latch, and went in.

The girls screamed at the sight of him, bloody nose, mangled hand dangling, pistol at the ready.

"It's okay. It's okay." He quickly wiped the blood dribbling from his nose with the back of his hand. It didn't help; it only smeared the blood, caking the lower half of his face, making him look like a gorging hyena. "It's okay." He tried again, grabbing his shirt and wiping, wiping, wiping.

The girls pressed against the wall, staring at him in horror, but their screaming subsided.

"Good." He tucked the pistol into his waistband and stepped closer, half expecting one of the twins to pop his head up from the tunnel. *I'll kick him in the face.* But they weren't coming from there. They were running down the street, and he didn't have much time.

He turned his attention to the girls who were tied to one another, a nylon rope viciously knotted around each of their ankles. The rope trailed away to an eye bolt sunk into the floor. Jacob pulled and twisted the bolt, but it held. He tried the rope itself, but it turned out to be just as stubborn as the bolt as it was looped in and around itself so many times it only got tighter the more he fiddled with it.

He turned to the girl closest to him. She was wearing a T-shirt with Goofy's grinning mug staring back at him. He pointed at the character as he inspected the rope around her ankle and said, "I like Goofy too." She mumbled something, but he wasn't paying attention. Her ankle was red and raw. The knot was complicated and tight. Her foot had turned a grayish blue. If his right arm had been functioning, he might've been able to untie it, but he could only look up at the girl and say, "I can't get it."

The girl searched the room, her shoulder-length hair fluttering with each flick of her head. Jacob followed her gaze, but there was nothing there. Nothing except the tunnel. He hurried over and peered into the darkness. He had half a mind to climb in and see what was hiding down there. Maybe a shovel? The blade, if brought down on the eye bolt hard enough, might break it loose from the floor. But he saw nothing except dirt and stone.

Jacob looked back at the girls. "The kitchen!" He rushed out and ransacked the drawers, frantically searching for a knife or scissors, the entire time expecting Vicente to jump up and attack him, but he was dead, or close to it. He might've been still breathing, but it was barely perceptible. The guy was fading fast, the last of his breaths being taken.

In a drawer above Vicente, Jacob found several knives, butter knives. "Fuck," he howled, but he still grabbed one before running down the hall to Morena. "Knives? Where're the knives?" He pointed to the back of the house.

She pointed at the silver in his hand.

"No," he groaned. He couldn't think of anywhere else to look or anything else to do. He'd have to go get something, an ax to split the rope or a crowbar to yank the bolt from the floor, but he didn't have time. The twins were coming. And Missy. *Missy* didn't have time. *Missy!*

That fat cop had been eyeing her the second they'd walked into the station. He had to go save her *now*. Then he'd come back for the girls. He dropped the useless butter knife to the floor. "We'll come back. We'll come back," he promised. "Come with me." Jacob pulled the Charger's keys from his back pocket and waved at Morena to follow him as he hurried out the door. The girl scooted off the couch and dashed after him.

The street was blissfully devoid of the twin spiders. As they ran across the sand to the Charger, Jacob tried again to reset his shoulder. He needed to regain some mobility for the fight that was surely coming. Yet no matter how much he wiggled and shifted it, working the bone around the muscles that were supposed to hold everything in place, nothing clicked or locked. *The movies are such fucking bullshit.*

Jacob unlocked the Charger. Morena climbed into the back as Jacob got behind the wheel. He tossed the gun he'd tucked into his waistband onto the passenger seat and took one more look at the house. In the dark, it looked like a squat, ugly little troll. He threw the Charger into gear and roared away down the street.

The light from inside the station cast a deceitfully welcoming glow over the Honda Civic parked by the front window. *The glow of an anglerfish.* Jacob approached from the west, slowly, and pulled the Charger to the side of the road a hundred yards away. He killed the engine. Morena leaned forward, poking her head between the front seats, and they sat in the dark, staring out, studying the quiet fortress. Jacob's princess was inside.

He grabbed the pistol, popped the clip, counted four bullets, and snapped it shut. *Four will put Sluggo down. Two could do the trick, hopefully.* If he was still the consistent fifty-percent sharpshooter he'd been while at the academy, two bullets would certainly have to do. *Who wouldn't go down with two?*

He looked at Morena and gave a reassuring nod. *Could use her as a distraction. Send her in. Get Juanqui up from his desk, waddling across the room, and blam! He'd jump through the door and put two into the man's chest.* That was an option. A decent option. But he needed to check the station first. Maybe there was a back door he could sneak through and blow Juanqui's head off while he slobbered over some previously hidden *Playboy*. *Blam!* For the life of him, he couldn't remember if he'd seen a back door. He needed to look. "Wait here," he told Morena.

She stayed perched between the seats and watched as he carefully stepped from the car, shut the door with only the slightest click, and hurried across the road, onto the gravel, around the Civic, and pressed against the station, just below the window. He desperately wanted to rise and peek in to see what he was dealing with, but he couldn't bring himself to do so. *If Juanqui sees me...* His right arm dangled against his hip like a wet sock. *If there's a fight...* He couldn't risk it. Not yet. The element of surprise was still on his side.

He pressed an ear to the warm stucco, listening for a clue from within, but only a quiet hum emanated from it. He pulled away and studied the facade. He had no idea how to read the age of stucco, but this, with its long vertical cracks and plate-sized chips, looked old and fragile. A more powerful gun could shoot through it and take Juanqui out before the officer could rise from his chair, but not the pistol. The stucco was old, but the pistol was weak. It didn't have the firepower to get a bullet through. And even if it did, the pathetically small metal slug wouldn't do anything more than gently squeeze out the other side and drop to the floor with a sad clink.

He only had four bullets anyway. Blindly firing into the wall was a fool's last resort. Jacob went left around the corner to inspect the rest of the building.

Away from the glow of the window and the lonely streetlamp down the road, Jacob stumbled and staggered, kicking at unexpectedly high piles of sand and prickly shrubs. On the opposite side of the wall was the holding cell. *I'm coming, Missy. Just finding the right way in. But hurry. Hurry!*

He rushed to the back of the station, where a knee-high cactus was waiting to gouge him as he turned the corner. The spines dug in with vigor, and he danced away, tripping over a thick clump of fountain grass. The pistol went sailing into the darkness as he twisted and flailed, trying to keep from landing on his dislocated shoulder. He'd surely scream out if that happened, but thankfully, he quietly face planted into the sand, his shoulder avoiding the brunt of the fall.

"Dumbass," he whispered as he picked himself up, legs now punctured a thousand ways to Sunday and his face covered with a crust of dried blood and dirt. He listened. The desert was quiet. He went about in the darkness, stumbling around, scanning the ground for the gun.

Panic welled in his chest. He had to find it; he whirled and spun in the sand, scampering around shrubs and cacti, searching, searching, but it was gone. He'd lost it.

He looked at the back wall of the station. There wasn't even a back door. Only a couple of discarded tires and an overstuffed garbage can. He'd lost the gun for nothing.

The trash looked like his only option now, so he

went to it, hoping to find something in the putrid mess to use as a weapon (*MacGyver that shit*), but when he got close, the pile moved and an unseen animal whined in warning. He scampered away.

On the far side of the station, there was an abandoned GMC Safari, its flattened tires half sunk in the sand, and a Ford F-150 police truck. *Bingo.* Juanqui apparently didn't think anyone would dare mess with his truck, because when Jacob tried the door, it swung right open. He climbed in and spent a good minute searching through the loose papers and empty soda cans that littered the cabin, but there was nothing inside capable of incapacitating the man holding Missy hostage. Jacob jumped out and checked the truck's bed and finally found something of use. He snapped open the toolbox and sitting right inside was a hammer, a box cutter, and a crowbar. He took them all.

A loud, whooping cough came from within the station. He had to get moving. He'd take a look through the window, find Juanqui's position, then rush in. *Shock and awe.* The fat man wouldn't even react. He'd certainly see Jacob burst through the door, yelling and hooting and waving the crowbar, but he wouldn't have time to stand up before he was smashed across the head with the stick of steel.

Jacob hurried to the front of the station and crouched underneath the window again. Shaking with adrenaline, he laid the hammer in the sand, pocketed the box cutter, and clutched the crowbar. He stood up, carefully, eyes peering over the window's ledge. The inside of the station came into view, the ceiling, then the walls, the bars of the cell, Missy curled up on the bench, and finally Juanqui scribbling at his desk. Jacob relaxed and dipped below the window, unnoticed. The element of surprise still remained his.

He let out a gentle sigh, relief mixed with terrible

doubt. *Rushing Juanqui is a mistake, isn't it?* He had no right to believe he could come out victorious. Even with the element of surprise, would he really be fast enough? Juanqui only needed to have a gun in one of his drawers to ruin the entire plan. "Fucking hell," he muttered as he took a moment to think things through.

Jason Bourne could do it. Not him, though. He needed a suit of armor. *Like Iron Man.* If he was Iron Man, he could just punch the heavy metal door off its hinges and step inside. Juanqui could take as many shots as he wanted. He'd be invincible. Then he'd raise a hand and blast Sluggo with the suit's repulsor. Mission accomplished.

Jacob looked around, searching for an answer to his utter lack of armor, but there was nothing. Just the Civic and the Charger down the street. Yet that was enough to give him an inspiring thought. He dropped the crowbar beside the hammer and hurried back to the Charger.

Morena was waiting for him in the back seat, and he instructed her to hop out. She dubiously peered behind him at the darkness of the desert.

"Just for a second," he assured her.

She shook her head.

Jacob looked back at the station. *Hurry!* "Okay. Fine." He told Morena to buckle up as he climbed behind the wheel. "Hold tight, okay?"

"K," she answered.

Jacob promised himself they wouldn't get that much speed. And she was buckled in. She'd be okay. They'd all be okay. Missy was off to the side in the cell. He had an airbag. This was the best option short of an iron suit. He pulled his seat belt tight and started the Charger. *I'm going to kill us all.* "Hold tight."

He floored it. The engine roared. Tires spun. Morena squealed. Jacob prayed.

As they approached the station, Jacob hooked the car right, into the desert for a moment, then jerked the wheel left, crossing the road. The headlights illuminated the small white structure, the giant star, and its blue metal door. The Charger rumbled past the Civic. Just before they slammed through, Jacob noticed how incredibly bright and focused the headlights became when shining on an object mere inches away. *Like Iron Man's repulsor.*

The Charger burst through. The metal door, the metal frame, and a spray of dusty stucco flew up and over the car's hood. The windshield exploded into a shimmering white web. The airbag deployed hard into Jacob's abused face, and his foot slipped from the gas. But it didn't matter. The stocky Charger surged ahead, across the room, and into the desk, sending papers and oak splinters flying. The car continued for several more feet, then hit the back wall and came to a stop.

Jacob's ears were ringing, and for a moment he thought he'd gone deaf, but then Morena began to cry. Jacob punched the airbag aside with his one good arm and looked back at her. "Are you okay?" He saw no blood, no awkwardly bent limbs. "You're okay?" She kept crying, but it wasn't from pain, just fear. "You're okay. It's okay." He let her cry.

The windshield was covered with rocky chunks and wood shards. Half of Juanqui's coffee mug was wedged under the right wiper. Jacob gazed out the side window. Rivulets of dust and smoke filtered through the station. The holding cell was within arm's reach, its floor scattered with debris. The bars had caught the larger projectiles, keeping Missy safe. She sat on the bench, hands in her lap, dust settling in her hair, a pile of vomit between her feet.

Jacob unstrapped his seat belt and shoved the door open. "Missy," he cried as he climbed out and crossed over the mess to the cell. He tugged at the door, but it was locked. *Of course it is.* "I'll get you out," he assured her. He looked around the station. "Oh, God." The place had been blown to bits. Starting with a gaping hole in the front wall, a path of destruction crossed the room to where the Charger rested, bruised and beaten, but victorious. Pinned between the car's crumpled hood and the back wall was Juanqui, or the body of the man formerly known as Juanqui.

The Charger's grille had struck the man squarely in the gut, plucked him clean from his chair, carried him to the wall, then crushed him, splitting him open at his side. The man's tucked shirt was just barely holding back what had spurted from his bulbous belly.

Jacob went to him. He'd have a set of keys. He had to.

The glistening, dripping fabric around Juanqui's waist draped over his utility belt. Jacob tried to gently move the mass aside, but with just the slightest touch, the shirt gave way, coming untucked, and handfuls of warm, rolling fat and shiny, pink tubing splattered across the dusty floor. Jacob retched at the innards' noxious fumes, but he refused to back off. As his feet started to slide from the intestinal contents seeping around them, he went in, searching Juanqui's now moist utility belt. There was a set of cuffs and the Taser (still without a new cartridge) but no keys. Jacob grabbed hold of the belt and shook it. There was a soft jingling as the keys clipped near Juanqui's crotch bumped against the Charger's disfigured hood. Jacob reached over and unclipped the ring.

"Missy. I got 'em." He rushed to the cell and went in. "Missy?"

She gave no indication he was even there.

"Missy, let's go. Come on, babe." He grabbed her hand and gently tugged. "Are you okay?" She looked okay, but he knew what Juanqui had wanted to do to her, and that wouldn't necessarily show. Jacob gave Missy another tug toward the cell door. "Come on, babe." She stood, but he didn't think she was registering what was happening. "Watch your foot," he said, eyeing her vomit.

She stepped in the yellowish goo.

"That's okay. Just come on." He let go of her hand, put an arm over her shoulder, and guided her from the cell. "Stand here a sec." He planted her near the back of the Charger, its taillights casting an unsettling red glow over her body. Jacob went to Morena, who was still in the car's backseat. Her crying had settled into a low mewling. "We're okay. We're all okay. Just like I said." He leaned in and gave her a one-armed hug. "You're okay."

She wrapped her arms around him, not quite able to lock her fingers behind his back but still managing to generate a powerful squeeze. His shoulder flared; he smiled.

Jacob pulled her from the car and carried her over the mess. She was barefoot, and he didn't dare put her down. "Let's go." He went to Missy. She was staring at the floor, lost in thought. "Let's go. It's over," he told her.

Missy glanced up and gave him a little nod.

"Are you okay?"

She nodded.

Jacob looked back at Juanqui, dead as ever. Beside the squished slug was the weapons safe. The Charger had missed it by half a foot. It was undamaged, not even the glass coffee pot atop it had been disturbed. "Come on," Jacob said as he ushered Missy through the gap in the wall. He gently lowered Morena into the backseat of the Civic then helped Missy to the front.

As he hurried around the car to the driver's side, he nearly tripped over the crowbar and hammer lying in the gravel. He picked them up and took them with. It'd be cruel to take Missy and Morena back there, but the other girls were there, still tied to the wall. And he had shot Vicente, so...

He put the tools in the back next to Morena. His phone was still there on the seat; he grabbed it and climbed behind the wheel. He turned to Missy, who was absentmindedly picking at a hangnail. He looked her up and down. No blood. No torn clothes. No marks on her face.

Physically, she looked okay. "Here," he said, turning on his phone. He brought up some photos of home and showed her. "We'll be back soon. Real soon." He scrolled through images of their apartment, Gold Medal Park, the Minneapolis skyline on a bright-blue day, and Quincy.

Morena climbed forward and peeked at the photos. Jacob turned the phone, showing her Quincy. She smiled a little. He scrolled to another photo: Quincy in the park, squinting up at the sun like a fool. Morena's smile grew. He found the close-up he'd taken of Quincy's curly-tailed butt, and she giggled. He smiled back, tears forming in his eyes, heartbroken he hadn't really thought about saving the girl for the girl's sake. It'd always been about his story, about his book, and getting it to the masses, but not anymore.

He handed Morena the phone, a sense of deep, visceral shame welling up along with the tears. "There's more if you want to look. Sit back, though. And buckle up."

XXIII.

Vicente came to and picked himself off the concrete that'd become sticky with his blood. He lifted his shirt. The small, swollen, inflamed hole was starting to clot. A single drop of blood formed and dribbled down to the already-soaked waistband of his jeans. He had to give the guy credit for pulling the trigger. He didn't think he had it in him.

There was a ball of discarded duct tape on the floor. Vicente grabbed it, tore off a strip, and slapped it over the wound. He'd get it taken care of later. That and the concussion he most certainly had from hitting the back of his head against the counter. He was a little dizzy, a little tired, but at the moment, that wasn't of concern. If he didn't get this brazen psycho under control, El Avispón would have his head, literally.

Across the room, the door was wide open. *If that shit went down the tunnel...* Vicente staggered across the kitchen and looked into the room, bracing himself against the doorframe, struggling to focus his vision, the world shaking in rapid jerks.

He closed his eyes, let a wave of nausea pass, then reopened them. The girls were still tied to each other, the entrance to the tunnel still dark. "Where'd he go?" Vicente asked. The tallest of the girls pointed out the room. Vicente spun his head around, thinking Jacob was standing right behind him grinning stupidly, but the kitchen was empty. The silence of the house split with the roar of an engine out front. He knew that deep growl. It was his Charger.

"Motherfucker." Vicente pushed from the doorway and slowly lurched through the house. The TV was showing cartoons in the front room, but it was entertaining no one. The crisscross-patterned couch was bare. Vicente threw open the front door. Bravo and Sleepy were crossing the dimly lit street.

"Which way did he go?" Vicente called out.

"Who?" Bravo clutched a black bag filled with the tools of their trade.

"That son of a bitch. Who the fuck you think I'm talking about?"

"Oh, shit," Sleepy muttered as he and his brother caught a glimpse of the blood covering Vicente. "Are you okay?"

"I don't feel it." Vicente lowered himself to sit in the doorway. "Get the old man's keys."

Sleepy looked from the dark stain over Vicente's hip to the street, where the Charger had been. He then took off running to the house next door.

With great effort, Vicente pulled his phone from his pocket and wiped some of the drying blood from the screen. He swiped and tapped. "Put a tracking app on his phone," Vicente mumbled, inspecting the map that popped up. "It's at the station." Vicente shook his head. "He just left. Sluggo must have it. I'm sure he's going back there."

"You're sure?" Bravo tossed the black bag over Vicente's head and into the house. It landed with a chorus of sharp, metallic clanking.

"Of course. He'll go back for his girl."

Bravo nodded and crossed his arms.

Vicente stared at the map of Tijuana and the little blue dot blinking in the vicinity of the station.

Sleepy returned, clutching a key ring. "He wants it filled up before we bring it back."

"Fuck that old man," Vicente groaned.

Bravo helped him to his feet, and they went to the rusty, thirty-year-old F-150 truck.

"The station?" Bravo confirmed as he climbed behind the wheel and took the keys from his brother.

Vicente settled into the middle of the cab, between the twins, and nodded. They were at least ten minutes behind Jacob. Vicente told Bravo to run the first set of lights. And every red light thereafter. They made up some time doing this, but out on the highway, a pair of semis, rolling side by side, held them at bay. A deadly drop-off to the right and a concrete barrier to the left prevented them from putting the truck's all-terrain tires to use for three miles as the road climbed into the hills. Vicente checked his phone. The blue dot hadn't moved.

At the top of the hill, the land came level with the highway, and Bravo swerved, passing the trucks in a flurry of dust before jerking back to the asphalt and racing down the hill.

When they reached the station, the three of them stared in silence, stunned at the destruction. Bravo parked the truck near the gaping hole.

Inside, Vicente's Charger rested like a beaten dog under a layer of dust, chunks of stucco, and slats of wood. They saw a portion of Sluggo hanging over the side of the hood.

"Wow," Bravo whispered.

The place was empty. Vicente checked his phone. Still, the blue dot hadn't moved. The phone was probably under the heaping mess the Charger was perched atop, he thought. "Fucker's gone."

As soon as the concluding thought had materialized, though, he spotted a refresh icon in the upper corner of the map. He tapped it. The dot shifted. It was to the west, back on the highway. He refreshed the map again. The dot shifted farther west. "We have to go."

XXIV.

The Civic raced from the station and through the hills and open desert. The road they were on would take them right through Nueva Tijuana. *Perfect.* He'd swing by the house, free the girls, and move on to the border. *But the twins.* They'd almost certainly returned to the house. How was he supposed to take them on? Especially now that they'd be on high alert. There'd be no sneaking up on them. *If they're even there.* They might've taken the girls and bolted. So maybe it didn't make sense to go back? He should just continue on to San Diego. Missy and Morena were safe. That was enough. He could make it so simple on himself if he just kept moving.

But that was always his excuse, wasn't it? Because it was simple. Because it was easy. And he liked simple and easy; he settled into it like Quincy settled into the plush comforter, closing his eyes and letting his pug troubles fade away. That was who he was. He knew it. And Missy knew it. Why else did she constantly chide him to "do whatever it takes"? He never really pushed himself or committed himself to anything beyond a moderate level of difficulty. *Which is why you haven't ever accomplished anything of significance, why you haven't ever made a difference.* He went from one middling deed to another. *But not now.* He turned down a narrow side street.

"What're you doing?" Missy whispered. "Stay on the main road."

"The girls at the house..."

"Stay on the main road!" Missy shouted.

"We *have* to get them."

"Oh, God." Missy started to cry.

"They're just kids, Missy."

She buried her face in her hands.

"We have to."

Exhausted, she said nothing.

Jacob turned to Morena, who was worriedly studying the back of Missy's head. He said, "It'll be all right. Those girls? They're in trouble. We need to help them. Right?"

Morena nodded. "Yeah."

"We'll help them. We will," Jacob said, managing to convince neither himself nor anyone else in the car, but that didn't matter. They were going to try.

Jacob had been back and forth through Nueva Tijuana so many times that afternoon that even under the cover of night, he had no trouble returning to the house, or more precisely, returning to a quiet spot just around the corner.

"I'll leave it running," he told Missy.

She'd stopped crying, but her face was red and puffy. She shrugged.

Jacob scanned the street. A flickering lamppost. A shrouded window. A passing truck's headlights. He saw no twins lurking about, but there were plenty of dark alcoves from which to take shelter. *No time to waste.* Jacob reached back and grabbed the crowbar and hammer. He looked at Morena. "Stay here with Missy. Keep her safe." Morena gave him a nod, and he stepped from the car.

No one paid him much attention as he passed the corner store and curbside food vendor. The sweet smell of roasted corn reminded him he hadn't eaten anything since leaving Starbucks that morning. He was absolutely starving if he let himself think about it, but he still had some adrenaline left, so he pushed the thought aside, kept his head down, and hurried around the corner.

The first two homes were fronted by cinder-block walls and security gates. At the third house, there was nothing. Jacob stopped at the wall's edge and peeked at Vicente's squat troll of a house, still and dark.

He knew the twins had returned, and then... *Then what?* Taken the girls? *No.* Because before that, they would've come across Vicente's body, and being the cartel, specifically the CJNG, they would've wanted revenge. They weren't letting him escape. And that meant they and everyone else they could gather were at the border, searching for him and the Charger he'd taken. *Yes, that's it.*

There was a shuffling of feet behind him, and then Missy's voice, "Jacob."

He turned as Missy and Morena scurried up beside him. "Why are you out here?" he hissed.

"I'm not sitting there by myself."

"You're not staying out here."

"We're coming with."

Jacob looked at Missy, at Morena, at the house. His courage shied away.

Missy yanked the hammer from Jacob's hand and clutched it like the weapon it might need to become.

"You're not coming," he muttered.

She glanced at the dangling piece of meat that was his arm.

He quickly tried to set it. Like before, there was nothing but wiggling, crunching, swearing, and burning. The bone wouldn't go back in place. "Fuck," he grunted, letting go of the shoulder and taking a deep breath.

"You need our help," Missy said.

Maybe he did. It was a terrible thing to take the little girl back into the house, but what choice did he have? His beaten body wasn't up to the task, especially if he was wrong about the twins being off at the border. At least with Missy by his side, they'd have something of a chance.

"Come on," he said in a hush, hoping his gut feeling was right and the twins were walking the long line of vehicles waiting to get through the crossing. He stepped from the safety of the wall.

The three of them crossed the sand and pressed against the house without sound. He remembered the iron door had a tendency to squeak. Slowly, slowly he pulled it open, giving the old hinges no reason to gain their voice. He braced the metal frame against his hip and grasped the doorknob, giving it a slight wiggle. Locked. *That's okay.* He had Vicente's keys and a crowbar. He was getting in one way or another.

As he lifted the keys from his pocket, Missy gasped. His heart stopped. He glanced at the street. A car passed without pausing. "Don't do that," he chided before going back to the lock. There were three keys along with the Charger's fob; he grabbed the middle of the three and tried it. *Wrong.* He quietly switched to the third key. It slid in with a satisfying metallic *shink*, and he gave it a firm, measured twist. The bolt slipped aside.

He paused. *Anyone coming to investigate?* All was quiet, so he grasped the knob and turned, quietly, slowly. When the turn was complete, he pushed the door open.

The front room was quiet and dark. Down the hall, there was a faint glow, too dim to be the kitchen light. It had to be coming from the back room, where the girls were, where the tunnel was.

He stuck his hand through the open door and waved it up and down, trying to induce a hidden assailant into striking out, but there was no reaction. He poked his head in, glanced around, and withdrew. *Empty.* He gave Missy a nod and went in.

Missy and Morena, wide eyed and terrified, followed.

"Stay by the door," he instructed. "I'll get the girls. They're just down the hall. Then we'll be gone."

Missy nodded, clutching the hammer like a shield.

"Almost done," he said to Morena, then went deeper into the house. The bedroom he'd spent most of the afternoon in was lifeless, but he still took a half step inside to look. Nothing. His FBI training told him he should close the door on the off chance he'd missed something, but there was no door to close, so he moved on. Missy would be watching his back, ready to give a shout if someone suddenly emerged from the room—he hoped.

Down the hall, the faint light shone on dirty lime countertops and wooden cupboards. Vicente's body was gone. Only a bloody black pool congealing on the concrete remained. A set of grim footprints led away from it. *The twins took the body away. Maybe they're at the morgue or wherever the cartel dumps their dead. They're not here.* Feeling more confident than ever in his assessment of the situation, he quickened his pace to the back room.

The three little girls were as he'd left them, scared and alone. He let out a sigh and hurried in.

This time, the girls didn't scream at his gruesome appearance. They just sat up and watched as he crossed the room and fixed the crowbar's claw under the eye bolt. "Going to get you out of here," he said, and gave the crowbar several hard jerks. But the bolt remained in place. He pulled the crowbar away and smashed it against the bolt several times, knocking it around, loosening it some, then he tried the claw once again. The bolt popped free.

"Okay. Be careful. Don't trip yourselves," Jacob told the girls. "Follow me." He turned to leave.

Missy stood in the doorway grasping the hammer so

hard her knuckles were white. "A truck just pulled up outside."

"Shit." Jacob told Missy to stay with the girls and ran to the front of the house. Silhouetted in the open doorway, staring at the street through the bars of the security door, was Morena. Jacob rested a hand on her shoulder and peered out. At the curb, a truck sat with its engine running and headlights on. The driver's-side door opened, and the cabin light illuminated the occupants: Vicente and the twins.

"Let's go," Jacob told Morena, pulling her into the house and shutting the door. He thought he'd watched Vicente die. He thought the twins were at the border. He thought... *Wrong. You were wrong. Now move!* Jacob clutched Morena's hand, and they ran down the dark hall, curled through the kitchen, and ducked into the back room.

Missy was on her knees, frantically tugging at the rope around the ankle of the girl in the Goofy T-shirt. "I got Noemi's off," Missy said, gesturing with a tilt of her head at the tallest of the girls. "They're just alpine butterfly loops. I use these to climb all the time. And now..." Missy tugged the rope loose. "...Sofia's too." Missy turned to the third girl. "Let me see your leg, Rosa. Quick." The girl stuck out her foot.

"There's no time." Jacob gathered the loose rope and dropped the nylon bundle into Rosa's arms.

"I can get it off," Missy argued.

"We have to go. She can carry it," Jacob insisted. He scanned the room, settling on the jagged, dark mouth of the tunnel. "I think we have to go down there."

Missy followed his gaze to the devilish void in the floor. "No. What is that? A dungeon?"

"A tunnel. It comes up in San Diego somewhere."

"We're not going down there."

"They're coming," Jacob warned.

"Where's the back door?" Missy peered into the

kitchen.

"There isn't one."

"Then a window or something for Christ's sake."

"Missy, there's no door. There's no window. We're trapped." He pointed to the tunnel. "There's just this."

The front door was kicked in with a boom, pulling air up from the tunnel like a breath, filling the room with a harsh, musty odor.

"Come on, girls." Jacob ushered the group toward the cavity and the ladder poking from it. "Missy'll go first. Just follow Missy."

"Me?"

"You want to be last?"

Vicente called out, "Where're you hiding, you piece of shit?"

Missy backed up to the ladder and stepped on the top rung. She glanced at Jacob and the girls. "Follow me."

"Okay, who's next?" Jacob feigned extreme excitement and got the tallest of the girls, Noemi, to step up as a volunteer.

A thin, yellowish light flicked on from within the tunnel. "It's only like six feet," Missy announced.

Jacob helped Noemi get her feet set on the ladder, and then down she went. He turned to the others. "See? Easy," he declared and held out a hand to Sofia with her grinning Goofy shirt. "Think you can get down faster than she did?"

Sofia nodded and hurried to the tunnel's edge.

"Turn around, turn around," Jacob coached. "And there you go. One foot down, nice and easy." He watched her descend.

There was a loud pounding on the wall to their right. They all jumped. "Knock, knock, knock," Vicente yelled.

Jacob hurried across the room and closed the door, flicking the lock despite the gaping hole he'd kicked in the door. *Better than nothing.* By the time he stepped back to the tunnel, Rosa, the slack rope slung over her shoulder, had already helped herself down the ladder.

"Okay, great." Jacob turned and smiled at Morena. "Saved the best for last."

She stepped over, turned her back to the ladder, and gave him a hug.

"Are you ready, Captain?" he asked, squeezing her tightly.

She drew away and nodded, a spark of hope and trust in her eyes. Her yellow ribbon gave a fluttering wave as she went into the tunnel.

"Hey, there, Boy Scout," Vicente said.

Jacob glanced over his shoulder. Vicente's face grinned through the hole in the door. *Like the fucking* Shining.

Vicente pulled his face away and replaced it with the barrel of an assault rifle.

"Oh, shit." Jacob jumped into the tunnel, and bullets ripped over his head.

Missy was right. The tunnel was only six feet below them, but he landed awkwardly and crumpled to the earth. He knew his ankle broke the moment he hit. It was the same one that'd gotten twisted in the holding cell at the station. He tried not to let on. A light bulb was hanging from a wooden beam, spotlighting his face, and he forced an agonized grin for the girls. *Tada!*

He then pointed into the darkness behind the group. There was another dim, yellow light way off in the distance. There was no telling how far away it was, but that was their destination. "Go, go."

Missy didn't hesitate, and the four girls quickly fell in step behind her.

From above, Jacob heard the lock click and the door swing open. He turned and grabbed the ladder and tugged it loose, pulling it down into the cramped space.

"You little bitch," Vicente groaned.

"I'll fucking blow your head off if you come down here. Got a shotgun from the station," Jacob yelled before hobbling away into the darkness.

"Try it," Vicente chided. He fired the assault rifle into the hole.

With bullets pinging off stone and earth behind him, Jacob quickened his limp, continuously catching his head against the many wooden beams wedged across the ceiling. By the time he caught up with Missy and the girls, he was seeing stars and a trickle of blood was sliding down his temple.

Missy huffed on. "How far is that light?"

"Don't know. Not far. Can't be. Just keep going."

And she did, they all did for what seemed like an eternity but couldn't have been more than ten or twenty seconds.

"You're not getting out," Vicente bellowed, his voice loud and clear. He'd jumped into the tunnel.

Jacob glanced over his shoulder. Near the entrance, three flashlights flicked on. They'd *all* jumped into the tunnel: Vicente, Bravo, and Sleepy.

Jacob was about to shout another hollow warning, but he bumped into Morena. She quickly steadied herself and carried on, but Jacob did not. His feet crossed, and he went down with a pathetic whine.

Morena stopped. Missy and the others, oblivious to his plight, kept going.

"Go," Jacob instructed of Morena. "Keep going." His ankle was aflame. The pain in his shoulder had expanded to encompass his entire right side. He picked himself up but lost his balance and clattered to the ground once more. Wiping his brow of sweat and blood, he took a breath and made another attempt to stand when a set of small hands, firm and stable, clutched him around his waist and helped him to his feet. He patted Morena on the head.

"Come on. Let's keep running. Can't stop."

She gave a nod, lowered her head, and took off, pumping her legs as fast as she could. The others were well ahead of them now. Jacob placed his good hand on Morena's back, urging her forward, but she couldn't move much faster than she already was. She was trying her damndest, though. She was even starting to wheeze from the effort, and it broke his heart. If he hadn't been beaten half to hell, he would've bent down, scooped her up, and carried her to the others, but instead he could do nothing, and they were getting left behind.

The light in the distance was growing larger. It couldn't possibly be much farther. Hope rose in his chest. There was no way Vicente would catch them.

As if reading his thoughts, Vicente argued back, "You won't make it." He fired the rifle a couple of times into the darkness.

Jacob winced as chips of stone pelted the back of his neck. "Keep going, Morena. Keep moving."

Vicente howled at them, louder and closer, and let loose another round.

Ahead, Missy was nearing the light. She was nearly out.

"Don't stop. Keep running. Good job, girls," Jacob encouraged. "Don't stop. Never stop."

The girls quickened their steps a touch, but they were tiring.

"Just get to the end and climb out. Follow Missy," he directed.

Vicente and the twins were terribly close behind. The persistent slap of their shoes and the brisk rustling of their clothes was right in his ear. He cursed himself for losing the pistol in the desert behind the station. He cursed himself for not hitting the weapons safe with the Charger. Any of those weapons could have held these traffickers at bay. He could have camped out near the entrance, taking shots every time they tried to get down while Missy and the girls made their escape. *Now what do you do? Whatever it takes.*

Missy reached the light. "It's not the end," she yelled. "It keeps going."

"Keep going then," Jacob hollered back.

Missy ushered Noemi, Sofia, and Rosa around a bend before disappearing herself. Jacob kept his hand on Morena's back until they too finally reached the bulb and rounded the corner. They made another quick turn, and Jacob realized they'd only come halfway. A fresh string of lights, spaced much closer together, guided the way to a floodlight in the distance. They could all see the exit, but they weren't going to reach it. *No chance.* "Keep going." He gave Morena a final push. "Don't stop."

Then he stopped, quietly so as not to draw Morena's attention. He watched the little figure press on in the narrow space. *Do whatever it takes.* He turned back to the bend in the tunnel. The approaching flashlights made the wall of dirt and stone sparkle. Jacob took a knee, giving his broken ankle a moment's rest. He'd kneel until Vicente and the twins got there (which wouldn't be long), and then he'd give them the fight of their life. He had the crowbar and the box cutter in his back pocket. Maybe he could even catch Vicente by surprise and wrestle the rifle from him.

Jacob glanced up at the ceiling. The sounds of the girls—their bare feet slapping at the dirt, their troubled breaths—were fading. He stood and inspected one of the wooden support beams. They'd nearly knocked him senseless. They were thick pieces of old timber the size of his thighs. *But still*, he thought, *it's worth a try.* He reached up, sunk the claw of the crowbar into the top edge, and with his one good arm, pulled. The beam quivered. *That's something.* He yanked again, and the quiver became a slight slip. *Almost.* If it fell, the ceiling would collapse. Adjusting his grip, he tugged with everything he had, putting his full weight into it.

The beam came loose and dropped to his feet with a solid thump. Four small stones and a clump of dirt dribbled out. Nothing more. He scanned the ceiling. There were too many beams, too many support points. The removal of one didn't threaten the tunnel's integrity at all.

The tunnel around him was growing brighter, the flashlights drawing nearer. The space echoed with advancing footsteps.

Jacob stepped back, sunk the crowbar into the next beam, and pulled. It came down with a generous thud. A gentle stream of dirt sprinkled down from where it'd been, but the ceiling remained intact. He started to frantically claw at the earth. The stream of dirt became a waterfall. It still wasn't enough, though. He limped to another beam, coughing amid the cloud of dust filling the air. He gave the beam a vicious tug. The wood held, and he grinned. This one, wedged tightly against the walls, had to be holding a generous amount of earth at bay. If he could get it to fall, it would all fall. *And bury me?* He wouldn't survive that. It'd be his un-birthday. *But so be it, if it saves Morena and the girls.*

He extracted the crowbar from the beam, drew it back, breathed deep, and swung it hard into the wood. With all the weight and strength he had remaining in his body, he then wrenched the beam loose.

Vicente and the twins came around the bend, the hazy air glowing in the beams of their flashlights.

The heavy wooden beam lay at Jacob's feet, and the ceiling burst open. Shifting soil and stone came down with a glorious deep groan. Jacob, still grinning, stared at Vicente. *Whatever it takes.*

The earth above the tunnel's bend, from Jacob to Vicente, broke loose in a wave and came crashing down, burying them as Missy and the girls continued on.

EPILOGUE

CBP Assists in Human Trafficking Rescue
CBP Public Affairs Press Release - July 28, 2019
For Immediate Release

SAN DIEGO, Calif.—US Border Patrol agents responded to a request last night for assistance from the San Diego Police Department regarding the investigation of a cross-border tunnel in Otay Mesa.

On July 27th, at approximately 10:00 p.m., a woman arrived at SDPD Station #1 on Airway Road with four human trafficking victims. The victims were taken to Sharp Chula Vista Medical Center while the woman led SDPD officers and border patrol agents to a one-bedroom home on Via de la Amistad where the tunnel's entry point was located.

U.S. Border Patrol agents entered and explored the tunnel, but their efforts were obstructed after discovering significant structural damage one hundred yards from the entrance.

The Border Patrol's "Border Tunnel Entry Team" (BTET) is currently working to reinforce the tunnel in order to prevent further collapse. It is believed there are multiple individuals trapped within the tunnel. BTET will be conducting search and rescue efforts in conjunction with Mexico's Federal Police, Policia Federal.

To prevent the illicit smuggling of humans, drugs, and other contraband, the San Diego Sector Border Patrol works in conjunction with Mexican law enforcement to detect and remove cross-border tunnels. U.S. Border Patrol welcomes individuals to report suspicious activity by calling 1-877-872-7435.

San Diego Times
July 28, 2019

BORDER TUNNEL ESCAPE
Minneapolis Couple Rescue Four

SAN DIEGO, CA: A major human-trafficking ring was recently uncovered after a young couple from Minneapolis alerted the authorities to the activity near the border in Tijuana. The couple managed to rescue four trafficking victims, all girls under the age of ten, from their captors late last evening and escort them to the Otay Mesa police station. The girls are currently at Sharp Chula Vista Medical Center as a precautionary measure, but sources say they are in good health and are expected to be released soon.

The girls are believed to have been under the control of the CJNG, a notoriously violent cartel that recently has been battling the Sinaloa and Arellano Felix Cartels for territory in Tijuana. As has been previously reported, the CJNG's Avispón branch, often identified by their use of a hornet's silhouette, oversees most of the cartel's Tijuana/San Diego smuggling activities, and while this branch has historically focused on the smuggling of illicit drugs, last night's events suggest they've expanded their operations into human trafficking. All four girls had the image of a hornet burned onto the back of their right shoulders. Authorities on both sides of the border, including Homeland Security Investigations, US Border Patrol, and Mexico's municipal and Federal Police, are working together to apprehend those responsible.

The rescue of these four girls, according to Chief Patrol Agent Tony Nickelson, US Border Patrol, San Diego Sector, "will hopefully lead to the apprehension of several key figures in the CJNG and hinder future trafficking efforts. While [the tunnel] appears to have been recently completed, it was clearly being prepped as a major artery for sending victims across the border. Because of the bravery of these two citizens, many lives will be saved."

The woman who arrived at the police station with the victims, Missy Chan, a digital marketing executive, said she and her boyfriend, Jacob White, a scientist with 3M, found the victims purely by chance while sightseeing in Tijuana and "had to take matters into [their] own hands."

While Ms. Chan and the victims survived their ordeal unscathed, Mr. White was caught in the six- by five-foot tunnel when a portion of it collapsed. He was found thirteen hours later by the Border Patrol's Border Entry Tunnel Team (BTET). He was alive, but he had suffered multiple fractures, a concussion, and a punctured lung. He is currently being treated for his injuries at Scripps Mercy Hospital.

BTET also reported that they recovered the bodies of three male individuals. The men have not yet been identified, but it is believed they were members of the Avispón branch and had been pursuing the group.

The tunnel's collapse opened a ten-foot-wide sinkhole inside the Plantronix manufacturing plant in Tijuana. No injuries were reported, and authorities say there is currently no danger to the public in regard to further collapse. The tunnel was reinforced to facilitate the search-and-rescue efforts, and in the coming days, it will be filled in with concrete.

Border cities like Tijuana have seen a rise in narco tunnels as the cartels have begun using new and faster excavating techniques. Nickelson said the techniques have proven effective—tunnels have been dug wider and longer—but collapses, such as this one, are still a real possibility, especially given the malleable clay-like soil prevalent throughout the area.

"This is a perfect example of the unscrupulous tactics these transnational criminal organizations will take to threaten the lives of not only immigrants but also the lives of everyone in the area," Nickelson said. "It's crucially important that the public remains vigilant in reporting suspicious activity so we can continue to prevent personal injury or death."

In addition to human trafficking, US Border Patrol reported that the tunnel had been used to recently transfer a significant amount of drugs into the US. There were more than 450 kilos of cocaine worth nearly $10 million inside the Otay Mesa house that authorities say was ready for distribution.

Jacob hadn't gotten out of bed in three days. When he and Missy returned to Minneapolis, he slept for twenty-four hours, then he laid in bed for another forty-eight, barely moving. Everything just hurt so bad. Today was the first day the pain felt somewhat muted, like background noise, so he figured he better take the opportunity to move around and stretch.

Quincy, curled up on Missy's side of the bed, raised his head and watched Jacob carefully sit up and lower his feet to the floor.

The apartment was quiet. Missy was at work, just not at 44th Parallel anymore. She'd quit. Google had offered her a job, and she'd zipped right over to their newly opened Minneapolis office in the North Loop, unable to wait the customary two weeks.

Jacob grabbed his phone from the nightstand, then pulled his crutches close. He took a breath and stood. *So far, so good.* "Come on, Quincy," he said as he hobbled out of the room. A bowling-ball-like thump indicated the pug was coming.

Missy had a box of protein bars sitting open on the kitchen counter, and Jacob swiped a couple on his careful journey to the balcony. Stepping into the sun was glorious. He let out a long sigh. *That's enough walking.* He lowered himself into a plastic chair and propped his broken ankle atop the other. Quincy sat near the railing, scanning the street.

Gold Medal Park was a deep, Minnesota green. In another six or seven weeks, the rich palette would start to morph into a spectrum of yellows and oranges and reds. That'd be about as long as it'd take for his ankle to heal. His shoulder was another story. It needed surgery, and that wasn't scheduled until mid-November. He'd absolutely destroyed the ligaments and tendons in there. A stiff wrap was holding everything in place now, but the muscles burned like a hot iron. The hospital had offered him painkillers (Oxy), but he wanted none of that. He couldn't trust himself with it. He'd manage with Tylenol.

He tore open a protein bar and bit down, chewing slowly, checking his phone in the hopes that there was an email from the adoption agency. He and Missy had been told it'd take a while given the circumstances, but he couldn't help wishing something would be fast-tracked, and their request to adopt Morena would be granted. The other girls, Noemi, Sofia, and Rosa, had all been reunited with their families at the San Ysidro Port of Entry. They'd been part of the migrant groups heading north. Morena had also been part of that group, but she'd come to Tijuana alongside a trafficker, not her family. No one actually knew where her family was, so she was currently under the supervision of the Office of Refugee Resettlement.

As she'd told Jacob, Morena had likewise told the government officials that her parents were dead. After a quick check, that appeared to be the truth. A couple in Mexico City matching Morena's description of her parents had been murdered in June; they'd moved from Guatemala earlier in the year. The Office of Refugee Resettlement was working with the Mexican and Guatemalan authorities to follow her trail back to Guatemala and locate an extended family member, but it was proving difficult, so for now Morena was stuck sitting in a San Diego detention center.

Jacob had a feeling they weren't going to find any family, though, and he hoped they wouldn't make her stay in the center for long, especially given that he and Missy were ready and willing to give her a home right now. He was already imagining the three of them heading across the park for double scoops of mint chocolate chip or strawberry or whatever sounded good to Morena. He'd get her whatever she wanted.

There were a few new emails, but none from the adoption agency. One was confirming his purchase of a giant plush SpongeBob for Morena, and the other read, "RE: Query." He almost didn't bother with that email. He didn't care anymore. But as he sat there, watching Quincy pant in the sun, the cherry eye as big as ever, curiosity got the best of him. He wanted to see which agent had taken so long to finally reply, so he tapped the screen.

Hi Mr. White,

Apologies for the delay. I'd be interested in

taking a look at your manuscript. Please send it in .doc or .docx format at your convenience.

Also, I read about how you rescued those girls in Mexico. That was incredible! Do you think you might write a book about that? I've represented a number of best-selling nonfiction authors in the last ten years, and I think your story would interest many major publishing houses. We should talk. This has potential.

Truly yours,
Simon Halloford
Literary agent
Reah & Luogini Literary Agency
@S.HallofordLITAGENT

Jacob smirked. He held a finger over "Reply", then shifted to "Delete".

ACKNOWLEDGEMENTS

First off, I'm fairly certain all the good in this book was inspired from other works, recent and old. As such, I'm eternally grateful to everyone and everything. You're all an inspiration, and I couldn't have written this without you. Alternatively, everything that you, the reader, find terrible in these pages was entirely my fault. I made mistakes, and I apologize profusely.

Second, for those who did not help, I'm disappointed in you. You know who you are, and I won't comment on the matter further.

Finally, if you've read to this point, thank you, truly.

ABOUT THE AUTHOR

Who am I? I'm not much. Just a guy drinking coffee and writing crime thrillers.

Find me on social media if you'd like to see for yourself.

www.Instagram.com/ChesterGattle

www.Twitter.com/ChesterGattle

www.ChesterGattle.com

Made in the USA
Monee, IL
04 June 2021